A Squid on the Shoulder

A FURTHER HANNIBAL SMYTH MISADVENTURE

MARK HAYES

Steampowered Books

Steampowered Books
11 Saltholme Close
High Clarence
TS21TL

Publisher's Note: This is a work of fiction. Names, characters, places, and incidents are a product of the author's imagination. Locales and public names are sometimes used for atmospheric purposes. Any resemblance to actual people, living or dead, or to businesses, companies, events, institutions, or locales is completely coincidental.

A Squid on the Shoulder:
Mark Hayes -- 1st ed.
ISBN 9798419740808

For Dad

The Hannibal Smyth Misadventures
A Spider in the Eye
From Russia with Tassels
A Squid on the Shoulder

A Ballad of Maybe's
Maybe

Other Novels
Passing Place
Cider Lane

Anthologies
Cheesecake, Avarice & Boots
The Harvey Duckman Anthologies Vol1 – 10

Contents

Is it me or is it getting warm in here?

"Gyroscopes Elonis."

The thing about Hettie Clarkhurst

Goodnight my darling

That knotty romantic slither

The brave die young and childless

Redemption from on high

Payback is a dull edged blade

'The Epilogue', or the things about death cells...

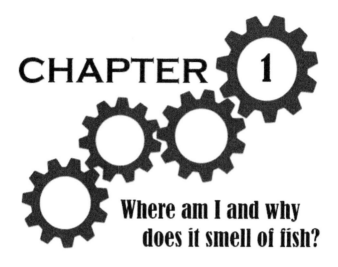

CHAPTER 1

Where am I and why does it smell of fish?

The first thing I remembered on waking, was falling to my death. So, when I awoke, the mere fact I had awoken begged questions…

There was of course the old favourite which literature has driven us to expect on such occasions. 'Where am I?' But in all honesty, the question that occurred to me when first I awoke was somewhat more prosaic, to wit… 'Why does it smell of fish?'

What I didn't ask myself was, 'Am I dead?' I was clearly not dead. It's not that I'm so arrogant as to believe I know and understand all the mysteries of the universe, nor do I arbitrarily dismiss the possibility of an afterlife, god, Heaven, the other place and all that, but wherever I was, it certainly wasn't Heaven. Now let me be honest here, I'm not much of a believer, not even in that 'I'm open to the possibility there may be a god', hedge your bets, agnostic, kind of way. Besides which, if there is any truth to the Church of England's version of the afterlife, which my Religious Education teachers tried to beat into me in a literal sense, then I suspect I'm destined for the place without the joyous choirs and gates of the pearly kind. But while I might not claim to know the truth behind the mysteries of the afterlife, I strongly suspect Hell isn't a small seven by four-foot room, with walls of riveted steel, painted a light but flaking vomit green. Nor were the doors in Hell likely to be of the airtight bulkhead, spin the wheel to lock, ocean going ship, variety.

Though then again, that could well be exactly what Hell is like. Maybe Old Nick's fond of the slowly rusting nautical motif, when it comes down to it, who knows? To my mind such are questions for the clergy, and as I abhor a cassock, I tend not to dwell on them.

Besides, questions of a religious nature didn't seem important right then. As I said, I was clearly not dead, on account of being alive. Which, I may add, is on the whole a state of affairs I'm greatly in favour of. You could almost say it's my reason for living, if that's not somewhat redundant, all considered.

So, I was alive, though I was damn sure I shouldn't be. Not that I'm one to argue with good fortune, particularly as recently it had been rare that Lady Luck deemed to smile in my direction. As such, if we are going to be all existential about it, I thought it best not to draw the Lady's attention to me still being in the land of the living. I didn't want her changing her mind, now did I?

I'd awoken laying on a bunk of some kind, and surprisingly, I wasn't restrained. That I feel the latter needs to be stated also said a lot about how my life had been going of late. To find myself unrestrained was rare when I woke up in unfamiliar surroundings. Strangely someone had taken the time to divest me of my uniform and dress me in unflattering, if neatly pressed, green grey overalls and put my left arm in a sling. I realised this meant I must have been out a few hours at least, though judging by the hunger cramping my stomach a good day or so must have passed since I'd plummeted, not quite, to my death from the Johan's Lament. My recently acquired ability to judge the passage of time by hunger alone probably also says a lot about my recent life.

Still it beats the most obvious alterative…

To top it off, I was feeling lightheaded and suspected I'd been sedated at some point, which was another of those odd things I'd learned to recognise recently. It worried me a little, one does hear stories about sailors after all, if you'll excuse the military humour… However, as I tried to sit up, I felt a burst of pain, the kind I associated with cracked ribs, which probably explained why someone had administered a sedative to me recently, pain aside given other possibilities this came as a relief.

Steeling myself, I managed to sit up carefully, easing myself over until I was sitting on the bed with my feet on the deck. An exercise that could have been easier, if my left arm hadn't been in that sling. The arm itself felt okay. I could move my wrist, fingers, even my elbow easily enough, but my shoulder screamed when I tried to lift my arm. I took a mental tally of my injuries, adding a dislocated shoulder to the broken ribs, along with assorted bruises, a headache that felt like a cracked skull, and blank spaces where my more recent memories should be.

All in all, I'd woken up in worse states.

I sat on the edge of the bed for a while, my eyes closed, trying to recall recent events. I could remember every detail

of my little scuffle with Saffron Wells on top of the Johan.
'Not Saffron Wells' I corrected myself. Saffron under the
control of one of Gates' Spiders. Her mind dominated by
The Ministry and the egregious 'M'. I recalled in vivid detail
'Not Saffron' shooting my own favourite Bad Penny, and
watching Penny take a swan dive into the ocean hundreds
of feet below. I also recalled the chill searing through me as
I stared down the barrel of the same gun while 'M' asked
me, through Saffron's vocal cords, three times where her
grandfather HG could be found. I vividly remembered
watching while her, or rather his, finger curled around the
trigger, sure I was done for and the cold determination
which came over me as I took my trusty cutthroat from my
boot. The familiar weight in my hand, thumbing the blade
out of the handle and the resistance of the safety cord as I
cut it and my own resulting swan dive into the Indian
Ocean. A dive from a height which I'd knew damn well
guaranteed terminal velocity was going to live up to its
name…

I even remembered the look on Saffron's face as I fell
away, seeing the gun go off, missing me I could only assume,
by my lack of bullet wounds, and falling… Tumbling
through the sky. My crippled airship rushing away as fast as
the ocean was coming up to meet me.

And then…

And then…

And then… well in truth then my memories become a
little fractured. I recalled something about drinking in a bar,
eating pork scratchings, and talking to a piano player from
Tadcaster about that time in the monastery when the little
black robe taught me a lesson in the rewards of avarice.
There was something about a talking cat as well of all
things…

And then… I recalled stepping back out of the bar and finding myself once more falling through the sky. Falling, then hitting water with the surface resistance of concrete, bright flashes of pain and plunging into darkness.

I suspect it was that impact that broke my ribs, dislocated my shoulder and cracked my skull. I also suspect this caused my somewhat wild hallucination about eating pork scratchings and drinking in an odd bar with a talking cat. It's strange the things the mind will do to protect itself from naked terror and agonising pain.

And beyond that? Well, I remembered nothing and all that was hazy to be honest, which may have been down to the bang on the head. Though, of all the things I could definitely remember, it was the saltiness of those pork scratchings, but a lung full of the Indian Ocean was likely to blame for that.

None of this, however, explained why I now found myself in a small cabin on some kind of ship. Clearly, I'd been rescued from certain death in the ocean. For which I'll admit to being grateful. But I could not recall seeing any ships when I fell and for all the fuzziness of my memory, the view of the ocean rushing up towards me was something I recalled all too clearly. I'd seen no ships, no islands, nothing but a huge blue expanse of ocean and the occasional shark's fin. Though in fairness the latter may have been the product of my overactive imagination.

I was still woozy and while exactly where I was and who had saved me clearly mattered, it wasn't all that high on the list of things I cared to worry about. Right then that list was very short. I could have tried the door, but I'd no doubt that I'd find it locked. People always seemed inclined to lock me in rooms. Of course, more often than not the rooms in question were cells, a tendency that might make a man question his life choices. Right at that moment, however, I'd also no desire to explore my many flaws. Besides, it occurred to me this room was unlikely to warrant a listing in the 'Good Death-cell Guide'. As a rule, few people go to the trouble of saving an unconscious man from drowning and patch him up, just so they can execute him when he recovers.

That said, I've met a couple of people over the years who'd do just that…

All the same, the room was still a cell. Though it's an understandable precaution, locking away an unknown man you'd fished out of the drink after they'd skydived without a parachute. I could've been anyone… I wasn't about to take offence at my rescuers for doing so. I'd have done the same. At least until I found out who I was.

Instead of trying the door, or alerting anyone to my return to consciousness, I took the opportunity to rest, not least because moving was painful. Instead, I sat on the edge of the bed and put some thought into what to do next. Not that anything beyond waiting to find out who'd plucked me out of the ocean was an option. So that's what I did, despite being conscious of a growing thirst and a buzzing headache causing my eyes to water.

It was perhaps because of the headache that it took me a while to notice the emblem sown onto the shoulder of the overalls they'd shoved me into, but eventually I did notice it and with noticing came a sinking feeling, if you'll pardon the nautical theme. It was an emblem I recognised. I'd seen it most recently, sown on the uniforms of guards working for my old 'friend' HG Wells. The guards in question being the particularly sinister-looking ones, with a penchant for rebreathers and no noticeable sense of humour. It was a strange, stylised squid-like creature, under which were written words in equally stylised Latin I'd never previously gotten close enough to read.

My Latin isn't entirely up to scratch. Dead languages died for a reason in my humble opinion. As they were only spoken by the dead, doctors and clergymen, I'd never seen the point in my learning them, much to my old house master's disgust.

As I may have expressed before, my firm conviction is that the only reason to learn any foreign language is so you're able to ask for a beer in a barman's native tongue. That and to get directions to the local house of negotiable virtue if you're on ground leave amid a three-month tour over the Nile delta… Though it has to be said knowledge of the occasional native swear word comes in handy. I, for example, can tell a chap to fornicate in a direction that could be said to be the opposite from my own in most European languages, Russian and thanks to my recent stint as an officer in the East India Company's air-arm, Hindi, but I digress…

My vision was still a bit fuzzy, even in my unnatural left eye, in the case of which just fuzzy was making a nice change. I struggled to read the Latin words below the insignia but as far as I could make out, they were 'Qui non solum mare'.

As I said, my Latin was not up to much. I'd done a couple of terms of it at Rugley School for the Sons of the Empire before my inability to conjugate the verbs led to the Latin master permanently excusing me with the words, 'Smith, sicut sis densissima sicut porcus stercore.' Doubtless I'd have been offended if I'd understood what he said but when it came to the formation of Latin I was, to use my native East End vernacular, 'as thick as pig shit'.

Besides, as I was banished to the study room, I used Latin lessons to study more interesting forms, such as the runners in the 2:30 at Cheltenham, and the illicit pornography the sixth form lads squirreled away between text books.

In any regard, I was ill-equipped to translate the motto beneath the stylised squid, though I could hazard a guess that it contained something about ownership and the sea. But whatever the motto, it didn't matter, what mattered was what that icon implied. To wit, whatever ship I was on, it belonged to those involved in the same conspiracy as Wells' little band of air-pirates. Somehow, I had managed to literally fall from the sky and land smack bang in the middle of the same web of insanity that'd had me fighting on top of that airship amidst a monsoon in the first place.

'Hell, what are the odds of that, Harry,' I found myself wondering.

I should have known better. If I was going to be picked up in the middle of an ocean by anyone, I could've lain odds it would be Wells' cronies or a British naval vessel, the latter of which would've gone worse for me. I doubted I was flavour of the month at Whitehall. Indeed, I was hoping Whitehall and The Ministry had me marked down as dead, all things considered.

Trying to distract myself from the ramifications of my discovery I took in the cabin that was my cell. Not that there was much to take in. The small cot bed I was sitting on, the wall with the door in it, two other blank walls and a final one with a small porthole. That, and the peeling vomit green paint, spots of rust, and nautical, which is to say part salt, part fish, aroma, was more or less the whole story of the room.

The porthole was a circle of darkness six inches across, so I made the reasonable assumption I'd woken from my stupor in the middle of the night. Clearly, I was going to glean nothing looking through that. My head was still pounding as well, so after a while I lay back down and closed my eyes. Sleep however eluded me. I ached all over, but was anything but tired. I dozed at best for an hour or so before restlessness led me to contemplate banging on the door just to see if I could raise anyone, but I decided to leave that as a last resort. I doubted I'd been forgotten about and as it was still pitch black beyond the porthole, I resigned myself to waiting.

The bed proving uncomfortable, I stood and walked around a little to stretch my legs, as much as I could in that tiny cabin. I'd also begun to notice the air tasted a little stale despite the ceiling vent supplying a slight breeze, and a steady drip of water through its rusty grill, pooling brownish water that smelled of brine on the deck by my feet. The ship was clearly old and perhaps not in the best state of repair. Though in my limited experience the same could be said of most ocean-going vessels. All this spender was bathed in the glow of electric filament from a single tesla bulb mounted in a bulky enclosed fitting, giving the room, with its sickly green paint, a strange ambience. But then I've never felt entirely at home on boats. Give me an air-ship any day of the week.

Pacing about, limited thought it was, was helping to clear my head, so I kept on going. Three steps to the door and three steps back. I must've done this a few dozen times before I noticed a tiny glow of light in the darkness beyond the porthole. Small and blueish, I mistook it for a reflection off the glass at first. Before I realised it was growing brighter. I wondered if it was a small craft of some kind moving out on the ocean, though squinting through the porthole I still could see no horizon line, no moonlight reflecting off the waves, nothing. It must be '*as still as a duck pond*' out there, I remember thinking to myself.

As I watched that little glow of light slowly moving closer, something else struck me… I couldn't feel any vibrations through the deck plates. Nor, now I thought of it, could I hear the tell-tale background hum of engines, or for that matter feel any pitch and roll. The obvious conclusion to this string of revelations was that if we were at sea, we were both utterly becalmed and not under power. I'll admit I'm no expert on ocean-going craft, but that struck me as damn odd. Then it struck me that the light was on, which required electricity, which again implied engines I could neither hear nor feel. If ocean ships were anything like airships, I'd have to be a long way from the engines not to hear their drone and feel vibrations through deck plates. How big a ship could this be?

Everything about the situation seemed a little off, a little out of kilter. Something, I realised, wasn't as it seemed, and while I considered all this, the small blueish light I could see beyond the porthole came closer still. But it wasn't until the last moment I realised just how small a light it was and where that light was coming from when I saw the jaws behind it. Massive jaws full of teeth. Jaws that gaped opened, then snapped shut violently. Jaws I'd never wish to see up-close again, even with the inch-thick glass of the porthole between me and them. As it was, I almost jumped out of my much-battered skin.

Once I'd got over the initial surprise, I realised this shock answered at least some of my questions. I was never a student of Ichthyology, which as you probably know, though I didn't at the time, is the study of fish. I can't say fish in general have ever held much interest for me beyond cod, haddock, and the occasion bit of salmon. But I've read the odd magazine article while bored at the dentist like everyone else, so I was aware there was such a thing as an angler fish and knew enough to know they lived in the depths, not in the shallows.

The deep depths…

'Well, that's a bloody turn up, Harry, we're on a bloody submersible,' I thought and then started wondering just how deep we were, fifty foot perhaps, a hundred maybe. I

knew the damn things didn't go all that deep. You'd need a diving bell for that. It wasn't as if as a technology it had much going for it, sea power hadn't been high on any government's agenda since the dawn of airpower. The senior service is now so senior it's in its dotage and has been since before Old Iron Knickers lost her virginity. Given her ever-growing brood of great, great great and great great great grandchildren, Vicky's cherry popping was so long ago it's achieved almost mythological status. Occasionally I've heard the theory ventured that the reason Queen Victoria is so keen on maintaining the empire is simply so there was room to keep that endless brood of chinless princes and prissy princesses out from under her feet.

They say, these days the civil list requires a whole wing of Whitehall to administer it. But I digress…

While I was still reeling from a close encounter with more teeth than a mouth had any right to contain, my left eye decided to wake up from its stupor and play its favourite game of 'let's make Hannibal see things he'd rather not'. Possibly due to the absence of any insects in the room, yaks to count the nostril hairs of, or anything else to zoom in and out on, the eye given to me by Professor Jobs deployed another of its tricks, one I'd been blissfully unaware of up to that point. Suddenly the world beyond that artificial orb became a strange greenish grey and in this new garish monotone everything beyond the porthole seemed to grow brighter and more defined. All at once, the ink dark depths of the sea were visible to me. As visible as a landscape illuminated by the sun in that dull twilight hour before dusk. In short, suddenly I was quite literally able to see in the dark through my left eye.

Later, when I'd had time to reflect on this new-found ability, I realised it could be a useful trick. Of course, it would've been a damn sight more useful if I'd any control over my mechanical eye. But I could think of a great many uses for such a trick. Uses to warm the cockles of my criminal heart. You'll have to forgive that my first inclination was to consider how useful it could be for a little late-night pilfering, but honestly can you blame me for that observation?

Right at that moment, however, the sudden unexpected ability to see in the dark came as a horrifying shock, one made worse for what I saw beyond that porthole. How to explain what I saw? Imagine the most alien of landscapes, visible in all its detail. A world of strange flora and stranger fauna. Of rocks encrusted with shellfish you would never pick at on a pier. Sandy dunes that have never seen the sun with creatures no man should ever perceive slithering across the them. Giant monstrous blind fish swarming and being hunted through forests of seaweeds that were as tall as any rainforest. Things scuttled over the sea bed that no plate had ever held. Eels that would never see jelly boiled in clusters, predators swam in circles of death, feeding on those smaller than they then darted away from beasts that could swallow them whole. All in a lightless netherworld which never saw the sun.

"Oh shit," I heard myself mutter as the implications of that singular view came to me. Whatever craft I was aboard wasn't, as I had assumed, fifty or a hundred feet beneath the waves. What was before me wasn't the floor of some shallow sea. This was the deep ocean bed. Whatever craft I was in must be hundreds, maybe thousands of feet down. This was a world beyond any I'd ever seen documented and with good reason. I may not have known a great deal about them, but I knew for certain that no submersible could ever achieve such depths. Nothing ever went this deep, even diving bells; the crushing pressure of the deep ocean saw to that. The only craft that lay this deep were wrecks. So, if I was here, in a craft this deep beneath the waves, I was on a ghost ship, a wreck. It was no wonder I could hear no engines nor feel the vibrations of machinery through the deck plates. I was entombed on the ocean floor. Entombed with nothing but death to look forward to. If by some miracle the pressure didn't rupture the hull and drown me, the stale air I was breathing would grow steadily staler, then run out completely. And if I was lucky enough to avoid drowning or asphyxiation? Well, starvation was always an option, if nothing else proved to be the death of me.

This cabin wasn't a cell, it was a death cell, the whole ship was a death cell. Both death cell and method of execution. If I'd not been in a state of panic as this all came to me, I dare say I would've penned another entry in my 'The good death cell guide'.

A submersible on the floor of the Indian Ocean

Basic accommodation good but inescapable due to crushing depths involved

Death guaranteed, admittedly interesting views if you have night vision but they soon lose their appeal, which is ironic as there is no opportunity for appeal once you are incarcerated within your roomy submersible cell

3/10, points knocked off for lack of hope

At this point, while I panicked and failed to scribble down an entry for the book I was unlikely to ever write, in fact just at the point I'd concluded both I and the craft I was on were effectively dead in the water, no pun intended, there came the sound of metal scraping on metal.

Turning to see what it was, and half fearing it was the hull rupturing, I turned to see the wheel on the hatchway rotating. This came as a relief, as it meant I wasn't alone in my sunken tomb. Though this realisation was tinged with the usual mild terror of realising I'd no idea who the hell was on the other side of that door…

As it was, behind that door was no one I ever would've expected. I mean, sure I expected guards in breathing masks with squid insignias on their shoulders, nor would I have been entirely astounded to discover it was one of The Ministry's Sleepmen sent to finish me off. Which is to say I would've been utterly petrified, but not at all surprised. I wouldn't have been greatly astonished if it turned out to be my favourite Bad Penny, because, god knows, she had a habit of turning up when least expected, and as I'd somehow survived the long fall into the Indian Ocean it seemed a fair bet she had too…

I will admit I might've been surprised if it had been Queen Brass Knickers herself, but even then, only to a degree.

What I didn't expect, could never have expected and wouldn't have bet a bloody farthing on, even at odds to make a bookie weep, was who was actually behind that door.

As the holding bolts were withdrawn and the door swung open, a voice which I'd only ever describe as feminine because I was aware its owner was, loudly and with a relentless brand of cheerfulness all her own, shouted through the opening doorway, "Hannibal, you old duffer, are you up and about yet, or do I need to chuck a bucket of water over you to get that lazy arse of yours moving?"

As I said, I knew that voice, knew it very well, in fact, and hearing it there and then, at the bottom of the Indian Ocean left me, quite frankly, stunned. However, one tries to make the best of things and get on, doesn't one? And so, without missing more than a couple of beats, I forced on my warmest, most welcoming smile and pretended not to be completely taken aback by the sheer force of personality stepping through the door.

Frankly this was mostly because I was afraid that if I did otherwise I'd never live it down.

Thus I replied in my best 'duffer' from the Gentleman's Club voice, "Hettie? What in Hell's name are you doing here?"

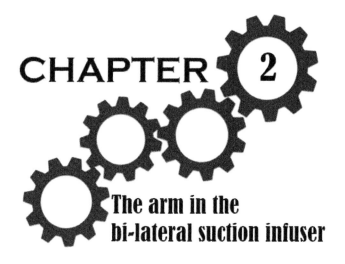

CHAPTER 2

The arm in the bi-lateral suction infuser

The answer to that question was to remain a mystery for some days. But to give you some perspective, when last I'd had the pleasure of the company of Henrietta Clarkhurst she'd been a warrant officer in the Queen's Royal Air Navy. 'Spanners' also happened to be a fellow member, in somewhat better standing than I, of 'The Ins & Outs', from whence she had acquired her nickname. Partly due to her rather precocious skills as an engineer, among other things. As such, while she may not have been the very last person I would've expected to bump into, in a submersible, in the middle of the Indian Ocean. It was a close-run thing between her and Pope Joan IV.

Last time I'd seen 'Spanners', a couple years before, wasn't long after I'd inadvertently found myself fighting a duel on Hampstead Heath one morning. A duel ostensibly fought to defend her honour, though no one, including myself, had bothered to inquire as to her opinion of the matter.

An oversight which proved costly for all concerned…

In the vaulted echelons of 'The Ins & Outs', more correctly referred to by anyone but those who frequent it as 'The Naval, Air and Military Club', that whole affair had been dubbed, thanks to one of the pretentious wags who hung about at the members' bar as 'The Cheesecake Dichotomy', or by those a tad less pretentious as 'the cheesecake incident'. Though, I should point out, it wasn't referred to in either way when Hettie was about. When Hettie was about, the incident was carefully not referred to at all.

While it is fair to say that, in general, members of my old club are less than renowned for their discretion. Some incidents cast long shadows over the members' bar. There are some events chaps just don't bring up when one of the chaps involved is about. There'd been many such incidents over the years and in the case of 'the cheesecake incident', the chap it was never mentioned in front of was Hettie.

Technically, of course, Hettie isn't an actual chap. She is, however, very much one of the chaps to the members of 'The Ins & Outs'. A chap deeply respected as a chap by all the other chaps, not least because she could out-drink, out-fight and probably out-fornicate the lot of us.

Unsurprisingly, no one thought twice about ripping in to me over my own part in 'the cheesecake incident', but I was unlikely to 'spanner' the living daylights out of them for mentioning it. Hettie almost certainly would.

Now, you may consider fighting a duel over a lady's honour to be somewhat out of character for yours truly. I can't argue with you on that score. Truth be told I was very drunk at the duel's inception and tripped out on LSD by the time I 'fought' it. Also, suffice to say, Hettie didn't thank me for the palaver involved and dealt with the whole situation in her usual brisk and direct fashion by threatening to give both myself and my fellow combatant, Charles Fortescue-Wright 'a right bloody spannering' if we didn't pack it in.

But that, in essence, is Henrietta Clarkhurst for you.

A few months after my abortive duel with 'Piggy' as Charles was generally known at the club, Hettie volunteered for some mission with the British Antarctic Survey. 'The Ins & Outs' threw her a rousing send-off, which I missed as I was on an extended RAN patrol in the Balkans, with on my part, a bit of light arms smuggling thrown in. Later, they told me her send-off had been a particularly uproarious boozy session. A session that ended with not one but two 'right good spannerings' that people very carefully never alluded to directly, as well as a trio of club members awaking to find themselves handcuffed to lampposts on the Mall, dressed as they came into this world. It also proved the old adage, a good night out should lead to questions on 'standards of behaviour in public life' being raised in the house of lords…

Well, that's not so much an adage, as a goal for members of my old club. I was rather put out that I missed it.

The BAS mission Hettie was seconded to was hush hush, and as such it was a subject of rife speculation in the members' bar for months, at least until the rugby season started in earnest when it was promptly forgotten. All that speculation amounted to very little and in essence the members' bar and by extension my good self, knew sod all about it. Why Hettie volunteered for a couple of years of freezing her… well, to be gentlemanly, let's just say a couple of years of cold weather in the company of penguins, I couldn't say. Such adventurous doings were, however, the members' bar agreed, exactly the kind of manly pursuits that a chap, who isn't a chap, like Hettie Clarkhurst, 'manfully' throws herself into. As such no one was entirely surprised she'd volunteered. Indeed, more than one of my old club mates was happy to admit they were a tad jealous that she'd got the opportunity not they. To me, the whole escapade sounded terminally dull, blisteringly cold, and likely to lack anything I'd ever deem as entertaining, but it was Hettie, so as I said at the time, 'good luck to her'.

None of this explained why she was now opening my impromptu cell door, on a submersible in the middle and quite possibly at the bottom of the Indian Ocean a couple of years later. But as I said explanations on how that came to pass were going to wait.

So, not to digress further…

The bulkhead door swung open and with a strange mix of relief and bemusement I found myself face to face with Henrietta Clarkhurst dressed in overalls matching my own, except her sleeves were rolled up past her elbows in the way of engineers the world over. They were overalls that bore the same squid insignia on the shoulder as mine and equally lacked any other markings. Except in her case there was a name patch sewn over her breast pocket, which was slightly strained as it was Hettie's breast pocket, bearing the legend 'Spanners'.

What her uniform wasn't, in any way, was British as it was noticeably devoid of a Union Jack or a royal crest. This immediately ruled out the possibility this submersible belonged to Old Iron Knickers' fleet, or for that matter was a merchant vessel belonging to subjects of the British Empire. My fellow brits are never shy when it comes to idolatry of the flag. The Jack was on everything, from ships to matchboxes. I doubt you could find the crew of a paddleboat in the empire whose uniforms lacked a Union Jack on them somewhere.

The lack of any viable Union Jacks wasn't my only clue to the allegiance of the craft I'd found myself upon. Hettie wasn't alone, she was flanked by guards in uniform. Uniforms I recognised, rebreathers and all. These were the self-same uniforms that had been worn by the guards forming HG Wells' personal retinue back in Nepal. Guards who, like the ones before me, had been armed with those strange harpoon rifles that not only looked downright lethal, but gave me the damn willies as did the men holding them. True though it was that those guards hadn't done Wells a whole lot of good back in Nepal, their presence either side of Hettie still sent a shiver down my spine.

"Ducking typical," a less than careful listener may have heard me mutter under my breath.

I was, as you may gather, cursing my luck. I'd escaped a mad man, a battle, flown a thousand mile or more in fear of my life, fought for that life on top of my own damn airship against a woman I considered a friend, vaguely at least. Sure, her mind had been taken over by a shadowy branch of the British Government bent on a crazy campaign against the mad bastard who thought he could travel through time, but still, she'd been taking pot shots at me. Then I escaped one fate by plunging to what I'd every right to expect to be my death. Done the belly flop to end all belly flops into the middle of the Indian Ocean. Yet somehow after all that I'd managed to get myself rescued by the same bunch of anti-Imperial nut-cases I'd just extrapolated myself from in the first place.

What are the odds, outside of the fevered imaginings of some hack of a paperback writer? It's enough to make a man fatalistic, I tell you.

"Hettie?" I said again, fully aware I was repeating myself. "What in Hell's name are you doing here?"

"Well, right at this moment? I'm checking to see if you're awake and ready to answer no one's questions, old boy.

What I should be doing is fixing the bi-lateral suction infuser on the port ballast tank as it's had a sodding metal arm dragged through it when it was running at full tilt. It's a wonder osculating manifold isn't just so much scrap, to be frank with you. You do know I'm having to overhaul the sodding influx cylinders, don't you? No, of course you don't, what am I thinking…? Well, I am. The gussets are completely shredded, and don't get me started about the state of my lubrication nipples on the central intakes… But no, it's not like I don't have enough on my plate. His nibs remembered you and I used to be drinking buddies so he asked me to pop along and give you a prodding. I guess he thinks you're less likely to need dragging before him if I come all the way up here to fetch you. I wouldn't mind but doubtless if I don't get the port ballast back up and working in short order, no one will give me an earful," Hettie explained, for want of a better word.

This was all said to me in her usual, jolly hockey sticks and engine grease tone of voice, which put me in mind of better times in the members' bar. That said, I tuned out a little in all honesty. Just about as soon as she started talking about things mechanical. I understand that stuff about as well as an American understands the difference between third slip and silly mid-off. So, in fairness I might be misquoting her here, but whatever was the issue it definitely involved nipples, lubrication, gussets and an oscillating manifold, because engineers…

In essence, something was broken, because reasons, and Hettie was in charge of fixing it. Fixing engines is Hettie's happy place, being dragged away from her happy place to talk to the likes of me was doubtless a cause of vexation. Which is to say she was a tad annoyed and the cause of her annoyance was yours truly. If anything, this cheered me, as it was in its own way a dose of normality amidst a less than normal day. However, it has to be said, as I more or less blanked out when she started her mechanic talk, I entirely missed the most important part of what she'd told me.

But there you go, somethings never change.

"Sorry about all this," I said, which was apology by rote, I'm aware. It was always wise to apologise to Hettie if you'd by chance annoyed her. While as firm a friend as a chap could desire, she could, and would, knock a chap to the deck with one punch if she ever felt the need.

"Oh, don't worry about it, old boy. It's been an odd twenty-four hours what with arms in the intake valves and stopping to fish people out of the drink. But now you're up and about, I must get back to replacing fingernail shredded pipes, so I'll leave these lads to escort you up to the captain. He's rather keen to have a talk with you, so best not delay. We can catch up over a bottle in the mess later. You can stand me a drink as it's your bloody fault I've been elbow deep in filter sumps for hours fishing out fingers. You know something, Hannibal, it never ceases to amaze me what an utter pain in my backside you can manage to be. Anyway, off you pop, old chap. See you in a bit." Hettie gifted me an amused smile. Then with half a wink she turned away and strode off down the corridor.

I stood in the hatchway, watching Hettie's ample 'part I was a pain in' depart, and felt like I'd just been 'spannered' for want of another word.

CHAPTER 3

Meeting no one

As Hettie Clarkhurst disappeared through a hatch at one end of the corridor beyond my cell, one of my two guards prodded me not entirely gently with the business end of his harpoon gun and motioned me to start down the corridor in the other direction.

Lacking options, I took the hint and started walking through what turned out to be a maze of confined corridors, hatches and occasionally ladders. My escorts said nothing, just kept prodding me along in one direction or another, leaving me wondering if they could speak at all. You'll note I didn't wonder if they could speak English. As an Englishman, I of course was firmly of the opinion that everyone should speak English. We ruled half the damn world, after all, so why shouldn't they?

The corridors I was shoved along were narrow, too narrow to take two abreast easily, and they were lined with similar hatchways to the door of my cell. All of them were painted in the same vomit colour that someone who'd never seen the ocean would've called sea green. Tesla lamps lined the walls, flickering within bulky cases and offering a modicum of light best described as dingy. Even so, as I went along, I couldn't help but notice each door had the same squid-like icon stencilled upon them, each with a different set of numbers stencilled below. Whatever the craft was, I realised, it clearly belonged to some form of military. Only a military mind is ever that utilitarian in decor.

Though the craft was a submersible, I found much of its design reminded me of an airship. It had been designed with the same conservation of space in mind, producing a compact environment. The ceilings were a maze of pipes and conduits, running just inches above my head. The metal deck plates on the floor were designed to be lifted out, and would doubtless reveal more service voids below them. Yet familiar though the design was, the materials used were vastly different. Airframes are predominantly aluminium, or hollow steel. An airship's bulkhead doors are flimsy sheets of metal on a frame. Everything on an airship is designed with weight conservation in mind. Here, in contrast, every consideration centred around pressure. The doors were solid lumps of steel, hung on hinges thicker than my forearms. The walls were plated steel, studded with rivets. Each compartment was designed to be sealed individually. As such, every hatch you opened had to be sealed shut behind you. Locked tight with heavy wheels that slid bolts into the bulkheads, the same way a good safe does. If they were sealed, it would take more than a blow torch to reopen them. Should the worst happen and a compartment rupture, then woe betide any unlucky sod stuck the wrong side of one of those doors with water pissing in. It was a death sentence.

Joyfully, as a consequence, none of the corridors were very long. Every couple of dozen yards or so, we would come to another hatch and the guards would prod at me, to encourage me to open them. This was far from easy one handed, those locking wheels were as stiff as an upper lip should be. I struggled with each one manfully, with only a little ungentlemanly language. Luckily for me at least it was the second guard who had to shut the damn things behind us.

These hatchways too were numbered in white paint, below that ever-present stylised squid, which I was already sick of seeing. As we progressed, I tried making some sense of the numbers. Each was a set of three, but whatever code they displayed escaped me at the time. Later, someone or other, explained their significance to me. The ship, I was told, was divided up in a three-dimensional grid. The numbers signified your location by deck, aft to stern and port to starboard. It was a clever idea, I'll admit that much. Had I understood what I was seeing, I would've realised that it spoke of the organised mind behind the submersible's design, but right then I found it all baffling.

After the third successive short corridor, I opened a hatch that led into a square chamber with similar hatches in each wall. In the centre of this chamber was a four-foot hole in the floor that matched another in the ceiling above. In the middle of the hole, a set of ladder rails ran through the room, granting access to other decks. I groaned inwardly as I perceived this, opening hatches with one arm had been difficult enough, climbing ladders one handed was going to be painful.

One of my guards, obliging fellow that he was, grunted at me through his mask and prodded me once more with his weapon while motioning for me to climb. Given he was only going to keep prodding me with the tip of a rather sharp harpoon rifle, it seemed wise to just suck it up and do as instructed. So, climb I did.

It was at this point I got a vague inclination of what the painted numbers were. I realised each sequence I had seen so far had begun with zero-seven, a number which was also painted in a somewhat larger stencil on the walls in the ladder chamber. The one I climbed into was zero-six. That gave me my first real clue as to the sheer size of the vessel I was aboard. Zero-seven had to be the deck number, and given the ladders went up as well as down, this was a fair indication there were more than seven decks. The ship was, I realised, bigger than I'd imagined. Perhaps the size of a reasonable airship, envelope and all, if there were at least eight decks. I risked a look down the hole, which proved inadvisable, as I realised the hole went down several decks below me. The craft was a damn sight larger than any submersible I'd ever heard of. Not that I knew much about them. As I said, as a technology they never really caught on. Sure, they had some limited value for defence but even traditional navies were hardly of great strategic importance in the age of airships. I could think of no government that would willingly waste money on a submersible of this size when they could construct a small fleet of airships for the same cost.

That said, of course, government budgets are ever a dark art...

Climbing a vertical ladder, with three broken ribs and a recently dislocated shoulder is no picnic. It was slow going and bloody agonising, so it was a relief when I stepped off the ladder onto deck zero-six. I stood, trying to catch my breath and trying to ignore the burning in my shoulder as I waited for the guards to ascend, which they did in quick time of course. Except when the first of them stepped off onto the deck next to me, he pointed back at the ladder and upwards. I am, however, nothing if not a man willing to swallow down pain and soldier on regardless with a stiff upper lip.

"Ah you bloody kidding me?" I berated, between bitter breaths.

"Avant," came the reply, in what my rigorous education told me was definably foreign and probably French, a revelation which just added to my general unease.

"Avant," he barked a second time.

I swallowed a sharp reply and proceeded to climb once more, cursing elaborately under my breath, each rung I scaled causing another spike of jarring pain in my side.

"Bloody frogs, snail eating, poncing superior, up their own bloody arses, bastard frogs," I may have muttered under my breath. It's fair to say, like any true Englishman, I hate the French. If there is one thing that we as a nation, rich or poor, can agree on, it is our universal distaste of the bloody garlic eaters. This abhorrence stems from knowing they believe they're culturally superior to the English. A belief we are only too aware of because they take every opportunity to tell us so. The British may have an empire that spans the globe, while they cling to bits of Africa and the scrappy parts of Asia no one else wanted, but according to every Frenchman I've never met and a fair few I have, the French remained superior to the English in every other way. They believe they have more culture, better art, superior food, wine you can actually drink, and of course, bloody existentialism.

And of course, like any true Englishman, my real hatred of the sodding French stems from my innate fear they're right…

But I digress, and do so in a way which paints me a bigoted arse, so as I was saying…

Three more arduous climbs lay ahead until I finally stepped off onto deck zero-three. Climbs accompanied by many a muttered comment alluding to the parentage of our neighbours across the Channel bridge. But finally, I got some respite.

My companions ushered me through a large open hatchway into a section of zero-three that was positively spacious compared to the claustrophobic corridors below. The large chamber spanned the whole deck, port to starboard. It also dispensed with the utilitarian military motif of the lower decks. Inlaid wooden floors instead of deck plates, ornate brass fittings on the walls that had delicate-looking glass lampshades. A set of large wooden chairs with green leather padding were set around a leather-inlaid coffee table, while sturdy bookshelves sat against the walls with what my eye for avarice told me were expensive old hardbacks, and other items of value, on open display. Large portholes lined both outer walls, each a good two feet across, with the glass blistering outward, offering a panoramic view of the ocean depths beyond.

The far inner bulkhead was a huge map, made of polished wood, with the continents set out in relief, while the oceans sank inward. The land masses were a uniform dark teak, but the oceans were layered in a way that reflected some close approximation of different ocean depths, the wood of those oceans stained in various shades of blue, from a light aqua around the coastlines to a blue so dark it was almost black in places where the deepest ocean beds lay. Even I could admire the workmanship that had gone into such a design. Polished wood and brass were everywhere on this deck.

If it wasn't for the slight curve to the oak panelling on the outer walls and those porthole blisters, you could have taken it for a gentleman's study, complete with drinks cabinet, reading lamps and a large desk that doubled as a chart table in front of the map wall. Though everywhere I looked there was that same squid motif.

'*Someone has a real thing about tentacles, Harry,*' I remember thinking, that and that whoever had designed the craft had that most worrying of combinations, a hugely inventive mind and a decidedly one-track imagination.

As I stepped further into the room, the last of my shadows stepped through the hatch behind me. There was an odd rushing sound, like breath over a bottle, and the doorless hatchway closed behind him, six sliding sections rotating inward like fan blades until they sealed over the opening. The blades were each painted with tentacles, so that once they rotated into place they formed a now familiar motif. Etched and inlaid in the stainless-steel blades, the largest stylised squid yet.

The two guards took position either side of the iris hatch, facing me. I was almost amused by this. Why guard the exit? It's not like I'd the faintest idea how to make the damn thing open. The only purpose their presence could serve was to intimidate me, and frankly they'd already succeeded in doing so. Of late I'd developed a bit of a complex when it came to guards wearing breathing masks. True these were not quite as intimidating as The Ministry's Sleepmen, but they weren't far off the mark. Their compatriots in Nepal had hardly inspired warm and fuzzy feelings either. HG Wells had those guards beat me senseless on a couple of occasions, albeit with good reason at the time. But I was all too aware these two had shock batons hung on their belts, not that their harpoon rifles weren't intimidating enough.

So, while I was almost amused, it was a bitter amusement… But when one is in the brown stuff, the only thing that really matters is the depth. As such I did my best to ignore my guards, put a brave face on things, and pretended to be taking in my surroundings unperturbed.

I'd no doubt that I would be waiting a while. Hettie had warned me the Captain wanted to see me, so it was no great leap of mine to realise this was his stateroom. Who else could command a room on a vessel like this that took up the whole width of a deck. There were doors on either side of the map wall that doubtless led to the rest of his quarters. At first, the amount of space given over to the captain's comforts struck me as bizarre, even on a vessel as large as this one. He could host full dinner parties in here should he wish to do so. With a string quartet. But as I waited, as captains always make you wait, I realised it seemed odd to me because I think in terms of airships. Space as well as weight is always at a premium on an airship. Even a fleet admiral could command no more than a small cabin at most. A submersible the sheer size of this vessel obeyed different rules, clearly. Yet even so, that this much space was given over to its captain's vanity proved difficult for me to fully comprehend, and left me wondering what kind of man the captain was.

I pretended to peruse one of the bookcases, then wandered closer to the relief wall to study the map, marvelling at the detail of it even from a distance. For a moment, I even contemplated wandering over to the desk to read the papers scattered on it, amusing myself with the thought that my old employers, The Ministry, would doubtless be interested in whatever I found upon it. Not that I cared one iota what The Ministry might find interesting, all I really cared about right at that moment was how much pain I was in between my headache, busted ribs and buggered shoulder.

'Sod it, Harry,' I thought to myself, 'if the captain's determined I wait on him, I might as well make myself comfortable,' and with that thought I decided to take myself over to one of the leather-backed chairs and sit down. It was in doing so I discovered the furniture was bolted to the floor. It made sense, I realised, considering where we were, but seemed a tad inconvenient. However, as I was now sitting, I decided to stay where I was. It did at least afford me a fine view through one of the portholes, though I suspected the view would be much improved had there been anything to see.

I'd still no idea of the depth we were at, but just like the porthole in my cabin, what lay beyond was nothing but the inky blackness of the ocean depths. My artificial eye deciding not to start playing tricks again, it remained so. Though on occasion as I stared out into the darkness, I saw the merest hints of movement, which would've been fascinating no doubt if I cared at all about the world of fish, whales, and the ocean in general. But my stomach was growling and the only fish I cared about was a battered one on my plate with a generous helping of chips.

But still, there was something mesmerising about the depths of the ocean seen this way and there was little else to see. So, I stared through the porthole and my thoughts drifted back to Hettie Clarkhurst. More exactly, I found myself thinking on what she had said. I had a nagging feeling amongst all that technological babble about bi-lateral induction sucker filter thingummy what's-its, whatever they were, she said something I should've picked up on. Something important, more important than wondering why she was on board this strange submersible.

'*What was it she said?*' I wondered, but the more I thought about it, the harder it was to get a grip on it, as is so often the way. Until… 'Oh…' Realisation struck me, she'd said 'an arm'. Specifically, 'a metal arm' had been dragged through some mechanical gubbings. That's why she was doing running repairs on something or other. Something that had been damaged when it sucked in a metal arm…

'*Oh shit, Harry,*' I berated myself, as I knew someone with a well disguised but assuredly mechanical arm. Someone who had also fallen from The Johan's Lament.

Someone who might not exactly be a friend, but wasn't exactly an enemy at the same time. Someone who had a propensity to turn up at the most annoying regularity, just like a bad…

"Mr Smyth, I believe," said a voice, which in case you were expecting the obvious, was not feminine. As I had just thought of my proverbial friend, this came as a relief. Penny's habit of turning up unexpectedly was matched only by her propensity to inflict pain upon my person shortly afterwards. So, you'll forgive me, if I was glad it wasn't her. The voice was a mans, and if my ear for accents could be believed, a Frenchman at that. Which at least confirmed one of my suspicions.

Though I'd never heard any about the French government building a craft like this, I wouldn't put it past them. It was just the kind of shifty thing the French would get up to. Sneaking about under the waves struck me as a very French sort of idea, but my bias may be showing there.

As it was the respectful thing to do, as this was doubtless the captain of the ridiculous craft I'd been picked up by, I rose to my feet and turned to him.

"And you would be the captain of this remarkably fine vessel, I take it, sir. It is a pleasure to make your acquaintance. I owe you my most sincere thanks for rescuing me from the waves," I said, laying it on thick and offering him my hand, as he strode towards me, all the while trying to take his measure as swiftly as possible.

To be fair the 'captain' was simple deduction, common crewmen wouldn't dress as he did. He was wearing an expensively tailored uniform that had more than a hint of military about it. It had enough tassels even my old 'friend' Vladimir couldn't have helped but be impressed. His uniform also sported a polished steel shoulder guard over his left shoulder, styled into a giant squid with articulated tentacles wrapped around his arm and across his chest, which I can only describe as ostentatious. As was his narrow beard, trimmed to perfection, while his equally narrow moustache hung over a narrow, far from welcoming smile.

"Indeed, I am, sir, and aboard this ship my word is law, my justice swift and I balk no lies. You should bear this in mind as I feel compelled to ask you if you were the one that shot my daughter?" he said, coming to a halt a few feet before me and raising not his hand in welcome but a small harpoon gun, pistol sized, and while doubtless less powerful than the rifles his men carried, at that range it didn't need to be.

As you would expect, my alarmed eyes were drawn to his pistol. It took a moment for me to tear my gaze from the barbed tip pointing my way, and meet his gaze. But what I saw in his eyes did little to ease my alarm. I realised at first glance putting a hole through me was something he'd not the slightest compunction against doing. At second glace I realised something else as well. His eyes had a look about them I recognised all too well, not just because I've seen it on many faces over the years. There was also a familial resemblance. His eyes were remarkably similar to those of another who was in the habit of pointing weapons in my direction. Both guns and other things as sharp as the tip of the pistol's harpoon. Eyes which told me all I needed to know, and what I needed to know was if I gave the wrong answer, a sharp object was very definitely about to come into contact with my body at a high velocity…

Typically, of course, at this point my augmented eye did its favourite trick and narrowed its focus in that familiar vertigo-inducing way on his trigger finger. A finger already tightening on a trigger, it was one wrong word away from pulling.

"Your daughter?" I heard myself enquire, but I knew exactly who his daughter was. It was her eyes I could see in his. I suspected however that he, unlike I, didn't habitually refer to her being his own personal Bad Penny.

In reply, I saw his trigger finger twitch in a most alarming way...

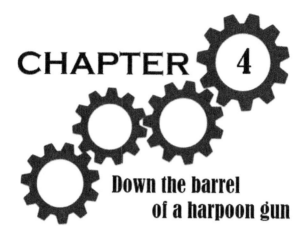

CHAPTER 4

Down the barrel of a harpoon gun

You'd think, when you have found yourself staring down a barrel at certain death as often as I have, you might develop a laissez-faire attitude to such situations. After all, when people threaten to shoot you at the drop of a hat, it perhaps would be only natural to become a little blasé about it. Frankly, I rarely meet anyone who doesn't threaten to shoot me, stab me or bludgeon me unconscious.

Familiarity, as you may have heard, tends to breed contempt. So as I say, you might well imagine that finding myself staring down the wrong end of a harpoon pistol, watching a trigger finger both figuratively and actually, twitch on the trigger, was something I took in my stride. As it were, just another day in the office. No more fear-inducing than a hearty breakfast, or a Sunday afternoon stroll in the park.

You'd be wrong of course… I was terrified.

"I asked you a question, Mr Smyth. When I ask questions, I expect them to be answered," the captain said, with a calm assuredness, at odds to how I felt.

"I didn't shoot Penny," I told him. Which resulted in him narrowing his eyes at me, and his finger itching a little more.

"That is not her name," he said, a response which it seemed was a hereditary comeback.

"I know," I admitted, trying to gather what you might laughingly call my wits about me. It was clear he required a broader explanation from me. Which was fair enough, as I was happy to provide one if it helped avoid me being turned into a kabab. I did so, fighting my base instinct to exaggerate and lie, as I took him through the events atop The Johan's Lament. That fight was a rear-guard action, of course, and I may've tried to paint myself in a slightly better light as I did so.

The version of events I outlined did have me in a more… 'heroic' role, you might say. In this version, when Saffron Wells shot at his daughter I'd leapt to her defence, manfully trying to intercede between her and the path of the bullet. As I told it, it was to my mortal regret I failed to act quicker, and wished I'd taken the bullet myself. The most I'd done was manage to shove her to one side, but I was sure my intervention saved his daughter's life as the bullet would have certainly struck her in the heart had I not intervened. And of course, it wasn't a mere pistol that The Ministry's diabolical influence had caused Miss Wells to level at his daughter. Not, it had been a machine gun, one of those heavy steam-powered ones which could shred a man to ribbons in but a moment. But, while I raged at this indignity, I'd done all I could to protect his daughter's life and keep her safe. I swore to him that it was ill luck and ill luck alone that proved my undoing. But for foul luck, why, I'd have taken down our assailant single handed to defend his daughter. I was mortified, truly, truly mortified, when 'Penny', as I call her – a pet name, he should understand, that stems from a mutual fondness of each other – had plunged over the side. I, of course, had leapt after her, trying vainly, it saddened me to say, to grasp her outstretched hand. The final twist, was that, as our beseeching fingertips almost touched, that was the moment we were finally undone as Miss Wells, slave as she was to the machinations to the maniacal 'M', cut our safety lines and I and his fair daughter plummeted through the sky, to the unwelcoming depths below…

"How much of the cheval-merde do you expect me to swallow?" the captain asked, his tone still even regardless of his words.

I noted though, with some relief, his pistol did lower a little.

"I make it a point not to lie to a man pointing a gun at me," I lied…

The captain laughed, a laugh both cynical and measured, then he smiled thinly. "Let me put that another way, Mr Smyth. How much of your 'entertaining' story will my dear Vivienne collaborate when she awakens?"

'Ah,' I thought, this I will admit was a minor flaw to my gambit. I'd failed to consider in my elaborations of events, somewhat lamentably, that the captain had said, 'shot' rather than 'killed'. Isn't it always the way, these little nuances occur to you, a moment after you've dug yourself a hole, thrown yourself in it, and invited the other person to bury you…

"Most of it… Well, some of it… I mean, it was Saffron who shot her, she'll confirm that certainly…" I told him, backtracking faster than a raw squaddie who'd just discovered the lady of the night in the Vietnamese brothel his 'mates' had set him up with, wasn't entirely a lady…

The captain's eye's pierced my own, his nose twitching at me, then he seemingly came to a decision of some kind and placed his pistol on a table by his side, before picking up a small bell that sat beside it. This he rang twice, before returning it back where it came from and standing with his hands clasped behind his back, waiting.

It was at this point it occurred to me to ask a question. A question which would doubtless have been wiser asked when he first entered the room.

"How is Vivienne?" I inquired, for once politically astute enough to use Bad Penny's real name, given the circumstances. I'll admit it didn't slip between my lips easily. I'd been thinking of her as my own personal Bad Penny for some time. In truth, I've never really taken to her real name. Her father may have been remarkable in many aspects. But he and her mother clearly lacked a measure in the department of taste, least ways when it came to naming their children.

Not that I've ever been called upon to make such a decision, but I've always felt appellation alliteration is a spiteful burden to place upon a child's shoulders.

You can, as I'm sure you will, infer from this that I'd deduced the good captain's name. His real name, that is. Further to this, his real identity. I can claim little cerebral credit on that score, I'd learned Bad Penny's real name some time before. And if you wonder why I've reneged on sharing that information with you, dear reader, well you must allow for a little dramatic licence. Besides, I'm somewhat fond of the non de plume I gave her, as you've no doubt realised by now.

"My daughter is recovering, though as of this moment she is heavily sedated. Fortunately, my surgeon informs me she is no longer critical, luckily for you."

I didn't like the sound of that 'luckily for you' one bit.

But he continued, "Unfortunately, her arm was shredded by machinery shortly after her… landing. Luckily not her real one, but the interface between the mechanical and flesh is… Delicate, shall we say. She fared worse than you in the fall. Which is somewhat remarkably. You seem to have avoided much the way of trauma, that she did not. She will be on opioids for a while, and it will be some time before she is fully recovered. My dear Vivienne is a delicate flower."

While telling me all this, he motioned at me to retake my seat, though he showed no inclination to do the same. He also kept his pistol close at hand, leaving me in no doubt that he'd take it up again if I was fool enough to assault him. Not that I was fool enough to do anything of the kind. But his caution may have been down to knowledge of the spiders and what they did. He might well suspect I wasn't entirely free of The Ministry's control.

For my own sake, I hoped he was wrong on that score.

Taking my seat, I tried and failed to think of my proverbial Bad Penny as a delicate flower. Fathers are ever blind to the truth about their daughters, I suspect, as I came up rather short on that score.

Another seaman entered the salon, through a door at my rear. He was dressed much like my guards, but without the half-mask, and his uniform had a more decorative quality to it which suggested he was a junior officer or ranking NCO with special duties. I deduced from this he was likely the captain's valet. Not that he'd the aspect of a man born to any role other than thuggery, he was, however, carrying a silver tea service on a matching tray, and his manners seemed impeccable despite his visage.

"Ah Philippe, please serve my guest tea. I shall take my café, of course," the captain said robustly, which I suspect was for my benefit, his man clearly knowing what he was about. "You take tea, of course, Mr Smyth. Being as you are an English Gentleman?" he added, turning to me, a tinge of the snide in his tone as he said those last two words.

This had all the hallmarks of a test of some kind, though I wondered if his vitriol was directed at me personally or the nation of my birth. I suspected the good captain was no anglophile, though few Frenchmen are in my experience. I've seldom met a Frenchman who lacked a certain bigotry towards the subjects of our seldom amused monarch. Honestly, how a whole people can hold so much vitriol against neighbours separated by the smallest strip of sea, I will never understand. But in my experience, it's typical of the bloody frogs. They're all soft cheese eating, snail botherers, in my opinion.

Okay, yes, I know alright. What can I say? My hypocrisy should hardly come as a surprise to you by now…

"That would be most kind," I replied, with a smile, not to rise to the insinuation in his words.

'Philippe' placed his silver tray on the small table beside the chair. Then, to my unbridled horror, he poured a dash of milk into the cup… before pouring the tea.

I swear I detected a thin malicious smile pass his captain's lips. For a moment I locked eyes with this blighter 'Phillipe', unsurprised to see he lacked the blank visage of a true valet. Indeed, his own grin matched that of his captain, leaving me in no doubt that this heinous act had been perpetrated deliberately in order to get a rise out of me.

Regardless of this deliberate insult, and, even if I say so myself, in a fine display of English reserve in the face of infamy, I managed to hold myself in check, limiting myself to merely narrowing my eyes and gifting him a momentary twitch of my moustache in my rage as he then poured the tea.

"Sugar or lemon, monsieur?" the valet inquired in the condescending tone of a waiter of his native land.

"Neither," I replied tersely.

"Very well, monsieur," the swine said, with a neat little bow of the head, placing the foul concoction of pre-milked tea before me. He then turned to his captain, nodding his head with all due reverence and moved off to the back of the room once more.

With a measure of distaste I tried to hide, I sipped at the tea and returned my gaze to the captain. By the second sip, I was feeling a little nonplussed as the tea apparently tasted perfectly fine. This despite being poured by a Frenchman, and the product of an act that my old mum in her short period of religious fervour with the cult of Gloriuiana, would have sworn was heresy. Though even discounting those frankly barmy cultists that worship Old Iron Knickers as a demigoddess, taking the milk first, well it's just not done. The Queen's butler adds milk after the tea is poured, such is therefore the only correct way to do so. As it was even in the dark times before her ascension to primacy in the court of St James. It is just the civilised way. After all, how else can you know how much milk is required to make the tea to your taste?

The captain studied me a moment or two while I drank, then with a slight nod towards the back of the room, he spoke once more.

"I am No One, Mr Smyth, Captain No One, a monogram I chose, for I will I serve no nation and no cause, but my own. I reject the notion of national borders and the false deities of colonialism. Thus, I set my old name aside and I have become No One…" he explained to me in a way that sounded a little too rehearsed. I can't say I followed his logic. He reminded me all too much of HG Wells. But that, I guess, is of little surprise. Wells was as mad as the proverbial hatter, so why would his co-conspirators be any different?

"I see, Monsieur Verne," I replied steadily.

This was, I shall admit, was a rather foolish riposte on my part. But damn it all, I'd fallen from an airship, taken a swim in the Pacific, suffered a clout to the head, had his guards point their lethal-looking guns at me, had them force me to climb up through his damn rust bucket of a submersible with a recently dislocated shoulder and to top it all off, he'd had some bastard pour my tea the wrong way.

I was feeling petulant…

"Indeed, Mr Smyth, indeed… But, do we not all sometimes choose the names by which we go, 'Arry'," Captain 'No-One' replied, in a two can play at that game, kind of way.

"Even so," I said, checking my temper, then gifted him a genuine smile. I was long past the point where discovering people knew the name I was given at birth surprised me. So instead I bought myself a moment by sipping at the irritatingly excellent tea, before changing tack with a tad more delicacy.

"If you will pardon my question, why chose the name No One? Even accepting your wish to unfetter yourself of nationalistic concerns, it seems a strange moniker to adopt," I asked, which was perhaps a little direct, I know, but I was trying to weigh the man. He was my latest captor after all. Besides which, he struck me as a man in love with his idea of himself, as all lunatic radicals are, so there was a chance I could learn something useful about him by encouraging him to explain.

'Offer a preacher a pulpit and you'll get a sermon every time,' as an archbishop's ageing dominatrix once told me over a sherry between clients.

Mags was a sweet old girl who rented a room at 'The Elves' when I was a boot boy there. She was always a little disparaging of the clergy, who made up rather a large percentage of Mrs T's client base, though reputedly she was also devilish with her cane whenever she had a cabinet minister on his knees before her.

But I digress, so reminiscences of my childhood aside…

"Perhaps it seems so, Mr Smyth, but it suits my purpose," he replied stiffly, then his eyes softened for a moment, lost in early times. "I've a fondness for the name. I used it once in a novel, though I used the Latin version of the same. It was a jest on my part. One that only the clever reader could discern. In that novel, he was the captain of a vessel not dissimilar to my own. And so when this craft was constructed and I took on the mantel of captain, I thus became No One, my own creation. It is a useful subterfuge at times."

"So you were a writer, like Wells? One of his contemporises?"

"As you are no doubt already aware, Mr Smyth, my good friend Herbert's loose tongue on such matters is fabled, but it is of no matter. I can hardly berate him while he lays in the hands of our Russian friends," he said, managing to infer I knew more than I actually did. But I could live with that. It is always better they think you know more than you do. Whoever 'they' happen to be. People are far more likely to tell you things if they think you already know.

Unless of course 'they' are torturing you for information you don't have, which is another of those unfortunate things that I have learned over the years…

"I see. Well, I must thank you once more for the rescue. I presume you were tracking The Johan somehow? Hence you were on hand to pull me and your daughter out of the drink?" I asked, as it seemed the reasonable assumption. I had a vague recollection of overhearing Penny say something along the lines of 'No One will help us' a few times to Saffron back aboard The Johan while I was recovering from the fallout of Nepal. Worryingly, I recalled the whole 'No One will help' was a bone of contention between them. Though what I remembered were merely snippets of conversation heard between bouts of consciousness, which seemed at the time to be Penny bemoaning our fate, not speaking of a possible rescuer. That said, there had definitely been something of resignation in her voice. I may have misread it at the time but it led me now to suspect that everything wasn't sunshine and roses between her and her father. That didn't bode well. Bad Penny vexed is a state that seldom ends well and often who it didn't end well for was yours truly.

I tried not to worry myself about that little nugget. Of course, as it proved, I didn't worry myself anything like as much as I should've, but I'll not to get ahead of myself…

"Indeed, Mr Smyth, we had planned to rendezvous with The Johan at Musk Island. But as your ship was drifting off course, I took it upon myself to 'dog your footsteps' as you English say," the captain explained.

This was news to me, save for the drifting part. The Johan had been down to a single, poorly maintained engine. An engine that was itself strained to its maximum and on the verge of breaking down. Our instruments were all over the shop and several damaged beyond repair in the battle. We'd also been leaking precious lifting gas for days before our doomed attempt to stifle our descent. So, of course we'd been drifting. What was news to me was that we'd even had a destination planned to drift off course from. I felt mildly aggrieved by this new intelligence if I'm honest. I'd been the Johan's captain after all, even if in name only. Admittedly the only direction I'd cared about at the time was any direction that led us away from Nepal, and between bouts of unconsciousness after our escape from the temple, even 'in name only' was vague. I wasn't exactly a trusted colleague and confidant of Mistresses Wells and Verne, and they were the ones really in charge.

I guess it's no surprise the two ladies chose not to take me into their confidence. You're doubtless as unsurprised by this turn of events as I... But still I felt somewhat bitter to discover just how little they had shared with me, on my own command.

"Musk Island?" I inquired, vaguely and left it hanging. The name meant nothing to me, though there are thousands of remote islands littering the Pacific, so that was hardly a surprise.

"It's listed under another name on most charts, Malay, I believe," the captain explained. "The Dutch built a naval station there in the seventeenth century, then the trade routes all moved north of the Sunda strait, so it served no purpose and they abandoned it. It was in fact roundly forgotten by the world, which served my purposes for a while. Now however, it's the solo province of an 'associate' of mine. Doctor Musk. Technically I leased it under another name from the Dutch government some years ago, though I doubt they are even aware of its existence anymore. It was to them a worthless little rock, with little remarkable about it save a good quantity of pumice they could get elsewhere. The 'good' Doctor asked to take over the island as it lies close to the equator, which makes it ideal for his purposes."

There was something in the captain's voice that betrayed a degree of personal resentment towards the 'good' Doctor, as he put it. I wasn't inclined to push him on that, but stored the little nugget away at the back of my mind, in case it became useful. As it was, Verne was proving unusually open with these little snippets of useful information. Yet that very openness worried me, call me paranoid, cynical or both, but in my experience, you only get such openness from men like Verne when they have a grip on your privates and not in the pleasant ways inspired by a whole other kind of openness...

From where I was sitting, I could see his guards, their expressions unreadable thanks to their rebreathers, but their eyes remained trained on me like hawks. Their presence didn't make me feel entirely welcome in the captain's salon, neither did Verne. I was sure if I'd fallen into the ocean in less exalted company, Captain 'No One' and his crew would've sailed beneath me without a second thought. As such, I was a less than welcome 'guest' aboard this vessel, and knew it. Though given the alternative, I was delighted to remain so, until some other option presented itself. *'Perhaps this Doctor Musk chap will be amenable... tropical island, could be worse places to end up,'* I remember musing.

"Hum..." I uttered, while pretending to contemplate the map wall. Then, thinking more was required of me, I feigned some careful consideration of matters before I continued. "Well, The Johan is likely to have come down before she reached anywhere. I doubt she stayed airborne another day... Thinking on that, how much time has passed since you pulled us out of the drink? She might be downed already."

In truth, I'd not a clue where we were relative to anywhere else on the map. How far we had travelled across the Indian Ocean or where I had taken the swan dive. The instrumentation on The Johan had been shot, literally in some cases. But what I did remember, all too well, was the already leaking air frame being shredded by Penny's claws as she tried to prevent her fall. So The Johan, crippled as it had been, was never going to stay aloft for long. Thinking of the fate of my old command, I took on a grim expression that wasn't entirely acting on my part. Then added, "There were a lot of people aboard her. Poor sods will probably drown, unless we can do something about it."

I wasn't entirely sure why I said that last bit. The only person that would have still been on board, that I'd cared a wit about, was Saffron Wells and she wasn't exactly herself anymore. I guess if I was cynical, I said those words because sounding concerned for the fate of others is just something one does. Particularly when you're trying to present yourself as a gentleman to a man pointing a gun at you, which the captain may as well have been. Then again, perhaps I was being entirely genuine for once. Looking back, I'm not sure which is true. It's strange, is it not, when our own motives no longer seem clear even to ourselves.

Maybe I was becoming a better man, and what a dreadful thought that is…

Either way, given all the events that followed, suggesting we seek out survivors of The Johan's Lament proved to be a damn foolish suggestion, but I wasn't to know that at the time.

"Indeed, Mr Smyth, as a fellow captain, I of course understand your concern for your crew. Let me assure you, once we're repaired, we will be continuing our journey. Perhaps we shall yet discover the fate of The Johan's Lament. If, of course, it hasn't been swallowed by a whale…" Verne laughed at his own joke. A nasty little laugh, it seemed to me, with less humour than spite in it. A laugh which reminded me once again of both HG Wells and the malignant M.

"Besides," Verne continued, "I require the facilities of Musk Island to put my sweet Vivienne back together after the accident, so our course is set for now. In time, of course, we must find a way to release my compatriot from Russia's grasp, but one step at a time, wouldn't you agree, Mr Smyth?"

I swallowed hard, and gave a little cough to hide the queasiness that suggestion inspired in my stomach. Trying to spring someone from the cells below the Kremlin, assuming that's where they were holding Wells, didn't sound like a job for someone who enjoyed a long-life expectancy. The casual way Verne brought up the subject just drove home the realisation I was still in the middle of the whole Wells, Ministry situation. I had a sudden sinking feeling all this was going to lead to me finding myself press ganged into something ridiculously dangerous again. But as hope springs eternal, and you never know your luck in a rusty old submersible several fathoms down in the midst of the Indian Ocean, I found myself asking if…

"I don't suppose you could drop me off somewhere on route, could you? Perhaps, I don't know, you could let me off at this Musk Island, or something?" Yet, even while I asked those questions, I was sure it was a somewhat vain hope. Though an equatorial island, miles from anywhere, sounded rather inviting. Particularly, I considered, if there was a steady supply of rum. And who knows, maybe the odd native girl or two, running around in grass skirts, lei garlands and little else…?

Captain Verne, or No One as he preferred, laughed, that same nasty little laugh. Then told me, "I doubt you'll want to stay with my 'good' friend Elonis, Mr Smyth. He is, how you English say, a little eccentric… but we shall see… Maybe you'll wish to join him in his plan to colonise Mars. Yes?"

"His plan to what?" I asked incredulously, though he was clearly pulling my leg by this point.

He chose not to reply however. Clearly, he was done with me now. So, he turned to the door and waved over his guards before instructing them to 'escorte-moi jusqu'au medecin du navire' which I grasped enough of to realise he was sending me to the ship's doctor, presumably to have him look at my injuries once more, now I was conscious.

That was something I suppose. I've generally found people don't bother sending you for medical attention if they're planning to kill you later.

Most of them anyway…

"You have the run of the ship, Mr Smyth, but don't go anywhere you shouldn't," the captain informed me as I was escorted back to the iris hatchway.

I stopped for a moment, to my guard's disgruntlement, but as it seemed prudent to do so, I turned back and asked him, "How will I know if somewhere is a place I shouldn't go?"

At which Captain No One, or Jules Verne if you prefer, laughed that nasty little gallic laugh of his, and smiled at me. "Oh, I expect when you're shot, you'll know… Good day, Mr Smyth."

"Good day, Captain.," I said, with all the pleasantness I could muster. Despite the laugh, I found myself entirely sure he was serious. Call it an instinct. The instinct that develops when you spend a lot of time around people who make a point of threatening to kill you. Eventually, you get attuned to the difference between an idle threat and a genuine one.

Just that once, I'd happily have taken an idle threat for a change.

CHAPTER 5

The Hettie Clarkhurst experience

As I may have eluded in the past, I, like any right-thinking Englishman, hate the French. It is, I will admit, a lazy kind of hatred, little more than a certain distaste for the gallic, if we are honest. It's the kind of distasteful hatred you adopt through osmosis in your youth.

That is to say, it's a hatred born of cultural influences. The kind of instinctive dislike that is hard to quantify as it has no real reason behind it. It is just a truth you accept because to you the reason has always been patently obvious. You hate the French, because hating the French is just the British thing to do. As such, this hatred of the French is a very human thing. Which is to say, flawed.

In essence, it's both trivial and wrong headed by any margin. And if you are honest with yourself then frankly a better man would rise above such things. The better man would in fact put such childish petty distaste behind him as he gets older, and wiser. I'm sure you agree…

I'm not the better man.

In my defence, however, I've found the French don't much like the English either. Something I was painfully reminded about by my visit to the ship's surgeon. He was, shall we say, less than gentle. Whatever the French equivalent of 'first do no harm' apparently didn't cover poking broken ribs with a pencil and yanking about a recently dislocated shoulder. He did this while calling me, and the English in general, a variety of colourful insulting names, which were not covered by my schoolboy French, but ones my brothel and bar room French understood perfectly well. Then he strapped my ribs back up again with bandages, causing me more than a little pain in the process, tightening them so much it felt like he was strapping me into a tart's corset.

If nothing else, this gave me a new-found appreciation of the brutal proclivities of female fashion.

Then, once this indignity was over, he forced a box of painkillers into my hands, for which I was somewhat grateful, though I presumed they were as much for the pain he'd just inflicted as for that of my residual injuries. As the surgeon spoke no English, he explained I needed to take them twice a day by first pointing at the bottle, rising one finger and tapping on the bottle with it. Then he vaguely waved his hand in a crescent motion which I suspect was meant to imply the passage of the sun. Then he raised a finger again, repeated the whole passage of the sun mime, tapped the box. After this odd bit of street theatre miming, he raised two fingers in a way that could've been an insult, or was stressing I needed to take two a day, or both.

I suspect the former.

After this I was ushered out of the surgery, so I grabbed the bottle and left. My chaperones then indicated where I should go with the point of their harpoon rifles and as I make a point not to argue with men carrying weapons that can impale you without even being fired, I did as instructed.

The guards marched me down a level, which meant ditching the damn sling again while I climbed, more pain, and having to suppress the desire to argue with the men with pointy guns. But thankfully it wasn't long, or far, before they left me to my own devices after they showed me to a mess hall.

I thanked them for being "so jolly helpful", which earned me a grunt as they turned away. But as just this once I'd not been beaten senseless by the mask-wearing thugs that had been instructed to deal with me, I was almost being genuine in my regards. So I waited till their backs were turned before telling them they could both take two a day, as the doctor almost certainly hadn't meant… And entered the galley in search of something to line my stomach before I ignored the doc's advice and took a couple of days' worth of pills.

Pleasingly, the ship's galley-hand had a few words of English, though most of these were curse words, which he directed at me as he dumped a tray of stodge in front of me that could only be called edible by the French. However, despite my reservations about what I assumed was fish in some kind of white sauce, I was ravenous. Besides, I was aware there is a certain wisdom to eating before you take an excessive amount of painkillers. So I grinned my best idiot grin, nodded politely to him and ignored the insults. Then taking the tray in my good hand, I made my way over to an empty table.

About five minutes later, while I was forcing down a lukewarm fish dinner, the whole galley shuddered violently for a moment, then as this tailed off to a steady vibration in the deck plates, an equally steady 'thrumming' pitch filled out the background noise in the mess, causing every conversation to become a little louder. Between the vibrations and the dull thrumming, I realised the engines must have come back on line. It was at once both a familiar, welcoming, sensation and a disturbing one to my airman's senses. The pitch was erroneous to my ear and the vibrations disquieting as they were off slightly. It is hard to put into words, but it was a sense of the familiar and the unfamiliar in tandem that made me slightly nervous. Like listening to a song, one you know well, being played slightly out of key. As such, I found it disconcerting and it made me feel ill at ease.

Of course, being aboard a ship full of Frenchmen carrying harpoon guns wasn't helping either.

Despite my unease, I struggled on, manfully masticating what was on the plate before me, while trying to ignore the flavour which wasn't nearly bland enough. I had managed to almost finish this unappetising repast by the time Hettie put her head around the mess room door. Seeing me sitting there, uncomfortably eating my last morsel of cold fish, she sauntered over.

"There you are, you reprobate," she said, plonking herself down opposite me. Her face unsurprisingly covered in grease marks, she treated me to a broad grin. Grease marks that were also prevalent on her arms and overalls, come to that, while her hair had clearly fought a battle against the Alice band holding it in place, had defeated that foe and run riot. You could say what sat before me was in essence the full Hettie Clarkhurst experience. Right down to the tool belt that hung low around her ample hips.

Hettie had, I assumed, come straight from the engine room, clearly having asserted her authority on assorted lug-nuts, gears, and bolts. Knowing her, she'd wrestled the engines back to life single-handedly. The smile and her demeanour certainly suggested she had been in her happy place. Elbow deep in an oily gusset, or some such thing.

With a wave, Hettie grabbed the galley-hand's attention, exchanged a nod with him, then turned back to me, still smiling brightly. "So how did the meeting with the old man go?" she asked.

"Well, he didn't shoot me. I take that as a good sign," I replied with a smidgeon too much bitterness to my tone, judging by the way she narrowed her eyes at me.

"The thing you need to realise, Hannibal, is the captain's very protective of his daughter," Hettie, the font of all wisdom, explained, with an unusual seriousness.

"I noticed," I said, and pushed my now empty tray away. I was feeling tetchy, my aching head no better for eating, and as I rubbed my eyes, a fresh stab of pain when I raised my arm reminded me of the pills in my pocket.

"She was in a hell of a state when they fished the two of you out of the drink. No One wants answers and he doesn't know you from Adam. Good thing too. If he knew you half as well as I do, old lad, he might have left you in the water," she said, though she smiled broadly as she did so, which suggested she was joking. Though it wouldn't have surprised me if she wasn't. "Anyway, he wants answers. Truthfully… I can't say he is alone. What the hell were you doing with Vivienne Verne?" she asked, using my Bad Penny's given name.

"It's a long story," I told her. I didn't want to get into it right then. In part because while I was eating, it had occurred to me that Hettie hadn't been in England at the time of my arrest. It was possible, by extension, she was blissfully unaware of my recent fall from grace. So, for selfish reasons I'd determined the longer that remained the case, the better. I was happy to find myself reacquainted with an old friend from 'The Ins & Outs', but I was under no illusions as to what would happen when she learned I was persona non grata back home. Our relationship would swiftly be under more strain than one of Old Brass Nipples' corsets after a state banquet.

Besides anything else, after my trial, I'd supposedly been strung up on a New Bailey gibbet. My avoidance of that fate was a secret to all but The Ministry, an organisation that itself didn't technically exist. My continued existence might therefore take some explaining, and some rather elaborate lying into the bargain. Which wouldn't normally be much of an issue for me, it's true, but lying to an old drinking buddy like Hettie, particularly Hettie, would have left a bitter taste in my mouth. Even more bitter than the dreadful fish I'd just eaten.

That all said, I wasn't sure my escape from the noose was much of a secret anymore. Not after Nepal and everything else. It was fairly safe to assume neither Hannibal Smyth, or even plain old Harry remained listed as 'On Her Majesty's Service' anymore. Though I didn't doubt The Ministry would have me on another list should I ever surface and draw their gaze again. I knew full well should I returned to any part of the Empire then I would have to consider myself lucky if I was merely arrested. Though I doubted The Ministry bothered with such nuisances as trials.

"I'm sure it is, you old dog. She's a bit of a wild cat by all accounts, just your type in fact…" Hettie ribbed at me, with a dirty grin that had little to do with smudges of engine grease.

"She is not…" I snapped back, perhaps a little too quickly, judging by Hettie's laughter.

"Sure she is, just like that barmaid down Stratham. The one from The Nag's Head. What was her name?"

"I assure you that Miss Verne is nothing like Lilly Little," I said, defensively, but that's what talking to Hettie does to you. She has a way of wheedling the truth out of a man.

It's the cheerful enthusiasm that gets you.

"I don't remember anything little about Lilly…" Hettie joked, her eyes alive with humour.

This was all, in fairness, true enough. Mr Little's daughter wasn't a girl who embodied her name and she'd definitely been a bit on the wild side. I remember one night she came at me with a broom handle after I mistakenly rolled into The Nag's half cut with some chaps from the club. Which was a damn fool thing to do considering I'd blown off several dates with Lilly, by telling her I was on an extended patrol over the Balkans.

I was also seeing a delightful half Italian waitress called Liza d'Poca from The Elves at the same time. A relationship which also ended badly, with me dodging a rack's worth of freshly polished boots being slung with some venom at me across the bar room. Frankie had to ban me from the establishment for a month, and I was left nursing a black eye caused by the heel of a size nine cavalry boot. I was just thankful the boot in question had been bereft of spurs at the time.

It was also around then I learned a plethora of Italian swear words, as well as the Italian, for of all things, 'little'. As well as a vital life lesson. This being, if you're going to carry on behind the backs of two girls at once, you should make sure they're not related… Apparently, Lilly and Liza were not too distant cousins. It turned out only one of their fathers had changed the family name when the brothers d'Poca had moved to England in their twenties. It also turned out that a week before the barrage of boots incident, Lilly and Liza had been comparing notes about their respective boyfriends at a family wedding.

The same wedding I'd managed to blow off two invitations for, with the same vague excuse about duty, service to the crown, and patrols over the Balkans… which

I had managed to do without realising it was the same bloody nuptials.

I wasn't actually in the Balkans of course. I'd been on a rugby club piss up in Bath, trying to chat up a delightful west country bar maid whose name was probably Sandra Small, though I'm damned if I can remember, and I woke up alone in a hedge as far as I recall.

Good times…

But anyway, over-complex reminiscences aside, Hettie was among the chaps I rolled into The Nag's Head with the night Lilly took at me with a broom. She'd also laughed as loudly as the rest of them when I'd beat a hasty exit through the lounge bar with Lilly Little chasing me in earnest. Needless to say, I had to stop drinking in The Nag's after that night. This was a shame, for an Italian Mr Little kept a surprisingly good stout…

Begrudgingly I shared the joke, then shrugged. "Well, that's true enough but no, it's nothing like that. Me and Penny were working together, that's all."

Hettie gave me a look that suggested she didn't entirely believe me, and she knew me too damn well. "Sure, that's why you've a pet name for her and everything, right?" she needled.

Not wishing to get into that minefield, I tried to steer the subject away from Captain Verne's daughter. "Look, let's put my Bad Penny on one side, shall we? What the hell are you doing on her papa's ship? Aren't you supposed to be in the Antarctic, making charts, or doing something unnatural to penguins, or whatever?"

Hettie's joviality slipped away, a hard look replacing the easy smile. "That's its own long story," she said to me, coldly.

It occurred to me then, considering where we were, Hettie might have her own secrets. Ones she had no more desire to share than I my own. I wasn't entirely devoid of sympathy on that score.

"Fair's, fair, I guess… Perhaps we can trade stories at some point," I told her, trying to sound dismissive and keep my curiosity in check. If nothing else, our mutual reticence on the how and whys each of us came to be sharing a table in a submersible a few hundred feet beneath the Indian Ocean, put us on a common footing. Though my interest was piqued. The Henrietta Clarkhurst I had known in London'd had no business mixed up with the likes of Monsieur Verne and HG Wells. Though all considered, the same could be said for me.

Sometimes life happens… Things get complicated.

With conversation stifled for the moment, I pulled the bottle of pills from my pocket, ostensibly to examine it, mostly to avoid more awkwardness. I was though wondering, in the absent sort of way one does, if they were the sort of pills you shouldn't take with alcohol. You know the kind, the ones that reacted with drink to send you into a stupor. But as everything written on the label was in forcign, I couldn't tell. 'Probably,' I concluded anyway. They almost always are. I've long suspected that pharmacists purposely put something in pills to make that happen, just so doctors can delight in telling a chap he can't drink when he's on them. Spiteful buggers in my experience, your average sawbones. Still, if in doubt the wise course would obviously be to avoid strong liquor while taking painkillers, as I was well aware.

"Don't suppose you know where I can get something to drink on this tub, old chap?" I asked Hettie.

She eyed the bottle of pills, raised an eyebrow at me and chuckled. "I've a half decent single malt in my cabin, but balls to wasting that on you if you're just gonna chuck it back up," she said, smiling again. "What are the pills for?"

"Painkillers from the quack," I explained, then corrected myself. "At least I think they are, blighter didn't speak a word of the Queen's…"

"He does, you know. Speaks it like he was born in bloody Clapham." Hettie smirked.

"Then why the hell didn't he say so? He just waved his arms at me and prattled on in French."

"Oh, the doc hates the English, so he likes winding us up." She laughed.

"Typical bloody Frog!" I raged.

"Keep yer voice down, you prat, and don't say the bloody F word around here if you value your hide. I swear, you haven't changed a lick, Smyth, have you?" she scolded in hushed tones. Rightly, I realised. Glancing about, more than one of the gallic faces in the galley were giving me the hard stare.

"Sorry, sorry," I said loudly, raising my hands in an act of contrition to placate the snail eaters. My apology though fell well short of easing the sudden tension in the mess.

"Ignorez-le, il passe une mauvaise journée," Hettie told them, whatever that means. It had the desired effect whatever it was. As one, they turned back to whatever they'd been doing as, while they may have cared little for me, Hettie clearly had their respect. Knowing her, it was respect she'd battered into them by the brute force of her personality and where that failed her fists. Hettie's never been anyone's wilting wall flower when it comes to expressing her dissatisfaction with anyone who gets on her wrong side.

I cleared my throat loudly, in a vain attempt to hide my embarrassment. Then in a somewhat measure tone, I asked, "If the doc hates the English so much he won't speak the language, how do you know he does?"

"Because he tried that bullshit on me when I joined the crew. I needed some tablets for…" she began explaining before breaking off a moment and lowering her voice in a most un-Hettie way. She also went a shade of red for a moment and choked down a cough to hide equally her un-Hettie-like embarrassment. "Well, that is… I needed some painkillers for… well… There're times a girl… Look, my French wasn't up to explaining woman's… Wasn't quite up to explaining what I needed and when he started miming stuff at me, I lumped him one."

I managed to choke back the laughter. In all honesty, for fear she might lump me for laughing. The thought of her spannering the doctor was causing my amusement. I'd have given much to witness the look on his face just before the punch landed.

What I wasn't laughing at was her embarrassment. Never that. If Hettie Clarkhurst had one blind spot, it was to do with womanly things. She never liked talking about her monthly visitors. She'd happily converse on absolutely anything else to do with bodily functions or anything to do with sex come to that. I've seen Hettie make grown men blush on more than one occasion. Yet when it comes to that one subject… Well, my guess is Hettie suspected it's the one subject that would make the chaps treat her differently, which let us be honest here is probably true.

Most chaps tend to shy away from the particular subject, myself included. That said, I've occasionally mused that our reluctance to discuss a woman's menstrual cycle is a little odd, because if chap's had 'monthly issues' we'd turn them into a glorified pissing contest in no time. The changing room banter at the rugby club would swift make a bloke getting his mensie's a rite of passage. We'd be competing with each other when it came to stories of how we fought through the cramps and soldiered on despite a tidal flow of epic proportions every month…

'You wouldn't believe the flow I had,' 'Talk about the red army on the march,' 'High tide, more like rip tide, and the cramps, oh the cramps… You couldn't take it, I'll tell you that for nothing…'

All without ever mentioning that in reality each of us curled up on the bathroom floor in agony, screaming for our mothers in secret for three days a month. Gods no, we'd never admit it to another bloke.

But I digress and frankly as digressions go, this one is a tad distasteful even by my standards.

"Good to see you've not changed, old chap," I said to Hettie, with a smile, in an attempt to ease her embarrassment.

She eyed me with suspicion, before switching her glance to my bottle of pills, with a thoughtful, somewhat sly smile. Then she chortled to herself, which I found slightly unnerving. "Well, you're still not having my single malt, but as it happens, I'm chief engineer on this boat, and well, as you know, I'm a good engineer…" she said, before getting to her feet and grabbing the pill bottle off the table. Then the chortle turned into an almost girlish laugh that seemed utterly out of character as she motioned me to follow her, saying, "Come on old lad, let's get you sorted out, shall we?"

In my defence, I was still a bit dazed and under the weather, so it took me a moment or two to catch on, but as light dawned I found myself smiling as I rose to follow her. Hettie was chief engineer on that tub, I remembered. If there was always one person you could be sure could find booze on any ship, be it ocean going, an airship, or doubtless something even as unconventional as a submersible, it was the chief. Admittedly, engine room hooch is only called booze because if they admitted it was drain cleaner, you wouldn't drink it… But as it had been a long day and I felt like Hell, I was prepared to take my chances that it would get me drunk before it killed me.

What's life without the odd foolish gamble…

With the prospect of poisoning myself in mind, I fell in behind Hettie as she led me down through the ship, giving me a short tour into the bargain. She explained how that strange numbering system on the bulkheads worked, though I struggled to follow the logic at the time. Hettie's explanations were as ever brisk and to the point. She assumed anyone could understand the things that came simply to her, provided she explained things is a forthright vocal manner. More lecturer than school mistress. Not that I followed a great deal, but luckily there was unlikely to be an exam afterwards. A question did occur to me though, as I followed her through the maze of bulkheads and hatchways.

"What with all the squids?" I asked.

By this time, we were two decks down and making our way aft wards. Hettie stopped for a moment, and raised an inquiring eyebrow at me, so I pointed at one of the ubiquitous squid icons that were on every door.

"Oh those, because of the name of the ship," she replied.

"The ships called The Squid?" I furthered, which caused her to chortle.

"Not as such… She's The Oegopsida."

"The what now?"

"The Oegopsida. It's Latin," she explained, before grinning somewhat conspiratorially. "The captain, well, he has a thing about Latin."

"Okay, but Latin for what?"

"It's the Latin for the genus of, well, squid," she admitted.

"So she is called 'The Squid' then?" I said with a smirk.

"Technically… But I wouldn't let anyone hear you calling the old girl that. They're all fairly proud of her. I am myself, truth be told, but I'll let it go this once… Just this once…"

Hettie smiled and managed to not make it sound like a threat. But I knew Hettie, and the way she felt about her machines. Let's just say I wasn't entirely sure it was a jest and I wasn't about to push my luck on the subject.

I shrugged, patted a bulkhead with faux affection, and let her lead off once more. Whence she started climbing another ladder, which at least availed me of a view more entertaining than that of bulkheads painted with squids.

Eventually, after more climbs up and down ladders, which was as painful as ever with my shoulder, but at least Hettie wasn't prodding me with a harpoon rifle to go faster, we entered a large chamber which I assumed was the main engine room. Mostly because of the wave of heat and noise that washed over me when she opened the hatch. It spanned three decks and the half the width of the ship. It turned out to be one of a pair of engine houses that mirrored each other divided by a solid-looking bulkhead. Even with my fleeting grasp of engineering, this made a certain sense. If your ship was holed and your single engine room flooded, you were dead in the water. As 'The Squid' was a submarine, a couple of hundred feet down, that dead would be a quite literal. Dual engine rooms, each watertight and separate, just made sense. Last thing you'd wanted in a submersible was to find yourself at the bottom of an ocean without power. It was a design I heartily approved of, given I was currently aboard such a vessel.

Hettie led me down a metal stairway to the deck below, then back on ourselves, into a small office come control room, full of levers, consoles and controls I could never hope to understand. The two grease monkeys on duty gave her a nod of respect and she said something in French that sounded like a greeting. Then she led me to another small hatchway at the back of the control room leading to a second compartment, where, to my utter lack of surprise, a small still was bubbling away nicely to itself.

"Now, no telling the old man this is here," Hettie said with fake earnestness, before rooting around on a shelf to find a couple of marginally clean glasses. She pointed me to a chair, which I accepted with some relief. Then I watched as she tapped a couple of shots of cloudy engineer room moonshine.

"Oh, I assure you, you can rely on my discretion," I promised.

"That would be a first, Smyth," Hettie said, grinning and handing me a glass.

I gave her a hard stare but didn't bother to protest. Hettie and I had been drunk in each other's company too many times for me to waste my breath with false protestations. Instead, I shrugged, and said, "Well, okay, let's just say, I won't tell the captain about your still, if you don't tell him about Clapham Common…" and grinned. I was alluding to a drunken midnight foot race that involved me and several other members of 'The Ins & Outs' a few years back. A race we all undertook dressed as we came into this world. Which involved a second unexpected sprint after some of the naked athletes managed to attract the unwanted attentions of a couple of patrolling coppers.

That night I learned it's remarkably hard to make botanical assessments while legging it full pelt in the dark. I still have scars from all the scratches I obtained diving into a thicket that turned out to be a holly bush.

"Oh, he knows about the still, he just pretends not to. And no one should ever mention Clapham Common again," she told me sternly.

I agreed on the latter subject, but the former raised my opinion of Verne. There was an old saying we were taught at navel collage, 'A good captain must know everything about his ship,' a saying one of the tutors would always amend with, 'and know what he doesn't need to know.'

I downed the shine. It proved to be of the finest quality, as engine room gin goes. That is to say, it could degrease pistons and strip stomach lining with equal efficiency. It did, however, hit the spot. Though hit is possibly an understatement. Successive blows of that stuff would pummel the spot to within an inch of its life.

"Good stuff," I managed to wheeze, between coughs and splutters, before handing the glass back for a refill.

"Only the finest in my engine room," Hettie said with a grin. Then downed her own with no obvious side effect and commenced to refill the glasses.

"Cheers," I said, already feeling the warm glow alcohol gives you, though that might've been the heat from the engine room.

Hettie fished in her pockets, pulled out my bottle of painkillers and threw them over to me. "Best take one of those before you drink another," she said with sage-like wisdom. "Give them a chance to work before you hurl your stomach up," she added with a wink.

Catching the bottle, I groaned, but she was probably right. State I was in, drinking hooch and pills was a recipe for disaster. So, I put down the glass and fought with the cap, one of those safety ones you can strain yourself trying to open. But I struggled manfully, managed to make it pop open, and shook out a couple of pills. Which I stared at, as they lay in the palm of my hand.

"How am I supposed to swallow these?" I moaned. They were huge. The shape of torpedoes, almost the size of my little finger. "I'm likely to choke downing these buggers."

Hettie laughed loudly, then downed her glass of shine. She even managed to splutter a little in the process this time, though I think that was from laugher, not the engine room loopy-juice. Then, covering her mouth to stifle the giggles, she got up and somewhat pointedly turned her back to me.

"The doc's French, Hannibal," she told me.

"So?"

"So… The French mostly take their pills the other way… On the bright side, you're less likely to chuck them up at least," she said, over her shoulder. Which left me slightly bemused as to what the heck she was talking about. As well as why she was doing so while pointedly staring at the wall.

"What?"

"Well, the French… They… Let's just say they prefer to put a little spring in their step at the same time as they take their medicine," she said and started laughing again.

"I don't get you," I replied, still somewhat befuddled.

"Oh, for god's sake," Hettie cursed, turning back to me. Then she began to mime at me. Making an O with her thumb and forefinger with one hand, before slipping the index finger of her other hand through it. I thought, you'll doubtless be unsurprised to learn, she was miming something else at first. But then, with an utter lack of self-consciousness, indeed, in the most 'Hettie' way possible, she cleared up the confusion by means of loudly shouting, "You stick it up your backside, you wazzock!"

I was of course horrified.

Shaking her head at me, Hettie pointedly turned back to face the wall and began tapping her foot impatiently. Which was her way of suggesting I got on with it.

Hettie was, I later discovered, entirely correct. The French do indeed prefer suppositories. I suspect it is something to do with the gallic character. That or perhaps, as she said, they just like to leave the doctors with a spring in their step… Though as I downed trousers and took the damn things, in that tiny closet behind the control office, with Henrietta Clarkhurst stood only a few feet away from me, albeit with her back turned, it sure wasn't putting a damn spring in mine.

As to what I was thinking as I did the necessary…

Well, as I said earlier, I like any right-thinking Englishman, hate the bloody French…

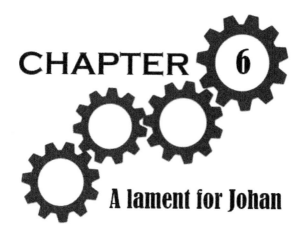

CHAPTER 6

A lament for Johan

I was awoken by a siren, wailing in the corridor. Such a sound is seldom good news on a ship of any kind. Added to this, the overhead light in my cabin came on of its own accord. Flashed brightly once, then the white light became a pulsing red, bathing the room in a worrying scarlet hue. This, I determined rather rapidly, didn't bode well.

As awakenings go, I've had worse of course. Particularly of late. But my head took this one as a cue to start pounding. I'd drunk rather more than was wise of Hettie's engine room shine and I only vaguely remembered making it to bed. I'd recollections of being shown to my quarters by some junior engineer Hettie had jollied into said task. I seemed to remember him being rather resentful about that, but he wasn't going to argue with Hettie.

Once I'd arrived, between the pills, indignantly taken though they may have been, and the shine, I was out for the count in no time. But on being awoken by the charming alarms and pulsing red of happiness that accompanied them, I found whatever painkilling qualities those finger-sized torpedoes may have had, they'd worn off.

Sitting up was agony, my ribs throbbing once more. This was not helped by my managing to catch my bad arm on the wall as I jumped up, which sent a profusion of stabbing pains through my shoulder blade. Gritting my teeth regardless, I struggled to my feet, trying manfully to ignore my pain. Instinctively though, I grabbed for the bottle of rectal torpedoes, only to think better of it. I was an Englishman after all. It was only pain. Stiff upper lip and get on with it. Bugger to painkillers, I didn't need the damn things…

A minute later, of course, I was struggling with the lid again and having wrestled it open, I 'put a little spring in my step' before grabbing my overalls and struggling to dress myself. I didn't know what was going on beyond my hatch, but what with the alarms and flashing lights, I felt the urge to find out. For all I knew, the submersible was under attack. Or worse, sinking in that unplanned way ships occasionally do. Frankly, I was a tad afraid right then. Fear only enhanced when a moment later the whole room started shaking violently. This was accompanied by a low-pitched booming sound that immediately made me think of the sound you got when you dropped a banger wrapped in tinfoil into a water butt. A sound I knew because it was one of those dumb things me and Frankie Burns used to get up to on Mischievous Night back when he and I were 'dirty faced little angels' as my old mum used to say. Or 'scruffy little hooligans' as almost everyone else called us.

If you wrapped tinfoil around a banger just right, and sealed it with wax, it had enough air between the tinfoil and the little firework, to keep the water out and the fuse burning for a few seconds after you chucked it in the butt. When you got it just right, the banger would still go off and water would explode up out of the butt. Occasionally, if you got a really good one, it would split the butt entirely. This was, of course, hilarious as far as me and Frankie were concerned.

Of course, the holy grail for me and Frankie were the outside toilet blocks up Crawford Street, where the old back to backs still lacked indoor conveniences. It is perhaps one of the greatest regrets of my childhood that we never figured out how to make a banger's fuse burn for a full ten seconds or so. That would have been long enough to pop it in after a flush, vacate the stall and have it still burning when the next person came in to use the facilities… We never quite manged to pull it off.

I will note, in our defence, we always made sure to flush first before we tried this. I mean, there're some lines you just don't cross… But not to digress further, and leave the wistful days of youth behind… The boom I heard after that during the violent shaking, put me in mind of the deep muffled boom of one of our water butt depth charges. Something that worried me, to say the least.

Once dressed and out in the corridor, I found myself almost trampled by a rush of seamen running past me for the hatchway at the far end. I managed to flatten my back to the wall just in time as they barged past, before doing my best to follow on their heels. I'd no clue where they were going but they were either running to their stations or away from something, and in the worst-case scenarios that were rattling around my head, away is always the best direction to head.

I followed them through the hatchway and got shouted at for my troubles. It took me a moment to realise the gesticulating seaman before me was waving his hands at the hatch. Realisation dawned that he wanted me to seal the damn thing. I'd have rather kept running, but despite the shouting, the look he gave me was one of exasperation rather than panic. I took this as some small relief, as if he wasn't panicking, I probably didn't need to, so I did as instructed.

By the time I'd finished with the hatch, the siren ceased, and the lights turned back from angry red to the pale white glow I associated with tesla lamps. I'd still had no idea why they'd turned red and the siren had been sounded, but as I was now firmly in the land of wakefulness, I just kept following the sailors as they made their way through the body of the submersible. Whatever was happening might not quite be the emergency I'd feared but I still wanted to know what was going on.

We climbed up a couple of decks, to one just below the captain's quarters, then they started down another corridor. This led, through several hatches, to a larger chamber with several sets of ladders all leading up to another deck. I made an educated guess these led to the bridge despite the fact that going up to the bridge was something of an alien concept to me. On an airship, the bridge is normally on a lower deck. But given this was a submersible, everything was a little topsy turvy in my mind and an upper bridge would allow for a direct connection to the captain's quarters, if my guess of the layout was anywhere near right. So it seemed a reasonable assumption.

As I stepped onto the ladder, however, I had a moment of doubt. True, the captain had said I could go anywhere. But there had been that 'apart from where I couldn't' he'd tagged on the end. As instructions go, that was a tad opaque, but entering the bridge uninvited could be one such no go area. It's always unwise to enter the bridge without permission no matter what kind of craft you're on. As such, I hesitated, but while valour isn't really my strong point, as I am sure you have realised by now, I'll admit I was curious. So while curiosity may be known to slaughter felines, I still wanted to know what was going on. After a moment of self-doubt, I decided to ascend regardless.

The ladder topped out in another of those square rooms, but the seamen I'd been following were already disappearing though a hatch. And so I followed them, and entered the most impressive chamber I'd seen so far on The Oegopsida.

Actually, I would go so far as to say it was one of the most impressive chambers I've ever seen.

The bridge, for that was indeed where I'd found myself, was almost as large as the engine rooms I'd seen the day before. But unlike the functional magnificence of Hettie's domain, the bridge of The Oegopsida was a symphony of wood, brass and glass.

Extending a full sixty feet or more from the entrance and two decks high, the walls were panelled in oak and ash. Long consoles ran the full length of the outer walls that curved inward as they approached the nose before meeting in a huge semi-circle. Those consoles sat a good dozen or more seamen to each side. The three I'd followed were already dropping down into vacant seats before god knows what monitoring equipment. Those consoles were a vast array of brass dials, leavers, toggle buttons and several small round porthole-like scenes that reminded me of those I had seen in Cairo in Gates' lab, which made me shiver on seeing them. A raised platform sat in the middle of all this with what looked like an old-fashioned ship's wheel mounted in its centre and a couple of raised signal levers, the likes of which I'd seen on older airships. These would be linked no doubt to the engine room by some mechanism or other, so they could signal down orders for speed changes, depth controls, and god knows what else.

A few feet back from the great wheel, his hands behind his back as he surveyed his domain, stood Captain Verne. No doubt with the same serious but detached look on his face that all captains have when standing upon their bridge.

I think they teach prospective captains that look at navel college, but if they do, I missed that class. Perhaps because I wasn't judged to be senior officer material...

The most impressive thing about the bridge of The Oegopsida, however, was all the glass involved. The upper sections of the hull that arched over the bridge were in effect one huge glass window, curved up to form a semi-dome sweeping back overhead. The steel superstructure of the observation window was immense. I'm no engineer, a fact you're probably painfully aware of by now, but even I had a working grasp of the enormous pressures the outer hull needed to deal with at depth. Each pane of glass had to be several inches thick in order to withstand those pressures. Each had to weigh several tonnes. The steel work holding them all together probably coped with more strain than Old Brass Knickers' corsetry after a state banquet.

Astounding as the dome over the bridge was as a pure feat of engineering, it paled in compassion to what lay beyond it. I've never seen a stranger, more alien sight in my life than sunlight on an ocean, from a hundred feet below the waves. It had the same eerie quality as sunlight through shifting mists. Yet within this mist was an abundance of life. Schools of fish darted through it in strange dances that twisted and turned, changing direction as one for reasons that defied comprehension, the filtered sunlight flashing off them as if they were made of quicksilver. A whale crossed before us then dived, revealing in its wake a school of hammerhead sharks, those erstwhile hunters of the deep swimming almost directly above us, darting into a shoal of fish that swung right just as the sharks opened their jaws. Other creatures swam into view and then out of it again. The water seemed to teem with life. Even to me, a man who would cheerfully admit the only fish he really cared about was the battered kind wrapped in newspaper, this was a sight to be seen. I was so entranced by the view, it took me a few minutes to realise those sunlit waves above us were getting closer and what that meant.

"Ballast," I muttered to myself. I spoke out loud. The booming noise I'd heard and the vibrations that had put me on edge when they followed the alarm made sense to me now. Airships and submersibles are not so different after all, for all they operate in different mediums. Both must shed weight in order to ascend or gain it to sink downward. The actual mechanisms to achieve this are vastly different but the principle remains the same. All that noise and vibration had merely been the ship venting ballast, the siren and red lights just a warning to the crew that the craft was going to surface.

"A man asks permission before entering my bridge, Mr Smyth," Captain Verne barked with no shortage of venom, the sound of my voice having alerted him to my presence. He turned my way, a look between indignity and indifference greeting me.

It was, of course, at this point I noted two of his guards stood flanking the hatch through which I'd entered, both of which obligingly bringing their harpoon rifles to bear on yours truly. Ready to make pointed interventions no doubt if the captain required.

"My apologies, Captain… May I?" I asked, in my most polite voice. Even without the guards either side of me, I, of course, would've been polite. Years of military training ingrains a certain respect for a captain's authority. But it is also my firm belief that it never behoves a man to be impolite to narcissistic loons with heavily armed flunkies on a tight leash.

Verne fixed me with an inscrutable stare for a moment, before turning back to face forwards, his hands slipping behind his back in a classic pose, also taught at navel colleges, I've no doubt, that is adopted by all captains everywhere. Meanwhile his guards stepped towards me, waiting to escort me in the gentle manner of guards everywhere. But then, with impeccable timing, just as I expected to be manhandled elsewhere, the captain finally uttered the words, "You may."

Verne clearly had a flair for the dramatic, but then he had once been a writer like Wells, so I guess it goes with the territory. I have long observed writers are ever full of themselves…

Somewhat relieved to be spared the indignity of being frogmarched off the bridge, by a pair of frogs, I stepped onto the bridge proper, moving to stand alongside the captain. This was of course presumptive of me. However, I've always found it's best to act the part of an honoured guest, rather than lurk in the background looking shifty. It also does no harm to let the men with guns get used to the idea of seeing you around. It makes them a tad less itchy on their trigger finger and disinclined to look upon you as one who needs introducing to the butt end of their rifles. A perception I was keen to encourage, after recent experiences.

"This is all very impressive, Captain," I said honestly. In truth, I was still trying to take it all in and found myself watching with mounting fascination as the crew went about the business of taking The Oegopsida back to the surface.

Verne ignored this comment. He just continued watching everything with an impassive expression I'd seen mirrored on many a captain's face in the past. And if they don't get taught that at navel college, then they all spent hours practising it in the mirror every morning. I know I had for the brief period when I was captain of The Johan's Lament. Admittedly, my 'stern impassive captain's face' hadn't garnered much in the way of respect from my crew. True, my crew had comprised a ragged collection of refugees from the monastery, my own Bad Penny and Saffron Wells, so I guess this comes as no surprise. I do though doubt it helped matters when Saffron looked over at me on the bridge when I was doing my best 'Stern Impassive Face' and asked, not entirely delicately, if I was 'feeling constipated'.

I'd given up trying to look the part after that.

"We're surfacing?" I said, more a general comment than a question. It was obvious this was the case, we were perhaps no more than fifty feet down now by my guess. I'd also noticed a long dark shadow on the surface off to port for the first time, along with a scattering of smaller shadows that surrounded it. As it grew closer, a suspicion started to form in the back of my mind which the captain all but confirmed a moment later.

"Very good, Mr Smyth. We are indeed, though with some caution. As it happens, your arrival is fortuitous. I was about to send a guard to collect you. I feel this will be of some interest to you, indeed of that I have no doubt," he told me, while never turning his gaze in my direction. His eyes were fixed on the surface above us.

"You've found The Johan then?" I inquired. It seemed the obvious conclusion. The looming shadow above us could be little else but an airship, all be it a wreck.

"Indeed…" Verne said then barked out an order, "Periscope depth if you please, Mr Hodges. Let's have a look, shall we?"

The Oegopsida continued to rise until it was thirty feet or so below the waves, perhaps less. It was difficult to judge distance through the prism of sea water as the ship levelled out and I felt an odd cessation of movement I hadn't realised I could feel as we rose. The remaining ballast was now holding us steady below the waves.

A small inverted dome on the ceiling separated into two halves and from it a device extended downwards on a hydraulic piston. I knew it was the periscope, of course. We used similar things on airships, allowing the bridge crew to get a holistic view of the skies around them. Though on an airship they projected downwards rather than up. This device wasn't entirely what I expected, however. Instead of a scope that one man could look into and rotate around the column to get the view they required, a large glass disc encased in brass folded downwards until it hung at eye level with the steers man, captain and myself.

I recognised the technology and suppressed a shudder because of who it brought to mind. "That's one of Gates' windows!"

"Ah yes, of course. You've met our dear William, have you not? The design is based upon his, yes. He built me a prototype ion-scope some years back, though this is for a somewhat less insidious use, I assure you," Verne explained. Though this didn't entirely set my mind at ease. The first time I'd encountered such a device, it had been relaying my own vison back to me, curtesy of Gates' spider. In truth, they set my teeth on edge. I can't say I felt entirely comfortable knowing Verne had associated with Gates at some time in the past either. Not that I was surprised. Gates, Verne, Jobs, Wells, all of them connected back to The Ministry in one way or another.

The big screen powered on with a burst of static. I watched, only half interested, my mind too busy racing to join up the dots. "So, you must have been part of it all from the start then, The Ministry, Wells, the whole thing?" I heard myself ask, perhaps unwisely giving voice to my thoughts.

Verne turned to look at me, his eyes narrowing as he caught my gaze. But he merely held it for a moment, saying nothing, his expression impassive, before turning back to observe the periscope screen. I was going to get no answers, not right then at any rate. He was too dispassionate to be so easily led into confirming my suspicions. Verne it seemed, unlike Wells, didn't suffer any desire to be candid with one whose fate remained undetermined. So, I checked myself, deciding against pushing my ever-woeful luck with further questions. Instead I simply followed his gaze and found myself looking over the shattered remains of my first and only command. The broken wreck of The Johan's Lament.

Only the air sack was visible, the gondola, engines, props and all, were fully submerged. Not that there was much left of the air sack either. Most of the substructure was bent and twisted beyond recognition. This told me that when she finally came down, she came down hard. The outer sections were in tatters, flapping in the ocean breeze. The only reason the whole ship hadn't sunk like a stone were the ballast bladders, the inner air sacks into which air was pumped or released to alter the craft's buoyancy. Ram enough air in and it compressed the outer gas while adding weight and you sank down. Leaching air out of the inner bladder lightened her and up you went. Simple physics even I could grasp.

Of course, once you got engineers involved, there were many different variations. Heating the air within the inner bladders could also cause extra lift and cooling it the reverse, for example. Once you got down to specifics, I soon got lost, along with my interest. But the same basic principles were always involved.

In any regard, while the main air sack was ruptured and deflated, one or more of the bladders had to be still intact, or she would have sunk without trace.

I was transfixed by the image on the screen before me, not knowing what to think, or how to feel. I'd not been her captain long enough to form any great attachment to the vessel. Only one flight, in fact, and her last at that. True, I'd crewed her for several weeks as first mate when I first got to India, but my time under Captain Singh bore no fond memories. Quite the reverse in actuality. The only part of her that I'd ever taken any pride in was the howitzer mounted at midships I'd spent weeks trying to get into some state of repair, and even that had just been a way to keep myself out of Singh's hair.

'*I never did get that damn gun cradle working smoothly...*' I thought to myself distractedly. Which may seem an odd regret, but it was one that struck me as I watched the images on the screen.

Yet, for all I felt little real connection with her, she had for a short time been my ship. Now she was nothing but a wreck that would slip beneath the waves once the last of her vital gases leaked away. It struck me as a damned waste. An ignoble end even if she'd been a belligerent ill repaired ship at best. I must admit to feeling a tad sorrowful at that.

I must have stared at her wreck for a good couple of minutes, as the periscope slowly panned the wreckage, lamenting her loss, before a question came to me that perhaps should've occurred to me sooner. "Where are the crew?"

"Where indeed, Mr Smyth," Verne replied, while I tried to remember how many had been aboard when we fled Nepal. Twenty maybe... thirty even. I tried to picture their faces, but I could hardly bring any of them to mind. It's strange how little you take notice of the people around you.

How easily they become just part of the background. I could picture no more than a couple. People I'd seen around the monastery, the mechanic, Penny and Saffron. That was it, and sure, they hadn't really been a crew, just a ragged collection of refugees, but all the same, as I stared at the remains of my ship through the ion-scope, I felt a sense of great incongruity. I'd been, no matter how briefly, their captain. I, of all people, should've known who they were. Known their stories, or their names at the very least. Someone should have, and if not their captain, then who?

Some damn captain I was…

"What's that?" I said. I'd seen movement in the water. I could barely make it out. Something or someone was hung over a piece of sub-frame still sticking out of the water.

Verne worked at the controls a moment and the viewer's image sharpened and focused in to where I'd indicated. Much in the way my mechanical eye sometimes did, with the same dizzying shift of perspective. I could half make out at least one person now, someone clinging to the sub-frame but not moving. Possibly dead, but just as possibly unconscious.

"A survivor?" I found myself asking, though who I was asking I don't know. The universe perhaps. Was this a slither of redemption? Did some at least survive? I felt a surge of hope I hardly expected to find within myself.

"Surface, Mr Hodges," the captain instructed, and almost instantly I felt the ship start to move upwards once more. As the periscope screen began to collapse back up into the ceiling, I watched with fascination as The Oegopsida broke the surface, the waters pouring back across the glass ceiling as she rose and then, with a lurch, burst forth onto the surface, to float , bobbing in the water, waves lapping at her side.

Looking up through the roof of glass, I found myself surprised how relieved I was to see the sky once more. With the sun beating down through the glass, I experienced a moment akin to elation. But only a moment, for as my eyes adjusted to the sudden brightness of natural sunlight, I saw the first of the bodies, caught up now on the outer skin of the submersible. A dead faced corpse staring back down at me through the glass, with lifeless eyes.

I tore my gaze away, not out of horror, but out of shame. When I looked back, I saw two more corpses strewn over the glass, caught by the steel framework as we broke the surface. One of these had been half eaten by something, only the upper torso remaining. The other had a telling chunk missing out of one leg.

"Sharks!" I uttered, bile welling up in my throat.

"Indeed," Verne said grimly, "but I would venture that's not what killed them, monsieur."

"Yes, of course," I reasoned, though it was small comfort. "They were probably killed in the crash." *'Better that than eaten alive,'* I added to myself, but even as I thought this, a niggling doubt formed in my mind. The Johan may have come down hard, but it was unlikely it came down so hard the impact alone would've killed everyone. There were no obvious signs of explosive damage or the flash fires, which were what did for you in an airship crash as a rule. Also, while I'd no real gauge of how far 'The Squid' had travelled since I came aboard, I suspect even if she was slower in the water than I believed, we must have travelled at least a hundred miles or more from where I made my premature swan dive into the drink. For The Johan to have come this far, she had to have come down slowly, relatively slowly. Hard enough for all the damage, but not so hard as to kill everyone. The crash alone couldn't account for the death of the crew.

This realisation got me wondering. Was Verne suggesting the alterative fate to being shark bait as a kindness, one captain to another. Such a gesture didn't quite tally with what I thought I knew of the man. The impression I had was of a man who was cold and aloof, except in matters concerning his daughter. But then, *'Harry, you judge people too harshly at times,'* I thought to myself and while I admittedly hadn't been especially close to my crew, this consideration on his part was appreciated. One captain to another. And in truth, despite the circumstances, it felt good that Captain Verne was treating me as an equal in this regard, by this show of compassion.

"Not the crash, I think, monsieur," Verne said, as impassive and cold as ever, "but not sharks either."

"What do you mean?" I asked him, puzzled as to what he was implying.

"Well, Monsieur Smyth, I have studied sharks for many years. I admire the beasts. Such single-minded hunters. Do you know they have found fossilised remains of sharks that date back beyond the Jurassic? Hundreds of millions of years, and yet sharks in essence have barely changed. Hundreds of millions of years. If your Mr Darwin was correct, and I greatly suspect he was, humanity back then were no more than odd little tree dwelling mammals. Not even proto-humans, not even apes. So imagine then, how much we have evolved over a millennia of millennia, to become what we are today. Yet in all those eons, sharks in essence have remain unchanged. They are today just as they were then. We must ask ourselves then, must we not, why this is so? Do you know why I believe that is, monsieur?"

"I must admit I've no idea, captain," I said in utter honesty, and in truth, natural history was never a subject I cared for. So what if we had evolved from the apes. Besides, frankly, I'd met a few bastards on the rugger fields in my school days who hadn't evolved very far from knuckle dragging gorillas in my opinion. The only biology and selective breeding that ever interested me when I was at school was in the final year when I was trying to convince the barmaid from The Five Flags to teach me a few lessons on the subject… This was a suggestion she sadly demurred at the time, which given I was a pimply fifteen-year-old drinking underage at the time, is probably understandable.

That said, the way she pulled a hand pump was an education in itself, I always thought.

"It is my opinion, Monsieur Smyth, sharks have never needed to evolve in all those eons because they had already reached the pinnacle of evolution for that which is a shark. Fast, single minded, perfect hunters, killers. They swim, they eat, they reproduce and that is all they do. Simply put, I believe nature has never come up with anything better at being a shark, than a shark…"

"This is fascinating, Captain, truly it is, but I'm not sure I am grasping your point," I said testily.

In my defence, I was standing under a glass roof with the half-eaten bodies of several of my former charge's strewn across it. Each of them noticeably bearing large bite marks and missing limbs. As such, I found a discussion on the relative merits of shark evolution a tad tasteless even by my wayward standards. Such circumstances would, I'd venture, make anyone testy.

"My point, Monsieur Smyth, is that," the captain said and pointed up at the nearest corpse, laying almost directly above us on the glass, its dead eyes staring back into the bridge below. I followed Verne's gaze, though it wasn't a sight I'd any great desire to examine in detail. The body had been in the sea for some time, a day at least by my estimate. It was bloated by sea water and as pale as ivory. A grim sight by any standards and one I wanted to tear my eyes away from, but I looked all the same. And as I did so, I finally I saw what he was pointing at. There was a hole in the corpse's head and two more in its torso. Holes that weren't caused by shark teeth. Holes I noticed just as Verne chose to give voice to his doubts.

"You see now, Monsieur? The point I am making is that over the passage of many eons, nature has deemed no requirement for sharks to move further along the branches of the evolutionary tree. What then is the likelihood that recently nature has seen fit to evolve sharks that use guns?"

I felt cold, even as I was bathed in sunlight. I started walking down the bridge, staring up through the glass at every corpse hanging over the sub, those caught in the wreckage or in the water. Each one I looked at closely I could see the same tell-tale bullet holes. A sick feeling welled up in my stomach and I felt the bile rising in my throat once more.

My mind was racing now. It was clear someone had shot what I would've otherwise laughingly called my former crew. But that made no sense. The only people who had been armed on The Johan had been a couple of guards, me, Bad Penny and… "Saffron!"

Even as I said her name, I was glancing around, searching, trying to find any sign of her among the dead. Then a flicker of movement within the remains of the airship sub frame caught my eye. A wave of trepidation took hold of me, given I was behind several inches of glass and steel, but as I narrowed in on a collapsed section of canopy, I saw a figure moving around upon it. A figure that then pulled itself fully upright, raised one arm and pointed something at the submersible. I didn't even bother to wonder what.

There was a flash that could only be a pistol going off, though the sound of it didn't penetrate the hull. An impact pinged off the outside of the glass dome. Several more followed in quick succession, until her pistol was doubtless expended. Yet she remained standing on a piece of substructure, arm extended, trying to shoot dry chambers, the hammer clicking away, the pistol barely wavering.

A pistol that I swear was aimed, through the glass, at me.

It was Saffron, still alive, and still consumed by incandescent rage. I felt a wave of nausea hit me and tried to bite back the panic I felt. With that panic, or perhaps the surge of adrenaline that it brought about, my artificial eye kicked back into life. My vison flickered, the focus of my left eye narrowing on her face. Suddenly it was as though I was looking directly into the eyes of the woman who'd once been Saffron Wells. One of her eyes was glazed over, as if weeping, the other was just a black pit. Her face, once beautiful, was a twisted mask of madness. She'd clawed out her left eye, the skin around shredded by her fingernails, bloody and bruised. Yet I could see tendrils of metal still hanging through the void that remained behind. Tendrils still moving of their own violation, the vestiges of Mr Gates' spider still vying for control of her mind.

From what I could see, they were winning, and any vestige of Saffron Wells' sanity was long gone.

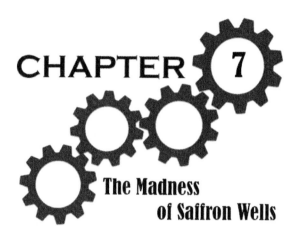

CHAPTER 7

The Madness of Saffron Wells

I am, as I'm sure you are aware by now as I've made no attempt to hide it, something of a swine. I'm something of a coward, a braggard and ultimately a man who looks only to himself. Every act I've imparted in these biographies which could be conceived by some kind-hearted myopic, in a dim light, as bravery, has, I assure you, been undertaken out of nothing more than selfish self-interest.

I have, however, never denied this is the case.

Yet, despite my 'honest' intentions to present you with nothing but the ungarnished truth, some among you, dear readers, may perhaps think I protest too much. Perhaps, somewhat naively, you think I'm too hard on myself, or that I purposely exaggerate my own inadequacies?

Well, if that is so, then I thank you for such open-minded acceptance, misguided as it may be.

But despite my many flaws, I regret little. Less than I should, some would doubtless say. I'm aware I've made mistakes, and if I've made one, I've made a hundred, but everything we do makes us who we are. As such, I've always been of the opinion that if you're the type of chap who regrets your past, then by extension you clearly must be unhappy with who you are. I may be a scoundrel, a liar, a thief, a coward and yes, a murderer on occasion, but I like who I am all the same. So, regrets, I have a few, but you will find, I seldom mention them…

But at the heart of the tale I've been imparting to you, there is one lasting regret. I regret that I was unable to take out a gun as I stood atop The Johan's Lament and couldn't shoot Saffron Wells dead the moment M's insidious spider took over her mind.

At its heart, this one true regret is not prefaced by any desire to have made my life easier. It hasn't even a slither of self-interest to it in fact, despite all that came later, all the events which might have been avoided by me doing so. In this one instance, my regret is for something I wished I'd done, but not to ferment any gain of my own. No, my regret at being unable to end her life on top of The Johan's canopy was inspired by a simpler unselfish desire. I just wish I could've spared her the madness that was to come. The madness I could plainly see in her face, as I stood there, staring back at her through the glass canopy of The Oegopsida's bridge.

Think of me anyway you wish, but if you think that regretful thought an oddly murderous one, believe me when I say it would've been as merciful a murder as one could ever wish to commit. No one deserves the fate of living that way, trapped within the tortured shell of shattered mind and that was the fate of what remained of Saffron Wells.

Verne sent his men out to drag her aboard, and to search, however vainly, for other survivors. There were none. Those that hadn't been killed in the crash or drowned, trapped in the now flooded gondola, Saffron had shot dead, in the water, or as they tried to scramble on top of the deflated canopy. She would've shot Verne's guards too, but for the lack of bullets.

I watched from the bridge as the crew scrambled over running boards hastily thrown between the submersible and the wreck to get at her. As they drew close, Saffron flew once more into a rage, dry firing her pistol at first, without seeming to register its lack of effect. Then once the first men reached her, she started using it as a club, beating them back as best she could. A dervish, flailing, kicking and screaming at them.

It took five of them to drag her aboard in the end.

Whether the link with M had been severed or just lay dormant I couldn't say, but it seemed to me that while the mind of Saffron Wells might very well be in charge of her body, that mind was lost to us. She fought everyone and everything, lashing out like the wounded, crazed animal The Ministry had made her. And all the time, she was screaming, oh the screaming, the voiceless screaming I could not hear through the glass, filled the air as they dragged her into the sub… There was nothing human about it, no words you might decipher, just a ceaseless primal roaring. All hatred, loathing and rage. Those screams cut right through me, as they manhandled her down through the conning tower. Those screams alone would have been enough to convince me that nothing remained of the beautiful strong self-assured woman that had once been Saffron Wells. She really was just a shell now, a feral creature, her consciousness shredded to tatters.

I felt the blood running from my face as I grew pale, watching them manhandle her along. The chief thought that kept occurring to me was, *'There but for the grace…'* as a more pious man might say. Unconsciously I realised I'd raised my hand to my left eye, fingers brushing what lay in the socket. That alien orb, the silver eye designed by Professor Jobs I hated so much. A replacement for my natural eye, which the same Jobs had wrenched out along with Dr Gates' damnable spider. Oh, but I'd hated Jobs for that at the time. But as I watched what the spider had done to Saffron, my maiming suddenly didn't seem so bad, faced as I was with the alterative. For what Saffron' s spider had done to her, my own could've so easily done to me.

'Oh, to be the man who only loses an eye,' as no one famous ever said.

They dragged Saffron down through the ship to the infirmary. There, the doctor wasted no time in trying to sedate her. Verne had followed them down, as did I in his shadow. So, I got to watch her flailing at her tormentors as they struggled to strap her down. There were four of them not including the doctor himself. She got an arm loose at one point and raked her nails across one of the guard's faces, ripping his rebreather clear of his face and leaving a track of gouged flesh hanging from his cheek. The guard responded by punching down at her, which caused me to winch if no one else. I feared he might have broken her jaw, so hard did he lash out. Not that the blow quelled her.

Needless to say, there was a lot of swearing going on. I may process no more than a disinterested schoolboy's grasp of French, but I didn't need to be fluent to grasp the context of the words. I can't say I blamed Verne's crew over much, considering the struggle she put up. I might abhor hitting a woman, gentleman or not, but they had little choice in the matter. More than one of them was going to be carrying bruises for days and the newly christened 'Scarface' was going to need stitches.

As they struggled to contain Saffron, they seemed somewhat aghast at her strength. No man or woman should've been able to put up such a struggle. But fight she did even when the doctor pumped her full of sedatives. Even with the first dose coursing through her veins, she managed to send one guard crashing to the deck with a kick and got her own back on Scarface for his punches by gouging at him again. I doubt they could comprehend just how she kept fighting back. They couldn't have understood it if she'd been twice her size, a man, and a prize fighter to boot. Not that Saffron was ever someone you'd have called weak to start with, but she was fighting them with a strength that she, nor anyone, should possess.

I knew why though. I remembered only too well how the spider in my eye had affected me when it wrestled control of my mind. How it sent me into mad, unthinking rages fuelled by massive unnatural bursts of adrenaline it sent coursing through my veins. When under one of Gates' spider's influence, pain and injury meant nothing. The resistance your own body imbued in your rational mind to prevent you pushing beyond natural limits was subverted. Nothing could stop those rages once the spider gained control, save severing its connection. That or being knocked from consciousness entirely.

Yet while I remember what it felt like when the spider took over you, my own spider had never gained the extent of control Saffron's had over her. Between it pushing her adrenaline glands into overdrive and the strength that madness gifts, I'm only surprised they didn't need to kill her before the sedatives finally took effect, and more to the point that she didn't kill one of them in return.

Finally, two injections of sedative later, they had her strapped to the surgery table. Even then she fought on against her bonds. I can't say I'd have been overly surprised if in a fresh surge of rage she'd ripped the leather straps free of their anchors. But luckily, for all concerned, they held and the doc managed to inject her a third time with sedative, and finally when that was still not enough a fourth.

There was more cursing and the doctor shouted something I assumed could be roughly translated as 'I've given the bitch enough sedative to put an elephant to sleep.' Because even a disinterested schoolboy would recognise the French for l'éléphant. This was as he was filling a fifth syringe which, as she finally sank down onto the bed in a troubled stupor, proved not to be needed, thankfully.

As she slowly quietened down, a couple of the guards slumped to the floor themselves, exhausted no doubt. The ones still standing didn't look much better. The doctor was clearly beside himself, trying to comprehend what he'd just witnessed. All the while Captain Verne had stood impassively watching on, his hands held firmly clasped behind his back, saying nothing. He may as well have been watching flower arranging for all the reaction that visibly crossed his features. Even when she was finally out for the count, the most reaction he granted was a curt little nod to his men and the doctor, before turning to make his way back to the bridge.

"She cannot stay here," I said as he passed me, which brought him up short.

He turned to look at me, possibly noticing my presence beside the hatchway for the first time.

"And why is that, Monsieur Smyth?" he asked calmly. As if he wasn't talking about the granddaughter of an old friend. A woman it had just taken five men and a bucket full of sedative to bring under control. His eyes however, as they bore into me, suggested he was not quite as impassive about it all as he wanted his men to believe. There was alarm and worry in them, and the moistness of a tear held back in the corner.

I took a breath. It struck me it may have been wiser not to have spoken up right then. But wisdom is often a matter of degrees and while I may have offended my host by speaking out of turn, the danger Saffron Wells represented was making my palms itch.

"The spider, the device they used to take over her mind, it's still in her. I doubt it can be removed without killing her," I explained.

"I fear you may be correct, but that does not explain why she cannot stay here for now," he said in a tone which suggested that while he might be holding his temper in check, there was no guarantee that he wouldn't lose it any time soon. This left me all too aware I was his guest only because he chose it to be so. He could be put off the ship any time he wished and right then, if I was lucky, that might only mean I'd have a hell of a long swim to look forward to. But nevertheless, I was committed now.

"The Ministry could take control of her mind again at any moment. They can contact the spider anywhere. If she is here when they take control then they will know exactly where the ship is," I explained, trying to make the danger clear and banking on his desire to remain anonymous to the empire. This was an assumption on my part but I considered it a fair one. Of course, my main concern, if I am being honest, was for myself. As far as the empire, or more specifically The Ministry, was concerned, I hoped they thought me dead. I'd been thrown off an airship. Doubtless they would have assumed that if the fall hadn't killed me, I'd have drowned, which but for Verne I would have. Thus they were unlikely to come looking for me, which I considered an upside to my current circumstances.

Small victories and all that…

The problem was, if Saffron remained aboard The Oegopsida, there was every chance The Ministry might discover my fate wasn't the one they'd assumed. Then I'd be right back in the middle of everything. Not that I was free of it all by any margin, but one less set of mad bastards trying to kill me had a definite upside in my opinion.

"Their transmitters are unlikely to locate her here, Monsieur. The hull of this vessel is somewhat thicker than that of an airship and we sail beneath the waves. Very deep beneath the waves. But it is a risk, I grant you. We shall be placing her in our most secure quarters, for now. At least until we can determine what, if anything, can be done for her. She is, after all, my old compatriot's granddaughter. I owe him that much," the captain told me, in tones that balked no rebuke.

"I hope you're correct, Captain," I said simply, turning back to look at the twitching form of a woman I... well, I'm not sure it would be right to claim she was a woman I cared for... wished to care would be more honest. But in that moment as I watched what remained of Saffron Wells, I swore to myself that if I ever got the chance to do so, I would kill that smug bastard M. Not for myself, though I had reason enough to do so, but for Saffron Wells.

In fact, I remember feeling most uncharacteristically determined on that score. Though in cold hindsight that became just one more reason to want him dead in the end.

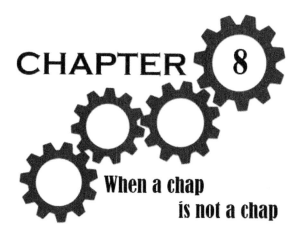

CHAPTER 8

When a chap is not a chap

With Saffron Wells firmly secured in the ship's surgery, Captain Verne sent men back out to strip everything of value from what remained of The Johan's Lament.

It didn't take long.

They found no one else alive and when men in diving equipment managed to cut their way into the submerged gondola, they found the bodies of those unaccounted for. Most of them must have drowned as the waters rushed in, in a desperate, unequal fight to escape the confines of what became a watery tomb. I can only imagine the horror of their final moments as they died trying desperately to free themselves.

The dead were left inside, welded back into their oversized coffin by the divers, for what solace such a tomb could offer them. They cut it free of the remains of the canopy and I watched through the observation window as the compartment sank into the lightless depths below.

Within a couple of hours, the canopy had been cut up and weighted down until it too sank beyond trace. By the time The Oegopsida dipped below the waves, it was as if The Jonah's Lament had never been there. A deep sense of melancholy settled upon me as we dipped below the waves. I felt as though we were turning our backs on the Jonah, and I on another pile of bodies left in my wake. Just like I'd turned my back on the train and Hiroshima. Just as I'd fled the monastery in Nepal taking with me those same poor sods I was turning my back on now. Those I had whisked away only for them to follow those left behind into the long night a few days later. Whisked away only to die in ways so much worse than the clean bullet to the head that might otherwise have been their fate.

Yet once again, somehow, I'd survived when so many others had not. This struck me as absurd.

Why did I, of all people, keep surviving these things…?

I don't believe in fate. I don't believe in some higher power guiding our lives. Saving perhaps she who resided on the throne of Great Britain, who'd been the only higher power in my life. Old Clockwork Ticker mightn't be a living goddess, as some mad gin-sodden fools like my old mum chose to believe, but she may as well have been. The empire Britain rules in her name shapes the lives of billions within its boundaries, so call her a higher power if you will, but old Sticky Vic doesn't shower favours on the likes of me. As for god, well, if there is one, it has always struck me that his ineffable plan is too damn ineffable.

No, I don't believe in fate.

Yet somehow, despite everything, I kept surviving from one disaster to the next. Surviving only for my actions to lead me to more disasters, more deaths to hang heavy on my soul. I could blame others. Say it was through no fault of mine. I could shrug my shoulders and claim myself as much a victim as those poor sods sinking beneath the waves in a welded-up tomb. But sometimes it's harder than others to gain perspective. Had I taken us west rather than east… Had I chosen to fly over land rather than heading out across the ocean. Had I fixed the leaking canopy when I first suspected the problem rather than wait till I'd no other choice. Had I… Had I… So many Had I's… So many other choices I could've made along the way.

But no, I made my choices with myself in mind every time, and somehow, despite everything, I was still around to think 'had I'.

These thoughts tumbled around my head. Each echoing the next. I was indeed melancholy, regretful and angry… But also, I needed a drink…

This was why before long I found my way back down to Hettie's engine room, and, on getting there, ignored the questioning glances of her engineering crew. I walked through the little control room and through the little hatch at the back. Making my way to Hettie's still and once there I tapped off a jar of hooch. Then started drinking.

I was still there a couple of hours, and a dozen or so glasses later, when Hettie found me. She must have had some inclination as to how I felt, or maybe she read it in my expression, as she didn't scold me for stealing her booze. Instead, she poured herself a glass and sat down opposite me in silence. A look of sympathy crossed her face as silently she sipped a little, while I drained my glass.

A lot of crap is spoken at times about chaps.

'A chap doesn't cry,' they'll say. 'A chap doesn't bare his soul and weep like a baby,' they'll add for good measure. But what they really mean is 'A chap doesn't do that in front of another chap…' It's part of the code. It's part of what's expected, because they are told, as we all are told, 'A chap keeps a stiff upper and doesn't blub…'

Hettie, as I have said before, was in many ways a chap. I mean, obviously, she wasn't a chap, but she was more a chap than most chaps could ever aspire to be…

And another thing they say is 'a chap doesn't break down in front of another chap,' no matter how much a chap has had to drink. No matter how black the day. No matter what burdens a chap is shouldering. No matter what.

A chap soldiers on and the most you should expect from another chap is for them to tell you to buck up and behave like a chap ought to, because it's just the done thing. A chap, that is, a man, well…

What it comes down to is a man doesn't cry…

Hettie didn't say a word, just sipped her drink and sat across from me, head bowed, not encroaching on my despair. Like a good chap does. Even a chap who is not a chap…

Hettie also didn't say a word when I started to weep.

Call it exhaustion, mental and physical, after all I'd been through in the last few days. Call it delayed shock. Call it the drink. Call it whatever you want. I sat there and I wept, tears streaming down my face, utterly distraught… And Hettie didn't say a word, she just sat there with me, like a good chap does. Even a chap who isn't a chap.

I wept.

And then Hettie put down her glass, picked up her chair, moved it next to mine, sat down again, put her arm around my shoulder and pulled me down onto her chest. And then she just let me get it all out, all that pent-up emotion, all the fear, all the horror, all the anxiety and dread. She let me just open the flood gates and empty the dam.

And all through this, Hettie didn't say a word. She just sat there with me, like a good chap does.

Even a chap who isn't a chap.

Because when it comes down to it, a good chap, a real chap… Well, a chap like that knows that all the horse shit that is said about what a chap does and doesn't do is just that, so much horse shit. Chaps sometimes need to weep, and chaps sometimes need another chap, even a chap who isn't a chap, to just sit with them and let them do so. Without all that 'A real chap doesn't do this' nonsense.

And you, dear reader, perhaps expect me to make a joke round about now, some irreverent witticism, some callow remark, some off-colour observation about resting there on Hetties's chest…

But no… Not this time.

Hettie sat with me, held me, and let me get all the welled-up guilt and sorrow of the survivor out of my system, and never said a word, because there was nothing to be said.

And afterwards, once I'd gotten it all out of my system, once I had moved past it all, once I was once more my usual callow self-involved self, Hettie still never said a word about it.

Because a good chap, even a chap who is not a chap, but is more a chap than most chaps will ever be, a chap like that knows when nothing needs be said. Instead, they just offer a smile of understanding, that nod of recognition that you need at that moment, and says nothing afterwards when that time is past, because nothing needs to be said. Instead, they're just there for you, in that moment when you needed them to be.

And sometimes a chap who is a chap, and a callow, bitter, sarcastic, swine of a chap at that, sometimes a chap like that just needs to know that someone gave enough of a damn to let them not be a chap for a while and just be a hurt, scared human being hiding in the darkness from those fickle gods of fate that chose to torment our souls…

CHAPTER 9

Chamber 17:2:4

The following day dawned, and its dawning brought with it the twin joys of a hangover and boredom. The former the worst of the combination. I can say this for Hettie's engine room hooch, it gets the job done. At least, if the job in question is seeking to avoid your demons by the liberal obliteration of brain cells followed by a loss of consciousness. There is, however, a price to pay the following morning. Hangovers were though hardly a new development in my life, so despite having no appetite due to a stomach as sensitive as a parliamentarian's press secretary on ministerial expenses day, I went in search of whatever the galley passed off as breakfast on Captain Verne's damn boat.

I knew that what my hangover cried out for, after years of dedicated research, was grease. To wit, a good old-fashioned English breakfast. Fried bacon, fried sausage, black pudding fried, fried egg, fried bread, mushrooms fried of course and all cooked with best quality lard. The kind of breakfast that sets you up for the day, not least because it takes a day to work off all the fat and gristle you just consumed. The kind of breakfast that settles in a stomach like half a pound of lead. Lead which on the face of it would probably be only marginally less healthy to consume than said breakfast.

If I was pushed, a cup of earl grey wouldn't have gone amiss either…

Unfortunately, I'd slept late. In my defence, my body needed the rest and felt like it still needed the rest. Cracked ribs and a recently dislocated shoulder don't heal overnight, and these were just the most recent depravations it had been dragged through in the last few months. The effect of multiple concussions had far from dissipated for one thing and while I'd popped another painkiller on top of everything that morning, it definitely wasn't 'putting a spring in my step' nor was it doing much for the hangover.

Sadly, however, when I got to the galley, they weren't serving a full English, partly because if the clock in the galley was anything to go by there wasn't much of the morning left. Partly of course it was because the majority of the crew were French or from the low countries, and their idea of breakfast wasn't designed to thicken the arteries and lead to coronary conditions in early middle-age. Instead, the morning repast aboard The Squid was mostly pastry breads, soft cheeses and fruit juice. Regardless, of course, when I finally stumbled belligerently into the galley, the chef and the rest of the galley staff were busy playing cards, drinking little cups of coffee and smoking those weird French cigarettes that are half as thin and twice as long as they should be.

I stood at the pass for a minute or two in the vain hopes one of them might take pity on me and offer me something, even if it was just one of their god awful tiny coffees. Apparently, however, pitiful though I felt, I wasn't near pitiful enough to entice any of them to give up their hand, or indeed so much as glance in my direction. It was clear soon enough that I was going to get no joy standing there and would have to come back whenever they were due to dish out the grub to the next watch. My stomach meanwhile was rebelling, all the worse for having been emptied at some point the previous evening down the latrine, so I shuffled off to find something to distract me from how bad I felt.

"Stupid Anglais," I heard someone mutter behind me as I vacated the galley through the hatch and right at that moment, I could find neither the strength nor the will to argue with that assessment.

I assumed it was going to be a couple of hours before there was any food in the offing and probably more, depending on how they ran the watches. If this had been an airship, there would have been three overlapping watches and meals would be timed around shift changes. But that was how RAN crews operated. I didn't have a clue if that translated over to the crew of an ostensibly French submersible. As such, I was just going to have to grin and bear it for the time being.

Unfortunately, while nursing a growling stomach and a pounding head, I was at a loss for something to do in the meantime. Boredom was already setting in. I'd no jobs to do. Verne might have decided to keep me aboard, but I wasn't part of the crew. Once again, I was a listless passenger on another's craft. Flailing around like a loose end.

It's odd, when you think about it, when I've a job to do I will move hell and highwater to avoid doing it. I'll happily shoulder work to another and skive off for an hour. Yet whenever I find myself without a job, I'm ill at ease, listless and almost always bored. This could be almost the definition of irony.

I was tempted to head down to the engine room and see if Hettie was busy, but I'd little doubt she would be. If Hettie has nothing more important to do, she almost without fail finds something to tinker with. Either way I'd just be getting under her feet. Besides which I'd no desire to make my only friend aboard sick of the sight of me. I'd imposed upon her good graces enough the night before and not entirely been myself at the time. As much as I appreciated what she had done for me, I wasn't quite ready to face her in the cold light of sobriety.

I could clearly rule out the bridge as well. Having entered uninvited once it seemed wise not to make a habit of doing so. My erstwhile host may have decided not to rid himself of me out of hand, at least until his daughter was in a position to verify my story, but there was nothing to stop Verne changing his mind as to my freedom aboard ship. I had no desire to encourage him to clap me in irons and stick me in whatever passed on this vessel for a brig. So I chose not to push my luck, which isn't exactly famed for its bounty, let's face it.

I even considered trying to look in on my own favourite Bad Penny, if only to see just how badly she'd been injured for myself. Not that I knew where to find her. She hadn't been in the infirmary when I was down there. In all likelihood, she was cosseted away in a room off the captain's chambers. She was his daughter after all. Looking for her in there uninvited struck me as even less wise than walking onto the bridge, so I dismissed that idea. Besides, what were the chances she would be pleased to see me even if she was conscious. Even after everything we went through together in Japan and aboard The Jonah, we weren't what you might call close. So, in truth visiting Vivienne Verne was a long way down my list of ways to pass the time.

But all that left me with what exactly?

Lacking any obvious choice of destination and having no desire to return to my cabin and just stare through the porthole into darkness, I decided the best I could do was stretch my legs a little and walk the ship. It was the best exercise I was likely to get for a while anyway; it wasn't like I was going to find a gymnasium on board after all…

Except actually, I stumbled across one later that day. It was of course small as these things go. Half a dozen yards across and twice that in length. There was though quite a lot jammed into it. A sparing square. A couple of punch bags and lifting equipment. Even a strange machine with a conveyer belt you ran on, driven by a drivebelt that came down through the ceiling from the engine room, like a never-ending road. Verne liked his guards to keep sharp and so they trained in small groups for a couple of hours a day. This was towards the back of the ship, and noisy as hell I may add, as the main engines were housed on the deck above.

If that seems unlikely to you, as it did to me before I stumbled upon it, then it is because you don't fully appreciate the scale of Verne's submersible. Nor did I up to that point, having never actually seen it from the outside. It was the length of a couple of rugby fields and not far off as half as broad as one at its waist, though it tapered off to each end much like an airship's gas bag. Beyond the engine rooms, it tapered even further until it came to an end at the two huge propellers forming the main drive. Each propeller was linked to one engine and could be driven independently, each of them over ten feet wide.

Of course, big as the ship was, it had a lot packed into it, all the mechanical stuff needed to make the damn thing work for a start. It wasn't just the engines, there were ballast tanks, fuel storage, weapons systems and god only knew what else. Then there were crew quarters, the captain's suite, the bridge, the stores, the cargo holds for whatever cargo a craft like this carried. Most of which I suspected was contraband of one kind or another. Perhaps it says something about me that I had leapt to the assumption Captain Verne wasn't above a little piracy. But even if he was, and I strongly suspected he wasn't, then he would trade with them. I mean, why have a submersible in the first place if not to sneak around. I didn't give a moment's thought to the possibility that Verne merely engaged in legitimate business.

This, at least, gave me something to work with. Pirates are just smugglers who don't bother to purchase stock they can acquire. Smuggling... well, that was a business I understood. While I wandered about, I gave some thought to how I might lean on my knowledge of shady acquaintances as a way to make myself useful to Verne. Though exactly how I might approach the subject alluded me. That you know a guy in the Balkans who might be interested in some acquired light arms isn't something you just bring up in casual conversation. Besides which, I was not entirely sure exactly which side of all the grey moral lines Verne actually stood.

I was contemplating all this as I wandered from deck to deck, stumbling over strange sections whose uses that escaped me. Like the hyperbaric chamber I found in the depths of the ship. I had a vague idea this was something to do with pressure, as the large dials on the side of it were something of a clue, but what its actual use was escaped me. It may have had something to do with the heavy-duty diving suits I found in the next chamber and the airlock, which seemed to be a far studier version than the ones used by engineers to enter an airship's gas envelope for repairs. This airlock, it seemed, was designed to be flooded and open out into the ocean so was built, like everything, to hold back immense pressure. I've seen bank vaults that were less sturdy in comparison.

It occurred to me when I came across the airlock that there was another way for Verne to finance his pursuits aside piracy. The oceans of the world are littered with shipwrecks after all. My mind, awash with sudden avarice, leapt to the like of sunken Spanish galleons in the mid-Atlantic, laden with Aztec treasure. Heavy pressure suits and a submersible suddenly made a lot more sense. Thinking on this naturally led me to consider the most pertinent of questions. Where exactly on The Squid did the captain keep his illicit hauls of Spanish gold?

You'll have to forgive my romantic nature. But thoughts of fortunes in little gold idols and Aztec head dresses, fired me with a new enthusiasm for further exploration of the maze of corridors and hatches in the bowels of the ship.

Not that I had to explore very far, because a few moments later I came upon Chamber 17:2:4.

17:2:4 was as innocuous a chamber as any other down in the bowels of The Oegopsida, save that the corridor leading to it was a little wider than most, and the hatch way, with 17:2:4 stencilled on it below the ubiquitous squid icon, looked almost as heavily reinforced as the airlock doors I'd discovered earlier. It wasn't, however, the heavy-duty nature of the hatch and the wide corridor that garnered my interest. What caught my attention was simply because other than the bridge, and the captain's personal quarters, it was the only hatchway I'd come across that was guarded.

Guarded and, I should add, a spit and a cough away from the airlock room, with a wide corridor leading to it… I didn't need my streak of avarice to tell me the most logical reason the captain posted guards on a chamber deep in the bowels of the ship. His crew was probably hand-picked, and doubtless he would claim to have faith in every one of them. But it was still a crew of privateers at best and perhaps one small step away from pirates. Such a crew doubtless had a few light-fingered fellows among their number. The guards therefore must be in place to dissuade anyone from helping themselves to an odd trinket or two. To my mind, therefore, it was obvious 17:2:4 was where Verne housed the valuable plunder they looted from the ocean's graveyards. I just knew it.

I knew something else as well… I knew I wanted to be in that room.

Of course, the guards with harpoon rifles at their shoulders were going to be a problem. Them and the heavy locks that said 'keep out' louder than words ever could. But these were merely problems to be surmounted. Right at that moment I wasn't trying to think of how to surmount them, I was thinking of the word doubloons.

I have always liked the word doubloons. I'm not sure what it is about it, but it just has a way of rolling off the tongue in such a satisfying way. Oh, I'm fond of words like pounds, dollars, francs, yen and the like. They are all good words, great words if they come at the end of a sentence like, 'Here's a thousand…' But the word doubloons, so often prefaced by the word 'gold' has a romantic appeal to it. It conjures up images of wild men with peg legs, thick black beards and tricorn hats. It's a word that suggests a brace of pistols and a cutlass or two. It suggests a skull and cross bones flapping in the wind. And maps to chests of treasure, overflowing with glittering, golden… doubloons…

Sue me, I'm a romantic at heart…

And so, with the word doubloons flittering across my consciousness, I strode down the corridor past the guards, giving them a smile that said, 'Hi, just out for a walk, don't mind me,' and kept on walking till I reached the next hatchway.

As I stepped through the hatch and closed it behind me, I risked a surreptitious glance behind me to see if the guards' eyes had followed my passing. The closest of them was just turning his gaze away, as I spun the wheel to lock the hatchway in place. I stepped back so I couldn't be seen though the small window in the hatch and stood there a while, watching them and trying to determine just how alert the guards were, considering a few dozen plans that might get me though that hatch.

Brute force was out, even if I could overpower both guards, which was a long shot, where would that get me but standing before a locked door. I could probably pick the damn thing, of course, it isn't difficult after all. All you need is a set of lock picks, which admittedly I didn't have. Though, in fairness, even if I had lock picks, I didn't have the first clue how you used them. While this is only a guess, I suspect it's not a skill you just picked up. It's more the sort of skill that requires a lot of practice and someone skilled in such nefarious activities to teach you. Which was a bit of an issue.

There was, of course, the old favourite of drugging the guards. The ship's sawbones would have plenty of high-grade sedatives, at least if he hadn't used them all up keeping Saffron Wells under control. My expertise in such things, learned from penny novels and ripping yarn magazines, told me a high enough dose of codeine would do the trick. Of course, I'd need a way to get them to ingest it. But then just how much codeine do you need, can you taste it in coffee should you bring a flask of the stuff to the guards and somehow convince them to drink? Knock out gas based on the stuff would be better… But would such a gas get past those respirators Verne's guards wore? And just how, when it comes down to it, would I steal a cylinder of high-grade seditives from the ship's surgery, get it down ten decks and across half the ship unseen, and frankly how exactly do those cylinders work? Cheap paperback authors are seldom realistic or forthcoming about such things. But if I could, well, it might work…

But then of course I would be standing before a locked hatchway again… Sans lock picks and the skill to use them.

It occurred to me that there must be a key. A key probably kept in Verne's cabin, because if I was the captain that's where I would keep it. So, if perhaps I could catch sight of where it was kept, and get to it. Well, I could make a copy. All you needed to do was press the key into some soap, then you could cast a copy. It didn't need to be a perfect casting; a needle file was all you required to sort out the rough edges and then, Roberta is your cross-dressing uncle's weekend name, I'd have a key…

True enough, I've never actually cast a key in a bar of soap, but I was sure doing so would work, I'd read it in a cheap novel once…

Except now I thought about it, wouldn't the soap just melt…?

Acid on the lock then, maybe?

But where would I get highly corrosive acid from? Unless Hettie's engine room cocktails counted and, in all fairness, her engine room hooch was probably not quite up to the job of corroding high grade steel in seconds… Though judging by my hangover, it would clean the surface off nicely.

I briefly considered that one sure way to get past the guards, playing to my strengths, would be to talk my way past the guards. All I had to do was find out everything I could about them and find a little common ground from which to build myself an in.

Perhaps they liked rugby…?

But no, unfortunately, a pair of Frenchmen and an Englishman talking rugby, well, it was an argument waiting to happen after the Seven Nations final three years ago. The French try that 'won' it was definitely a forward pass. Not to mention Macron's foot was in touch before he grounded the ball. Damn Russian touch judge… Why they ever accepted Russians into the tournament I'll never know. Besides, I heard from a mate in the know that the ref went on a two-week jolly to the Algarve after the match, paid for by the FFR.

Honestly, the corruption in the game's getting out of hand. Time was a brown envelope stuffed with a few fivers handed over in a pub round the back of the stadium was all it took to get the right decisions on the field…

But, not to digress further, I swiftly realised talking rugby with a couple of French guards wasn't going to go well.

The trouble was, as I rattled through a myriad of different possibilities, the more I thought about it, the more I came to realise that nothing I came up with would go well. The nub of the problem was all those cheap trashy adventure novels… They'd taught me everything I knew about getting past a pair of guards and into a locked room. But it was all either horse shit or required skills I just didn't have. This was a somewhat bitter realisation, and I felt some so-called authors owed me a refund…

Despite this shocking revelation, I stayed by the little window in the hatch, still watching the guards, for a while longer, steadily making my merry way through ever more unlikely plans and crossing them off one at a time. It was both a frustrating and distracting exercise. Which accounts for my utter lack of awareness of what was happening behind me.

"I believe, Monsieur Smyth, I was most clear when I explained there were parts of my ship it would be unwise to explore," said the voice of Captain Verne…

As I heard him speak, I felt myself tensing up in preparation for the blow to the back of my head that cheap novels and recent experience had taught me would come next.

My world, as you might expect by now, was about to go black…

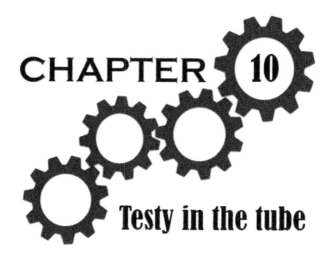

CHAPTER 10
Testy in the tube

Surprisingly the blow never came.

The captain, I suspect, felt no need to cosh me into submission, despite this being the reaction I was used to inspiring in people of late. For some reason, he felt perfectly happy just to stand behind me menacingly and wait for me to turn around. Which, of course, is what I did, after I let out the breath I hadn't been aware I was holding, somewhat surprised at still being conscious.

He was, of course, not alone. Two more guards were standing to either side of him with harpoon rifles pointed, somewhat pointedly, in my direction. Not that it is possible to point a harpoon rifle in any way that is not pointed... And barbed, I may add.

I can honestly say that the only thing worse than being shot by one of those things, assuming it didn't kill you straight out, would be trying to remove the bolt afterwards.

At least so I assumed. I hadn't had the displeasure at that point and was blissfully unaware of the small tesla generator unit that spooled up as the wire attached to the bolt dragged behind it, so when it embedded in the target it also delivered a high voltage electric shock so even a minor wound could incapacitate a horse. Blissfully unaware of that shocking detail though I may've been, having a pair of the damn things pointed in my direction was still intimidating enough.

"Captain… No One, I must apologise. I seem to have got myself a little lost," I said as quickly as my wits allowed. Given they were still in the grips of a horrendous hangover, my wits were a little slower than usual, and yes, thank you, I'm aware that may not be saying a great deal.

To this, the Captain merely raised a disbelieving eyebrow. Beyond that his expression remained impassive. His lack of response didn't help matters. I had no idea if he was about to have his guards arrest me, shoot me, or for all I knew, simply ask me to retreat to my quarters and leave it at that. Clearly though claiming to be 'a little lost', wasn't going to cut it when it came to explaining my presence deep in the bowels of his vessel, spying on a guarded chamber.

I groped around in the back of my mind for some common ground we might share with which I could appeal to his better graces. Unfortunately, I couldn't think of anything I had in common with a French expatriate aquanaut revolutionary with his own submersible. Except that was for a couple of common acquaintances.

There was that, of course, the obvious one.

"I was hoping to look in on Bad… on Miss Vivienne," I explained quickly, hoping that feigning concern for the psychotic death machine he called a daughter may at least buy me some leniency.

The captain continued to stare at me with an inscrutable expression. He was a man who knew how to stare someone down was Monsieur Verne. The full beard helped, I suspect.

A heavy moment hung between us before he spoke.

"I see, Monsieur… And is there a reason you thought to find Vivienne down here in the bowels of The Oegopsida?" he asked. Unfortunately, this wasn't an unreasonable question. She was his daughter, after all. Added to which the ship's medical facilities were on the upper decks, close to his quarters. But still, this all had a slither of plausible deniability to it, enough for me to grasp at, small victory though that might prove to be.

"I must confess, I was stretching my legs. I was feeling somewhat cooped up, you see, and so I was just walking the corridors of your wonderful vessel when I happened over the guards and thought to myself that must be where Vivienne is convalescing. 'What is more important to the captain,' I said to myself, 'than to guard the wellbeing of his daughter?'" I explained. This was laying it on a tad thick I know but occasionally I've found it's wise to play the hapless fool.

A role some doubtless would say I was born to play.

"There are many things and people on this ship I see fit to guard, Monsieur Smyth. Particularly when I have guests aboard whose merits remain questionable," the captain replied coldly. Then added with a note of suspicion seeping through, "Saffron Wells for example…"

That threw me a googly down the leg side. I'd not considered that the chamber beyond the locked hatch might be the ship's brig. It made sense now he pointed it out, of course. It's always wise to guard your prisoners. Without thinking, I found myself turning back toward the little porthole in the hatchway, those regrets that were barely buried coming back to me again.

"Has she become more lucid?" I found myself asking him, with no need to fake my concern.

"Miss Wells? Or my daughter?" he replied, guardedly, giving every me impression I was still on trial in his eyes, unsurprisingly.

I swallowed hard, turning back to his passionless visage. "Either?"

His eyes gave nothing away. He was obviously weighing me up, but then he always seemed to be judging everything and seldom gave any obvious sign of his impending verdicts.

"Miss Wells is sedated. I suspect she will remain so for some time. Vivienne at least is now awake, though not in a position to say a great deal," he said, then gave a vague smile that worried me, as he met my gaze full on, and appeared to reach a decision. "Come, I am sure my daughter will be overjoyed to see a familiar face. One who wishes to visit her in her convalescence. You are, after all, a friend to my daughter…"

There was a touch of malice to his words. A sarcasm I was all too familiar with, though usually issuing from his daughter's lips.

"I'd be delighted," I lied.

As I did so, I felt a cold sweat break out on my back. Despite everything we'd been through together, 'a friend' wasn't how I'd choose to describe my relationship with my ever volatile Bad Penny.

"Doubtless…" Verne said, and motioned to his guards to form up to 'escort' me. Then he turned his back, trusting his guards to keep me in tow, and started back through the bowels of the ship without further comment.

I was led along the usual maze of corridors and up several levels until we got to part of the ship I was more familiar with. It was on the same level as the surgery but further back towards the engines. My own cabin was two levels below but otherwise fairly close to the same section. The trek through the ship, for me, was accompanied by a feeling of impending doom that loomed closer with every echoing step on the deck plates. To call myself nervous would be understatement, what liberty I was afforded on The Squid hung upon the good graces of a woman with whom I had a complex relationship at best. That feeling of doom worsened when we arrived at a large hatchway twice the width of the normal hatches. A hatchway that incidentally was also guarded, which at least gave my earlier gambit some credence. Verne was indeed having his guards watch over his precious Vivienne. But as the guards nodded to their commander and set about opening the hatch, I had a distinct sinking feeling once more that was nothing to do with being on a submarine. The captain stepped through, not bothering to check that I followed, but then why would he need to, what else could I do?

Beyond the hatch was a large, dimly lit compartment bathed in this strange sickly yellow green glow that came from a large column of glass built into one of the bulkheads. It ran from floor to ceiling, must have been three foot across and was full of a luminescent fluid. It struck me as a strange way to light a room but nothing was exactly normal aboard The Squid. There were two more of these columns along the wall but only the one was giving out light. The rest of the room was full of strange equipment. What looked like an unoccupied surgical bed of an advanced kind was set up in the middle of the room with huge overhead lamps, that weren't lit, hanging above it. Several large racks of devices and tools hung on the wall, or were secured in other ways.

"I thought we were going to visit your daughter?" I asked, feeling a mite bewildered by what I was seeing. The room was clearly a second medical facility, but it looked more like Hettie's idea of paradise than a surgeon's.

Verne turned his gaze on me once more. "And so I have," he said, before raising a hand to point in the direction of the luminescent tank on the wall.

I turned my gaze as he directed and it was then I realised there was something in the tank. It took me a moment to realise that something was actually a someone. Floating, suspended in that strange glowing liquid.

Now, to be fair, you're probably thinking I was a little slow here. I mean, yes, of course there was someone in the tank. Of course, that someone was his daughter. Everyone knows what strange built into the wall medical tanks that give off an eerie glow are, right? Well, that's a fair point, except such things are just ridiculous fictions made up in penny dreadful novels, and as I established earlier, my faith in such things had been dented of late. No one is ever actually kept alive in a strange overgrown fish tank, are they...?

Except, I can tell you that in this case that was exactly what was going on. What had caused me to take a moment to recognise that a person was floating in the tank was that she was not entirely as I knew her. She was somewhat less whole for a start.

One of her legs ended just below the knee. The other just above it. Her left arm was not there at all, just a stub of flesh where her shoulder blades ended. Her chest and pelvis were wrapped in some linen-like material, which at least preserved her dignity, I guess. A breathing mask was strapped over her face, with multiple hoses going into it, occasionally unleashing a stream of bubbles that joined smaller ones that rose from the base of the tank, while her hair waved about in the water like some strange human seaweed.

I took a step closer to the tank, filled with a morbid fascination, and her head turned towards the movement.

Beyond the visor of the face mask, her eyes locked on mine and an eruption of bubbles came out of the mask. They were eyes I knew. It was indeed Vivienne Verne, or my own favourite Bad Penny as I still thought of her. Albeit less of her than I expected. I could see also see in her eyes a touch of hatred I knew only too well.

As she floated before me, there were several more large eruptions of bubbles which I thought it safe to assume were caused by several unladylike exclamations, muttered into her breathing mask. Then she raised her one whole limb and for a second, as hope springs eternal, I thought she was going to wave at me.

Instead, she turned her hand in the water so the back of it faced me and she made a fist briefly before extending one solitary finger in my direction.

And no, she was not pointing at me. It was the other one fingered gesture.

I found myself smiling…

That may seem irrational but after all that had happened in the last few days, Bad Penny flipping me the bird was actually a little dose of normality. There was a pleasing familiarity about it, a charm even. Like an old friend waving at you across a crowded bar room. That finger said all was right with the world, all was as it should be.

"She doesn't seem entirely pleased to see you, Mr Smyth," the captain said and gestured for his guards to take hold of me. Which they did, quite firmly, in a very professional brutal henchman way.

"She never is…" I told him, still smiling, because what other option was there at that point. At least I hadn't been coshed into unconsciousness, yet. Though I braced myself, sure it was coming. This was clearly the point where I would find out what The Squid's brig was like. So on the plus side, it seemed likely I was about to find out what lay beyond the hatchway into Chamber 17:2:4 after all…

CHAPTER 11

The horned mountain

As it turned out, that's not what happened. Instead, I spent the next couple of days politely encouraged to cease my wanderings by the lock on my cabin door and an armed guard beyond it. My cabin in truth became the cell I'd first imagined it was.

Captain Verne had decided I couldn't be trusted to wander about the ship, which was reasonably insightful of him, I'm sure you'd agree. However, while this was the case, he wasn't going to do anything else with me until he was able to fully converse with his daughter, once she had finished healing up in the tank, and presumably been put back together again.

The captain's guards, all considered, had been remarkably polite about it all, escorting me rather than dragging me back to my quarters, after I was dismissed. Given recent escapades, this was a comparatively new experience for me, that meant for once I found myself locked up but not nursing a concussion and further bruised ribs. But the lack of additions to my list of aliments did little to ease the boredom of being locked in a cell once more, with nothing to do but stare out of my tiny porthole into the dark depths of the ocean.

As I didn't find the occasional half glimpsed shoal of fish all that distracting, I spent most of my time laid out on my cot, trying to piece together all that had happened over the previous few months. That and counting the rivets on the ceiling, of which there were one hundred and thirty-seven. As that seemed an odd number, and an odd number seemed, well, odd, I counted them again, several times, seldom coming up with the same figure, but it did occupy my mind for a while.

It is astounding how riveting a man can find such mundane tasks when he has nothing else to do.

Food came regularly, which suggested I hadn't been forgotten, but I was getting sick of fish. What's that old saying, 'give a man a fish and you'll feed him for a day, give a man a fishing rod and you'll feed him all his life…' There may be some truth in that, but trust me, it would soon become a miserable existence if you don't also give him a deep fat fryer and a bag of spuds.

A bottle of vinegar wouldn't have gone amiss either.

At first, I'd hoped Hettie would bob her head around my door, but doubtless she'd been warned to keep her distance. Well, either that or she was just busy messing about with engines and hadn't given me a second thought, which knowing Hettie was entirely possible. Thinking of Hettie, I realised, I still had no idea how she'd come to be part of Verne's crew. Though from what I'd seen, she was living her best life mucking about with the inner workings of The Oegopsida.

All power to her, if you care for my opinion, but I ask you, would it have killed her to wander down and visit me, carrying a bottle of engine room hooch to brighten my day?

Instead, all I got was a regular delivery of fish stew and silence from the guards. Admittedly though, no one was spitting in my food, as far as I could tell, though I suspect that would've only improved the flavour. Nor was it being delivered by automaton geisha, which after Japan was something of a mercy. As cells go, in fact, beyond the boredom, it was relatively pleasant and non-life-threatening, though it did involve one hundred and twenty-nine rivets, according to the latest, and once again odd numbered count.

By the morning of my third day in isolation, having counted the rivets in the ceiling for the umpteenth time, and always ending up with an odd number, I woke when the lights switched from the nightly half-light to slightly less dim day mode and realised I was going a little stir crazy. What did it matter if the number of rivets in the ceiling was an odd amount? Just because they were laid out in a perfect grid and clearly should add up to an even number, didn't mean it was anything to worry about. So what if I was always counting one rivet short? What difference would one rivet make on a machine this size? It's not like the ship was going to sink just because one rivet was missing…

To distract myself from impending doom due to lack of a rivet, I started working through all the worst-case scenarios I could think of. By now, I'd no doubt the captain must have tried to get some sense out of Saffron Wells. That was a mine field of possibilities right there.

Then there was his daughter. Bad Penny had clearly been less than pleased to see me. We hadn't had the best of relationships to start with, even before the flight from Nepal. I suspected that floating in a cylindrical tank of iridescent water, or whatever liquid was in that tank, wasn't going to put my little pet psychopath in the best of moods.

Nor was being without her arm. I'd been aware her left arm was a prosthetic augmentation. Having extendable razorblades where her fingers nails should have been was a bit of a clue. But I'd never realised her legs were prosthesis too. In fact, I would have happily told anyone that there wasn't anything wrong with them, and to my eye a great deal right about them. But then, I conceded to myself, when Penny wasn't slicing things up with her fingernails, her arm looked perfectly normal too.

Not for the first time I found myself pondering what truth lay behind Vivienne Verne. I didn't know her lack of limbs was due to birth defects or if there had been an accident at some point in her past. If the latter, it must have been a miracle she survived at all. I've seen a man lose an arm and die of blood loss in minutes. To lose the better part of two legs and an arm, the shock alone would kill you. Either way, whatever the trauma of her past, it went some way to explaining her temperament. Though that said, I've met plenty of rage-fuelled bitter bastards who had all their limbs intact, and a fair few people who've lost a limb or two and are still better people that I will ever be. So perhaps making an excuse of her misfortune and blaming her psychosis upon it, says more about me and the presumptions I make, than anything about her.

But in her position, I'd be bitter, and if I was bitter and had razorblades for fingernails... well, there's a few eyes I'd be tempted to scratch out, I am sure.

The thing that got me about her augmentations however was that they were so advanced. More so than any I'd ever seen or ever heard about. Artificial limbs were normally very obviously artificial, these were the exact opposite. Vivienne Verne could streak naked at the Oval and no one would notice three of her limbs were artificial. They would notice plenty of other things, and I doubt one man in ten could be convinced to avert his gaze. But, until she started slicing the throats of Surrey's first eleven, no one would imagine she was anything more than the shapely example of womanhood she appeared to be, momentarily interrupting the day's play and giving the commentators something to talk about other than pigeons.

The Times would be outraged, and carry as many pictures as possible to convey its outrage as graphically as they could get away with, just this side of the public morality and preservation of standards in media act.

The level of sophistication in her prosthetics was therefore astounding, and what I had seen of her father's craft didn't suggest that level of sophistication. The Oegopsida was astounding in its own way, don't get me wrong. But the submersible was big, obvious engineering. Bad Penny's augmentations were a whole world of subtle in comparison. They were the fruits of the kind of science Professor Jobs and Mister Gates went in for. Verne had already told me we were heading for Musk Island, the name taken from that of its own resident 'genius', in order to get his daughter 'repaired'. As my recent encounters with 'mad scientists', hadn't turned out too well for me, I was far from inspired by this news. While I knew nothing about this Doctor Musk, the idea of crossing paths with another lunatic with a jeweller's screwdriver and the moral compunctions of a seven-year-old boy looking at his father's pocket watch while wondering how it worked, gave me a decidedly sinking feeling.

Having time to convalesce from my injuries was no bad thing, so being locked up for a few days did me no harm. But having time to think wasn't doing me any favours. By the third day, I was sick of my own company and when breakfast arrived, a depressing breakfast of fish which was decidedly not kippers, I found my appetite lacking as I resigned myself to another long day of counting rivets.

Then, just before noon, something changed. I didn't notice it at first, and though I felt a definite vibration through the hull as the first ballast tanks were blown, I didn't immediately realise what it had been. I did notice the water beyond the small porthole started to brighten a little, just before the surfacing siren went off a few minutes later. But once I realised we were surfacing, it suggested to me we were nearing our destination. As with many things that feel like impending doom, there is a certain relief when they finally arrive. That said, whether arriving at Musk Island was going to be to my good or ill, I could only speculate, and given my luck, ill seemed the likelier of the pair.

It may seem strange to you that a man would curse his luck having survived a fall into the Indian Ocean from a crashing airship and being rescued by a passing vessel. Perhaps you feel I was just being a tad pessimistic? Of course, with hindsight, if anything, I wasn't pessimistic enough...

As if nothing else it made a change, I stared out through my porthole as the ocean steadily grew brighter over the course of a couple of dozen minutes, until I could almost see the surface beyond a crystal blue filter.

It was at this point I heard the grinding of the locking wheel on my hatch.

I turned, not knowing who to expect and found myself greeted by a masked guard, who wasted no time in motioning me to follow him. I wasn't given much in the way of options to do otherwise, besides which, right then I was happy just to get out of my cell, so I did as instructed and found myself once more escorted through the narrow corridors of The Squid, towards the central tube that led to the upper floors. The climb up was arduous, but far easier than a few days before, my shoulder healing nicely with all the enforced rest.

When we reached the bridge level, I stepped off, assuming that was our destination, only for the guard to grunt at me and point upwards. So, I found myself climbing still further up towards the observation platform at the top of the small tower-like structure built at the centre of the ship through which the ship could be accessed when at sea. I was rather gratified to discover the hatch at the top lay open and beyond it I could see a clear blue sky for the first time in days. As I climbed through, I paused for a moment, taking long deep breaths of clean sea air. It was like drinking the finest nectar, I can tell you that for nothing. You'll be unsurprised to learn how close it gets aboard ship. The air filtration system may recycle the air inside, but it left it far from pure, a hundred or more sailors having breathed every bit of it at one point or another. You don't notice it over time, but my lungs sure had. The sudden influx of clean sea air led to a fit of coughing of epic proportions, which, by the by, announced my arrival on the observation deck.

"Ah, Mr Smyth has joined us," Verne said without turning towards me, no small humour to his tone.

I bit back the most obvious response about the lack of choice involved. Instead, I took a moment to recover myself and climb the last few rungs up onto the deck, then walked over to join him, offering respectful nods to the others on the deck none of whom I immediately recognised, but assumed were among the senior officers.

I settled myself at the railing and found myself looking out across the ocean at what was to be our destination. A large island, it was still some few miles away, from which distance it didn't look very impressive, indeed it was much like any of the multitude of small islands that litter the Pacific. It was part of one of those small island chains that were volcanic in nature. Like most such islands, a single large cone-shaped mountain dominated it, forming most of the northern side of the island. As we grew closer though, I started to realise there was something odd about its shape, not that I am an expert on volcanic islands, but as a rule I was sure they tended to only have one peak. The main peak was much that, a fairly traditional inverted V shape with sides that tapered upwards and got steadily steeper as they climbed towards the summit which must have lay just above what I first took to be the cloud layer. But when we got a little closer, it dawned on me that other than around the mountain top there were few if any clouds in the sky and those that were, were wispy trails high above, rather than the thick dense layer of cloud around the mountain top that looked more like smoke... the kind of smoke you got from...

"Is that an active volcano?" I asked no one in particular, keeping my voice steady. The thought unnerved me a tad, but I wasn't going to show it.

"Indeed, it has been active for some two hundred years or more. The smoke is from thermal vents on the mountain side. Luckily, they keep the pressure from building up to the point of eruption, unlike its sister to the east that blew a few decades ago," Verne explained, in an all too simple, matter of fact tone, for my liking. He sounded like a school teacher. I've never trusted school teachers.

"A natural pressure gauge, that's reassuring," I said, though I didn't find it all that reassuring at all. Still, if it had been happily bubbling away for a couple of centuries without blowing its top, what were the chances it would choose to do so at some point over the few days I expected to be on the island?

Yes, okay... But not get ahead of myself.

Verne, to my surprise, smiled at this, and at me. I took this to mean I was no longer in his bad books, for the moment at least. I could only presume he and his daughter had finally spoken and she had confirmed my story.

Surprisingly, this hadn't led to my being fed to the sharks, so, active volcanic island aside, things were looking up.

"The volcano is not controlled by nature alone, though a few of the vents are natural. The good doctor, I believe, has sunk his own vents into the mountain as well so he can regulate the seismic pressures with more precision," he explained, in his lecturing tone, as if someone regulating a volcano was a sane concept.

"This would be Doctor Musk?"

"Elonis Musk, yes," Verne said, and there was something in his tone that suggested there was friction between them. Not that I cared if they danced hand in hand through the meadows or spat at each other over the garden wall. But I filed this away at the back of my mind anyway. It's always good to keep track of these little tensions.

"It must take something of a genius to do something like that…" I said, just to dig a little deeper with that knife. Genius wasn't a word I would have normally used to describe anyone messing about with volcanoes.

Idiot springs to mind.

"Something like that…" Verne replied, in a dismissive tone that suggested his own opinion wasn't so far removed from mine. I took this as another hint that he and the island's resident mad scientist weren't entirely friendly. While that was good to know, I tried not to let that worry me, after all it was his problem not mine. Which just goes to show how little the last few months had taught me…

"How is your daughter?" I asked conversationally, mainly because I was all too aware my presence on his ship, rather than bobbing about in the ocean, was on sufferance only and depended on the good word of a woman with little reason to give one.

"Much healed. She has confirmed your version of events, I'm sure you will be glad to know. Though she has warned me not to place too much faith in you, Mr Smyth."

"That sounds like the Bad Penn... Ahem, Vivienne I know," I half muttered in reply, and stared off at the approaching island, silently wondering to myself if I could take the opportunity it presented to leave The Squid and end my involvement with all this HG Wells and The Ministry business once and for all. It says something, does it not, when taking up residence on an active volcano seems a viable alternative to any other options you have before you.

Not that what it says is anything good.

Thinking this and looking at the smoke rising from the mountainside, I noted again that something about the mountain looked decidedly odd. While for the most part the shape, as I said, was what you'd expect, on the northern slope there was a strange protrusion which I had first taken for a second peak. Now we were closer and at a better angle, I realised I was mistaken, for what stuck out of the side of the mountain seemed more like a horn on the forehead of some enormous beast. Think of the mountain as a rhino's head, and about a third of the way up its northern slopes there was the horn, sticking out at a strange angle somewhere akin to seventy degrees or so, pointing upwards until it was almost level with the flattered top of the volcano. As a rock formation it made no sense at all, though much of it was obscured by the smoke.

As we drew closer, The Squid started to angle its course back towards the southern side of the island, so I didn't get a better view of this strange protrusion, but I saw enough to be certain there was nothing natural about it. It was too uniform and straight to be made of rock, and I drew increasingly certain that whatever it was, it was man-made. If anything, it looked like some enormous pipe. I remember thinking momentarily that it could be a telescope but it seemed far too big for that to be the case. Eventually my curiosity won and I found myself asking the captain, "What is that?"

"That! That is the product of our host's obsession," Verne said.

I raised an eyebrow of inquiry, hoping to get a little more information on the good doctor's activities, because if I'd learned anything in recent times it was that it was best to know what the mad scientists are up. Then you know what you need to avoid. Not walking through the doors of a literal bullet train for example…

The captain kept his own council a moment and stared up at the mountain. I sensed a degree of anger in his voice, which, as this was Verne, was unusual as he never gave much away. Then after a long pause, his eyes narrowing slightly, he went further. "Doctor Musk is something of a polyglot, a big ideas man. His interests are… varied, but in essence he is an engineer with a single great obsession. That which lays beyond this world. All his other interests, and those he gathers to him, are to feed that one singular obsession. One of these interests is the augmentation of the human body, like the augmentations that allow my daughter to walk and do other things. Which is why, Mr Smyth, we're here."

"I see," I said, though I had a feeling there was something more at play here. Verne, it seemed, was harbouring a great deal of resentment, over something or other, towards our prospective host. *'This doesn't bode well, Harry,'* I remember thinking. Though of course I could just have been on edge because of the whole active volcano thing. But this was all starting to have the hallmarks of a powder keg…

Which is not what you want when the powder keg involves a volcano…

"Now, Mr Smyth, I must go below while we guide The Oegopsida into port. You should remain here, Mr Smyth. I'm sure the fresh air will do you good," he told me, which sounded like an order no matter how carefully phrased. Then without further comment, he walked over to the hatch and descended back into the heart of his craft.

This left me alone on the observation deck, save for a couple of guards and a petty officer who I assumed was charged with watching the ship from outside as she went into port. I didn't bother to question why I'd been summoned to the deck in the first place. I assumed it was probably due to no more than a whim on Verne's part. Unless he had a reason for wanting me to see the island as we approached it. Once that thought had occurred to me, I became convinced it was the case. Though as I couldn't for the life of me guess why that might be, I decided not to let that worry me.

Of course, if deciding not to let something worry you was all it took to stop something worrying you then life would be far less… well, worrisome, I supposed is the word.

To take my mind off this quandary I focus on the other one that was looming ever closer. I tried to piece together what I could from the snippets of conversation the captain had gifted me with but little of it made much sense. It found myself assuming from his comment on Musk's obsession with 'that which lays beyond this Earth' that my first and previously dismissed guess as to the mysterious construction on the north side of the volcano was in fact correct and that it must be some kind of telescope. Clearly this Musk was a budding Galileo. Though what a star gazer would have to gain from human augmentation I could not surmise. Still, I decided, a scientist, even a mad one, obsessed with stargazing through an oversized telescope, all be it on the side of an active volcano, didn't sound like something I should worry about overly…

Of course, as it turned out, I was wrong about that, on all counts.

CHAPTER 12

The Island of Doctor Musk

It is my opinion, and it's an opinion that I believe wholeheartedly is well founded, that excessive exposure to science rots the brain. Spend too many hours of your life playing around with strange chemical concoctions in test tubes and it does something to the mind. Perhaps it is something to do with the fumes. Perhaps it's being exposed to anomalous compounds. Perhaps it's all that tedious reading of academic texts and staring at fungi growing in petri dishes. In truth, I really couldn't tell you what it is about science that drives otherwise quite brilliant men off the deep end sanity wise, but drive them it does.

Every scientist I've ever met is mad. They all have something downright odd about them and every single one of them smiles too much…

Doctor Musk, I determined at first glance, was definitely a grade 'A' example. For a start he'd this inane grin, with too many teeth, that seemed to be a permanent resident upon his face. A face that was always too clean and just a tad too shiny. Too clean and a tad too shiny is the best way to describe everything about him. In fact, he sort of gleamed, in an oddly off-putting moist kind of way. Even when Musk was vexed, which I suspect as The Oegopsida pulled into harbour he surely was, he still smiled way too much and gleamed.

I've never been one to put much stock in crazy conspiracy theories. That's not to say I don't believe there is a nugget of truth in the notation that some secret cabal is running the world. I just don't believe that secret cabal is made up of lizard people dressed in human skin suits. However, if there was ever a man who gave credence to the lizard people theory, then it was Elonis Musk as his ill-fitting human suit was far less convincing than most.

But I get ahead of myself, slightly at least.

As we sailed closer to the island, rather than continue our course, The Oegopsida turned with sweeping grace towards the cliff face rather than further along the southern side where the land tapered down to the sea. I found this somewhat alarming. I don't claim to know a great deal about sea-bound vessels but heading straight for a cliff seemed an unwise proposition. Ships as a rule tend to work best in the water, and the water ended rather abruptly a few hundred metres ahead.

The guards and the junior officer alongside me showed no hint of concern, so I tried to put this development out of my mind. But as the distance between us and the cliffs narrowed ever more, I became increasingly alarmed. My alarm was not helped when I noticed The Oegopsida had begun sinking once more into the waves, until just the conning tower where we stood remained above the waves. That too sank slowly downwards several more feet until little more than the four foot of tower remained above the surface and all the while the cliff loomed closer.

I'd half expected we were heading to some unseen gorge or split in the cliff that had been hidden from view. But I saw nothing but rock. It wasn't until we got within a hundred yards or less that I realised there was a dark shadow right at the base of the cliff. As we got closer, I realised it was a cave mouth. A cave whose opening was only a couple of feet higher than the top of the tower on which I stood.

The petty officer stepped around me, as we drew closer, and as nonchalant as you like removed a pin that held the radio mast in place at the back of the conning tower, lowering it down until it rested horizontally, pointing out along the rear of the craft. Then he came back alongside me just in time to duck his head down as we began to sail under the cliff face.

I didn't need to take the hint as I had ducked down into the well of the conning tower long before we reached that point.

We sailed in and the world went dark as night in a moment. In the dark, the noise of the engines was amplified by the close confinement of the cave. On the conning tower it was almost deafening. Which meant I wouldn't have heard the creaking of steel on rock if The Squid was just a couple of feet or so out of alignment with the tunnel through which we were passing. I suppose that was some small mercy. What little light there was stemmed from a small illumination strip that ran around the inside of the tower's rails. The roof of the cave was passing overhead, close enough to touch, close enough to brain me if I stood up.

I've never been overly claustrophobic, but our passage through the mostly subaquatic tunnel seemed to take forever and frayed at my nerves. I felt an intangible sense of dread throughout the whole journey. It seemed inconceivable The Squid could pass through the tunnel unharmed. But then suddenly we passed beyond the tunnel mouth and the cave opened up into a huge gallery that went up some fifty feet or more above us and The Oegopsida started to rise once more from below the waves.

As secret harbours go, this one was impressive. Calling it cavernous would be redundant. The natural cavern had been machined out until it formed a space bigger than the average airship hanger. It was fully long enough to take a craft twice the length of The Oegopsida, though I doubted any other craft ever docked there, because only a submersible could. This island, I realised, may belong to this Doctor Musk, but this dock was clearly Verne's.

As my eyes adjusted to the light and I got my first impression of the submersible bay, it came to me that prospective international terrorists must read the same penny dreadful's and cheap paperbacks I'd indulged in as a youth. It was the only explanation I could come up. Wells had based his operation in that remote Tibetan Monastery. I'm sure the remote location had advantages of course, but a monastery, with Buddhist monks practising martial arts, lotus blossoms, et al… The brass Shogun's cliff top castle at Hamamatsu, with its clockwork rooms and automaton tea geishas also had shades of penny dreadful villainy about it as well, now I thought of it. Which would explain much of what Yamamoto went on to do when he rebuilt Tokyo years later. When Verne originally built these facilities on Musk's Island, which I suspected was the case as who else had a submersible of that size, then he too must have done so after reading those self-same penny dreadful's. What else would inspire a man to build a submersible base inside an active volcano?

Just once I'd have liked to find myself embroiled in an insidious plot that left me at the mercy of an international terrorist who, in defiance of tradition and peer pressure, built their secret base of operations somewhere with a descent hotel bar and room service that didn't involve masked guards with harpoon guns… Call me a dreamer, but I'd sooner be drinking a tall gin and tonic, after a relaxing sauna and massage with extras, than perched on top of a mechanical whale in the heart of an active volcano.

The only upside to the slavish devotion of international terrorists to penny dreadful clichés is I needn't bore you with a detailed description of the cavernous submersible base The Oegopsida emerged into. It was a cavernous submersible base inside an active volcano, like the ones you've read about in the penny dreadful's, built by international terrorists who have read those same penny dreadful's. Let's leave it at that.

We coasted into the dock, the ship rising once more as we did so. For a moment I feared we were moving too fast, but the backwash of water and a last-minute reverse of the engines brought us to a halt just as the bow gently touched home at the end of the main pier. It was an impressive bit of piloting, even I had to admit.

As we finally came to a halt, I relaxed a little, the tension of the journey through the tunnel seeping away. At least, until a moment later, when I heard a gargantuan rumbling noise. I'd sudden visions of the volcano blowing its top. What dumb luck was this? Arriving here just in time to get caught in an eruption… Shaken, I grabbed the hand rails as the ship began to shake violently. My heart was pounding and panic swept over me…

It was therefore a moment or two before I realised the sound was coming from a row of huge hydraulic compressors that lined one side of the dock. The noise of them just got louder as the rams they were feeding took the strain and started lifting the ship. I discovered we had come to rest over some kind of cradle. This allowed the craft to be raised fully out of the water if necessary. I couldn't begin to calculate the immensity of the hydraulic rams that had to be involved in such a feat. But what struck me more as they lifted The Oegopsida partially out of the water was just how enormous the ship was. Far larger than I'd imagined from my internal wanderings.

Eventually the noise of the rams tapered off, the vibrations levelled out and we came to rest. But just to finish off my frayed nerves there was then an ear-splitting hiss as a section of the hull below the conning tower split open, steam filling the air as a pair of vault-like doors swung open on the side of the ship, then a grating sound accompanied a metal gang plank ten feet wide as it extended out onto the dock.

As I was distracted by all this, I didn't notice the reception committee entering the sub bay through one of the heavy sets of doors that led further into the mountainside. But after I watched Verne flanked by several of his, noticeably armed, guards walk on to the dock, I looked up to get my first sight glimpse of our host, Doctor Musk, he too flanked by armed guards of his own. An uncertain tension hung in the air.

I gathered, from my perch at the top of the conning tower, I was witnessing a less than amicable reunion between the two men. My vantage point, now the cradle had lifted the ship, was some forty feet up above the dock. Too far away to make out what they were saying above the general noise of the bay, which was amplified by the constant echoes that ran through the cavernous hanger. But I didn't need to hear the words to know this wasn't a happy reunion. The body language and the nervous nature of their guards told me enough. Whatever relationship the two men had, it was clearly strained. Verne's guards held their harpoon guns at rest but with the kind of stiffness that said they could be raised any second. The guards from the base looked no more relaxed than Verne's.

I studied the captain and the doctor for a moment, but as they talked, I found my gaze wandering around the dockside. Trying to take it all in, I guess. But it was while I did this that I saw someone who scared me far more than Verne, Musk and all their guards put together. A figure standing a little further back, but clearly part of the doctor's entourage. A figure that made me shiver on sight.

Most of Doctor Musk's people were dressed and equipped in similar ways to Verne's, saving that the guards carried more contemporary firearms. This other figure though wasn't wearing a uniform. What he was wearing was a familiar heavy black coat, the kind that only adds to your bulk, and lends a certain intimidation factor sartorially. From my vantage point I couldn't see his face, his wide brimmed top hat saw to that, but I didn't need to. I'd seen men built like him before, wearing the same heavy dark clothing. I'd seen them all too often in recent months, not to mention in my nightmares. I knew that hidden beneath the brim of his hat would be the blank visages of a gasmask with dark facetted lens that always made think of insect eyes.

The figure stood silent and impassive, automaton like. It was a Sleepman, it could only be a Sleepman.

His presence could well explain the strained relations between Captain Verne and the doctor. Explain them all too well. Verne needed Musk, or at least something Musk had, to put his daughter back together again, but that need had brought us deep into the snake pit. Verne may have built the base originally, but I suspect he'd built it before he and Wells had broken ties with The Ministry. Given what Wells had told me in Tibet. But if there was a Sleepman here, even just one, then the island was likely still a Ministry base, and 'the good Doctor', as Verne had referred to him, worked for them. My mouth went dry as I considered that it seemed Verne had dragged me right back into the clutches of the one organisation I most wanted to avoid.

I stood on the conning tower, rooted to the spot, my eyes locked on the bulk of the monstrosity in black. As I watched, it slowly tilted its head upwards, its gaze scanning The Oegopsida. I had to suppress the urge to duck down below the balustrade as that gaze fell upon the conning tower itself and me. I was all too aware that had I reacted how I wished I would have stood out all the more, rather than fade into the background as just another member of The Squid's crew. But in effect this left me staring right back down at the Sleepman. Feeling like a rabbit staring back at a farmer's lamp, only unlike a rabbit, I knew the farmer was aiming his shotgun. And so, it took a moment for me to realise our eyes had met, and the significance of that statement.

Our eyes met…

The Sleepman, if that is what he was, wasn't wearing a mask. Instead, what looked back at me was a pale face I could only describe as bloodless. But it was a pale, bloodless face that was incomplete. He may not have been wearing a Sleepman's gasmask, but he did have a mask of sorts. A metal plate, that looked like iron beaten into something that resembled a human skull, lay over the right side of his face. It completely covered his right eye and across his cheekbone. While this wasn't a Sleepman's mask, it was no less terrifying a visage than theirs were. I was far from reassured. Not least because for all I knew, this amalgamation of white dead-looking flesh and iron was what they all looked like beneath their gasmasks.

My adrenaline, fuelled by my fight or flight response no doubt, must have been spiking. You start to recognise the signs when you have an artificial eye that likes to kick in at points like this. My vision in that eye cut out for a moment before flickering back in at high zoom. It was as if the left half of me was standing right before him. His own gaze, impassive and unmoving remained locked on my own. Yet I was sure I detected the slightest hint of recognition. As if he knew, in some creepy way, my mechanical eye was trained upon him. Then slowly the Sleepman, if that was what he truly was, nodded towards me. It was a nod that spoke of recognition and common purpose. The nod of a friend on seeing you across the bar. It was in fact an oddly human gesture, something I'd never previously associated with his ilk. I'm not sure that made me feel better or worse. Who wants a nod of recognition from an iron masked nightmare?

Around then, the business on the dock between Verne and our host came to a resolution of some kind. Whatever had passed between them, the tension of the standoff eased. What had been said and agreed I couldn't say, but the captain and the doctor stopped short of a handshake, I was sure. Yet they both started walking together towards the doors that led deeper into the facility, some of Verne's guards in behind them along with most of the doctor's men, though some of both groups remained on the dock, taking up quietly opposing stations from which each could watch the other. The tension may have eased, but it remained too palatable for my comfort.

As for the strange Sleepman, he too left the dock. Though as he did so, I felt unsure of my original assessment. While there was much about him that reminded me of The Ministry's goons, there was something else, something both remote and yet very human about him. Not that his humanity or otherwise was any guide to his intentions. If anything, the Sleepmen I was used to would've been more straightforward. I knew exactly what to expect from them.

I watched them, and him, go from the top of the conning tower with a degree of dread. This island was no Pacific paradise. Doctor Musk, I suspected, was going to turn out as mad as all his ilk, while Verne's sanity was something I already questioned. Yet there I was stuck between two mad bastards, inside an active volcano, having 'moments' with a Sleepman.

Still, as days go, I've had worse. I hadn't had my consciousness removed by a blow to the head in days, and for once no one seemed to be blaming me for anything…

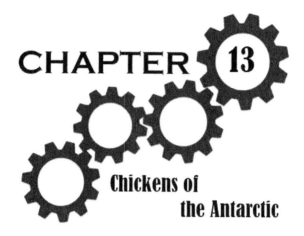

CHAPTER 13

Chickens of the Antarctic

"It's all your fault," Hettie told me, her eyes narrowing.

She'd been sent to collect me from The Squid and escort me to the guest quarters inside the facility. I went along with this because, frankly, what other option did I have? Staying aboard the submersible struck me as wiser, but my tiny cabin on The Oegopsida wasn't exactly what you would call welcoming. Besides which, it was Hettie who had come to escort me. She wasn't about to let me faff her about. So sure, she was dragging me into a secret installation in the heart of an active volcano, but what can you do?

In fairness, I probably sound over dramatic here. I mean, clearly it was safe and unlikely to erupt any time soon. People famously live within spitting distance of active volcanoes for centuries without incident. Whole towns grow up next to them. People raise their children, grow old, and watch their grandchildren play in the streets. All in the shadow of a burning mountain, gifting them with hot springs, a good living at the marble quarries, wealth and security. Hell, I'm sure the spa weekends in Pompei were famous...

That said, while I'd no desire to spend time hanging around waiting to become a footnote in a geology book, my actual concerns were more immediate than the possibility a mountain might decide today was the day to display the true power of nature. The Sleepman, or whatever he was, was a reminder that this island had once likely been a Ministry base. Sure, as far as I knew The Ministry thought me dead, a situation I was more than happy to perpetuate. I wasn't though quite ready to assume that was definitely the case and everything to do with The Ministry made my palms itch.

Verne thought himself safe from The Ministry, but I was far from sure myself. A little healthy paranoia is a good thing, or so they tell me, and well, you can't have too much of a good thing now can you...? Besides which, Wells had thought himself safe from the Ministry in Nepal, and you know how that turned out. All it took was one of Verne's crew, or Musk's men to be a Ministry mole and I was back in the whole sorry mess again. So as Hettie led me through the base, this streak of paranoia caused me to ask Hettie, once again, just how she'd ended up part of The Oegopsida's crew.

Sure, it struck me as unlikely that Hattie was secretly working for The Ministry or that she was even aware of its existence. Hell, she was as close to a friend in the world as I had right at that moment, certainly within a few thousand miles at any rate. Yet her being here was a Hell of a coincidence and I was starting to hate coincidences. So, while I went along with her into the burning heart of Doctor Musk's lair, it was not without a little trepidation.

And yes, I know the word 'lair' seems a tad over dramatic, but Musk, it seemed likely, was yet another mad scientist and his base of operations was inside an active volcano… Lair seems an entirely appropriate choice of words to me.

"My fault? How was it my fault?" I protested. I was feeling a tad on edge as I said, but this struck me as an accusation that was distinctly undeserved. There were, I'll admit, a great many things which could be laid at my feet, but Hettie's current employment status seemed an unreasonable addition.

Hettie laughed, her hearty laugh, at my confusion and just kept on walking.

We left the submersible dock and entered a maze of corridors. Then once we were further into the base she stopped, leant up against the wall and took out a silver tobacco tin.

"Piggy," she said, as if that explained everything.

Then leaned up against the wall, she locked eyes with me as her fingers rolled tobacco in paper with the same well-developed knack she had for engines, managing to produce a near perfect cylinder, without paying any attention to the process. Instead, she just held my gaze with a degree of expectation in her eyes.

"Piggy?" I asked in genuine confusion, as she offered me a handmade. Then as she rolled her eyes at me, realisation struck. "You mean Charles?"

"That's the fella, Charles bloody Fortescue-Wright, the f'ing turd," she said and started to roll one for herself. I must've been a tad agog, as I said nothing while she finished and tapping it on the lid after she closed the tin, as if to amplify her point, as she said again, "Piggy."

Charles Fortescue-Wright III was also, as you may have guessed, known informally as 'Piggy'. This was on account of him being an overstuffed, beady eyed oink of a man. He'd also once been a fellow member of 'The Ins & Outs', the

London serviceman's club both I and Hettie were members of. Though, I suspected, formerly in my case.

I'd not paid my subs in a while…

Admittedly there was also the small matter of me being convicted of treason, murder, and having been, as far as the world was concerned, hung, all of which may also have affected my membership. 'The Ins & Outs', however, were a very progressive club, they might overlook some minor legal infractions. As such, I suspect not paying my subs would be the nail in that particular coffin, at least on paper at any rate.

Back when I was a member, in moderately good standing, with my subs all paid up, 'Piggy' Charles had had quite a thing for Hettie. The kind of unrequited thing that causes men to act foolishly in front of their peers. I say this because to every other member of 'The Ins & Outs' Hettie, or Spanners as we generally called her, was one of the chaps. That is to say, even though she wasn't actually a chap, the members saw no reason to treat her as anything other than one of the chaps, on account of Hettie being… well, Hettie.

That had also been exactly how Hettie liked it.

Indeed, even if on occasion the chap, who was not a chap, spent the night with another of the chaps from the members' bar, and gave that chap a damn good 'spannering', she expected to continue being treated by the lucky fellow and the rest of the members, as just one of the chaps… And for all intents and purpose, she was.

With a degree of discretion 'The Ins & Outs' otherwise famously lacked, such liaisons between 'Spanners' and one of the chaps were never openly referred to. At least not if Hettie was about. It was common knowledge that more than one of the chaps had enjoyed a damn good 'spannering' at her hands, when she and a chosen companion were in the mood for a mutually enjoyable and mutually causal liaison of the physical kind. But there were somethings a chap didn't mention in front of the other chap involved. Particularly when one of the other chaps, wasn't a chap. 'The Ins & Outs' was a gentleman's club after all. Some common decency was to be expected.

Besides which, Hettie has a mean left hook. No one wanted to be 'spannered' by her in the other way for telling tales out of school about her occasional romantic entanglements. Admittedly, romantic was never a word associated with such liaisons. Bracing, athletic, punishing, energetic, and on one notable occasion the phrase 'been ridden like a grand national winner' were, but romantic never.

I myself had never had that particular pleasure, if that is the right word, but between me and Hettie there'd always been an understanding of sorts. While we were both members of the club in good standing, we were also both outsiders to an extent. Hettie because, when push came to shove, she wasn't actually a chap, and me because, well, I wasn't actually a gentleman. But not to get too side-tracked in telling a story I've told before, I'll try to explain the cheesecake incident as briefly as I can…

Yes, I know, I'm seldom brief, but just this once…

Charles 'Piggy' Fortescue-Wright III, sometime after he became a member of the club, started to have designs on Hettie. These were the kind of designs that eventually involved the proclamation of love, and the offering of engagement rings. Which, in of itself, was all well and good, if a trifle embarrassing for all concerned.

The problem was Charles also had an over developed sense of entitlement. A sense of entitlement which meant he wouldn't take no for an answer. Not least because the world view of Charles Fortescue-Wright III didn't allow for the possibility a girl, any girl, might have any answer to such a proposal other than the affirmative.

Suffice to say, Hettie didn't welcome his proposal, the proffered ring, or even the cheesecake he used to present it to her. This of course was where I, out of a very drunken sense of duty on my part, stepped in to preserve her honour, and save her from further embarrassment. As such, I managed to land myself in the utterly ridiculously position of squaring up at dawn on Hampstead Heath to fight a dual with 'Piggy' Charles. I was also, I should probably mention, off my head on LSD at the time. A state of being that was, in no small way, thanks to Hettie.

Hettie had rather firm opinions when it came to chaps fighting duels over her. To wit, if anyone was going to fight for her honour, it was damn well going to be her. Hence, she spiked my breakfast with drugs, called 'Piggy' a cretinous pillock, and threatened to give us both a damn good spannering.

It's fair to say this was one of the more memorable incidents of my time in 'The Ins & Outs'. Indeed, the affair took on somewhat heroic proportions in its oft retelling at the bar and was considered to have been 'a grand jape' in the vaulted opinions of my fellow club members. Much to the chagrin of Charles Fortescue-Wright III.

"Piggy… But didn't he resign from the club after the whole… 'cheesecake' thing?" I inquired, while trying to downplay the last as much as I was able. I knew only too well Hettie's opinions on the incident. She'd berated me about it on multiple occasions since.

Hettie gave me a slightly withering look as she sparked up a match to light the cigarettes. Then having done so, she took a long drag and blew a smoke ring at me.

"Of course, he did. He had to, didn't he. Fighting a duel… A duel with a lowly gunnery officer… It was beneath his dignity… And over a woman of all things…" she said, half spitting the latter half of that sentence. Not out of any contempt for her gender, quite the opposite in fact. She reserved her contempt for men stupid enough to do such a thing. I tried to ignore the fact that equation included me in this instance.

She drew another drag of her cigarette, buying herself a moment to calm her temper, before continuing. "Yes, Charles resigned from the club. But that was hardly going to be the end of it, was it? More's the pity. Piggy's a worthless sack of shite but his family, well... They're old money. So, it doesn't matter that he's fit for nothing but sucking on the family teat, his uncle's a brigadier-general, his father runs a ministry, and his family own half of bloody Surrey... Fighting a duel. Brawling with the lesser classes... All over some milksop of a girl... Well, it just wouldn't do. Stain on the family honour and all that tosh."

"Oh," I said, while trying to get my head around anyone, even herself, describing Henrietta Clarkhurst as a 'milksop of a girl'. Though at the same time, I was also putting two and two together and coming up with an uncomfortable four. It didn't take a genius to see where this was going. Regardless, however, I blathered on, foolishly. "But how's any of that my fault?"

For that fool question I was treated to another of Hettie's patented withering looks.

"Oh, come on, Hannibal, you must know I could've handled the whole thing quietly. Do you really think that was the first proposal I'd had from an idiot who thinks women are all just hanging around waiting for a man to get down on one knee and will fall over themselves to get dragged down the aisle? I could've gently dissuaded him quietly and he'd have forgotten he'd ever asked me in a couple of months. But no, you had to blunder around gallantly intervening, causing a fuss. Making a great damn mess out of it all... Me turning that pig-faced arsehole's proposal down, well that'd be one thing. 'So, some tart said no, probably for the best anyway, not the right sort of girl for the boy, easily forgotten, youthful spirits and all that.' I doubt his family would have batted an eyelid. But a duel… A duel over that tart… A duel with a scrag of a gunnery ensign… A duel that got Piggy drummed out of his club… Well now!"

"I thought he resigned?" I interjected, while not feeling entirely comfortable with Hettie describing herself as 'some tart'. Admittedly, I'd been in enough rugby changing rooms to know how certain conversations went. Hettie had her upper-class rugby club prig accent down to a tee. It was almost as if she'd spent as much time in those changing rooms as I had.

"Oh sure, of course he did… The alterative would've been getting kicked out by the committee, further adding to his disgrace."

"They didn't kick me out…" I protested.

"Yes, well, no one gives a damn if a poxy gunnery ensign with no family name does something stupid. You're not important enough. You don't have any connections that matter. Nothing you do embarrasses anyone important. Besides, let's face it, you're only a member in the first place because you're an entertaining idiot," Hettie explained. All of which was true, if a tad harsh when it was thrown in my face like that. "The thing is, Hannibal, no one is going to pressure the committee over anything you do. Besides which, no one really liked Piggy to start with. He may've had money, but he was never the right kind of chap, you know that."

I nodded along. She was right. Piggy was the kind of chap who joins a club because he wants to be one of the chaps, while at the same time despised everything about the club's members. Piggy had opinions. Opinions which in his view were the only ones worth having. Opinions that led to him looking down on everyone because looking down on everyone was what countless generations of his family had done for centuries. His family was of a class that considered the Sax-Coburgs to be nouveau riche. The type with family trees that stretched back beyond the losing side at the battle of Hastings.

"Anyway, all that, the duel, Piggy being drummed out of the club, the rest of it… Well, it was a whole different kettle of fish than a polite refusal. It was far more embarrassing for a start. The Fortescue-Wrights of this world take such embarrassments to the family name personally," she explained.

"What did Piggy do?" I asked, a bad feeling in my gut. I was starting to realise she might be right in apportioning some blame in my direction.

"Piggy, well, let's just say the fat little piggy ran all the way home… In this case, back to his father, with his little piggy tail between his legs. So, his father gets onto the air-marshal, who's an old chum because they fagged together at Oxford, apparently. The air marshal, well he gets on to the regiment, and a couple of weeks later I find myself in the CO's office being sold a 'terrific opportunity' to take up a position with the British Antarctic Survey." From the look on her face, I could see the 'terrific opportunity' was one of those 'terrific opportunities' you are offered with a strong suggestion the alternative would be another kind of opportunity altogether.

"What?" I asked, unable to stop myself as this was something at odds to the story as it was told by the chaps at the club. "We all thought that was a promotion. Didn't you volunteer?"

"Volunteer? Of course I did…" she said in a somewhat withering tone. "My CO spun me a line. He told me I was being offered a position as chief engineer on one of three airships chartered for a fifteen-month survey mission. They were off to chart some damn mountain range in the middle of the continent. Apparently, there is some really strange geology down there and some Americans out of Boston claimed to have found these odd prehistoric artefacts. The British Museum was in a tizzy about it and they were throwing this whole expedition together to placate them. Anyway, they wanted the best people for the task and my CO had recommended me. So of course, I volunteered, even if I wasn't being given much choice about it. Chief engineer on my own ship, the challenge of high altitude flying in the Antarctic, it was a wonderful opportunity."

Hettie looked slightly wishful explaining this. Personally, a year spent in the Antarctic sounded anything but a 'wonderful opportunity', but I knew why Hettie thought differently. 'Spanners' revelled in a challenge. Besides, while she'd never said so directly, I've always suspected Hettie also revelled in any opportunity to show she was as capable as any man and generally twice as stubborn. Though frankly in the case of the latter, she didn't need to convince anyone who knew her that this was the case.

"Okay, so Piggy's father had them hand you an opportunity you would've bitten their hands off for. I'm not sure I get it?" I said and Hettie laughed, a laugh tinged with bitterness.

"Nor did I. I mean I'd my suspicions. My CO… Let's just say he wasn't exactly enamoured of me. I mean, a female warrant officer who knew more about airships than his chief engineers. It rubbed a bit, so it all sounded too good to be true. Yet I can't say it crossed my mind that that was exactly what it was… I was too busy accepting the post. I thought he was using the expedition as a way to get me out from under his toupee. I hardly batted an eyelid when he said for the paperwork I needed to resign my commission temporally, because the British Antarctic Survey isn't technically a military endeavour. Civilians only, I was told, funded by civilian spending even if it was mostly government money either way. Besides, the bastard told me my commission would be 'waiting for me when I got back' and he sweetened thc pot by saying I'd get promoted to CEO before I resigned. My resignation, well that was just to keep the paperwork straight for some international agreement or other which bans military vessels from crossing the Antarctic landmass."

"So, they steam roll you out of the RAN, and out of the way for a year or so into the bargain, by wrapping it all up as a promotion…" I said, wishing I was shocked by this intelligence, but I wasn't. It sounded about right for the old school tie brigade.

"More or less, and I fell for it. Not that I realised that's what they were doing till later. By which time, the bastards had neatly gotten rid of 'the little tart' who'd caused them so much embarrassment. Clearly it was my fault that someone's cretinous progeny became besotted with me, but not to worry, they'd neatly gotten rid of the 'embarrassment' by packing me off to the other end of the world. I'm sure they found it easy afterwards to make sure the paperwork got lost, so I could be neatly forgotten about. The bloody hand-cranker's must have been pleased with themselves when they came up with that little plan."

"Yes, very neat…" I growled. I could feel my hackles rising because of how they had treated her. Which, as my being angry for her was what got her in a mess in the first place, was sadly a tad ironic.

"Very," she said bitterly. "Of course, I didn't find out the full extent of it all for a while, not until I was firmly aboard The Shackleton and it was well underway. The bastards let me think I was in charge of the engine room up to that point."

"The Shackleton?" I asked with my usual professional interest in airship names.

"Got its name from some polar explorer or other. One of those that died down there last century. It struck me as a bloody silly name for an airship if I'm honest. What kind of cretin names a ship after a guy who died on a failed expedition? But then, men do so love to name things after famous failures. Bloody idiots, the lot of you," she said half smiling as she did so.

I coughed, as much from embarrassment for my sex as from the cigarette smoke, and motioned for her to go on.

"Anyway, once we were underway, I found out the truth. Captain Wright, I was 'delighted' to discover, was a second cousin of dear old Piggy's on the non-hyphenated side of the family. I should've realised something was up when I first met the swine. He'd those same bloody piggy eyes. Not that the family resemblance was particularly strong, but then neither was his chin. But anyway, chinless wonder summons me up to his quarters, as we are heading out into the Atlantic, and was 'nice enough' to explain that I'd been fostered on him as 'chief engineer' by his uncle, but as far as he was concerned, my second, a festering crotch itch called Barns, was the man in charge of engineering and I should keep my 'pretty little head' out of the way."

I almost choked on my cigarette. I could see the distaste in her face as she spoke about The Shackleton's captain. Telling Hettie Clarkhurst to 'keep her pretty little head out of the way' sounded like as good an invitation to getting a right bloody spannering from her as anything I could imagine.

"Some harsh words passed between us at that point," she told me.

"I bet they did…" I said, fighting the urge to laugh. I could imagine how that conversation likely went.

"As it happens, I threatened to bugger him with a screwdriver. I'd a rather large one in my pocket at the time which I felt compelled to show him. All in all, it didn't go down very well, and Wright had me escorted to the ship's brig 'to cool off,' as I was 'clearly being emotional'…"

"Oh Christ," I swore, not needing to imagine the reaction a statement like enticed from Hettie. It wouldn't so much be like pouring oil on troubled waters as throwing a bucket load over them.

"Yer well, then the bastard comes down to see me a few hours later and takes great delight in spilling everything. It turned out the main funders of the expedition were the Fortescue-Wrights and Piggy's dear old dad had made that funding provisional on me being placed upon it. He'd been told to keep me on board at all times, nicely out of the way, and if I caused any trouble then he'd been told to dump me off the ship at South Georgia."

"Where in Hell's name is South Georgia?"

"The arse end of the south Atlantic. There's nothing there but a small survey team who study the penguins and get resupplied once every six months or so. Them and an old whaling station at the other end of the island."

"Sounds delightful… And captain chinless threatened to strand you there if you caused trouble? I take it… Let me guess, you caused trouble?" I said, and for a second, she feigned offence at the mere suggestion she would do such a thing.

"Of course I didn't. Not until we put in at South Georgia, dropping off supplies for the survey team. Then I decided to tell Wright I'd just as soon stay there as fly the rest of the way to the pole with a shower of shit like him and preceded to break his nose," Hettie said and burst into a sudden grin. "In two places… It seemed the least I could do under the circumstances. I broke that tosspot Barn's arm as well. Oh, and I threw a few spanners where they shouldn't be thrown, if you know what I mean. I imagine it took them weeks to fix everything I managed to break before they finally put me off the ship. I'd had time to plan after all, and it's amazing the little 'time bombs' you can leave if you just loosen the right nut here and take out the odd screw there. By my reckoning, they'd have been over the icecaps right around the time the fuel heater failed for a start. I just hope Barns could figure out how to get that going again or they were going to be in real trouble…"

"Jesus, Hettie…" I said, genuinely shocked to tell the truth. I don't know much about engines but even I knew that would cripple the ship. Hettie must have been really angry if she started damaging engines. She loved engines.

"Oh, they'd be fine. There were two other airships on the expedition, remember. All I did was make sure Barns and Wright looked incompetent. Serves the bloody bastards right if they were moronic enough to think I didn't know what I was doing in an engine room," she said, laughing now with genuine humour.

"Can't argue with you there. But that doesn't explain how you ended up on The Oegopsida?"

"Like I told you, there's this small survey team on South Georgia studying penguins. That's who they dumped me with, which I suspect was their plan all along. I sodding hate penguins by the way. That's all those tossers on the survey team ever talked about, penguins. All there was to see there was, well… Do you have any idea how tedious it is, watching penguins, all day every day?"

"I could take a fair stab," I conceded.

"Well, that's nothing like as tedious as the men who study them," she told me with a shudder.

I laughed, choking slightly on my cigarette which was down to the nub by now, so I stubbed it out on the wall.

"Anyway, I hung about around their camp for a couple of months, half praying something would break so I could at least entertain myself by fixing it. I managed to keep to myself for the main. I managed to get the penguin enthusiasts to keep their distance as well. At least, after I impressed upon them my lack of interest in sea birds and men obsessed with them. I think it was my willingness to express that disinterest with a lead pipe that finally discouraged the most persistent of them. But I was still stuck on a half-frozen rock with nothing but bloody penguins on it and their fetishizes for company. I wasn't what you'd call a happy camper. The next supply ship wasn't due for anything up to six more months and that promised to be a tedious six months at best. I was frankly bored to Hell by this point. So, I decided to go exploring for a while, not that there was much to explore. It's mostly just barren mountains and glaciers, but one of the twitchers told me about the old whaling station a couple of days' hike over the island from the penguin watchers' camp. I thought, 'what the Hell', took a week's worth of supplies and a tent, and had it on my heels. I guess I thought the worst that could happen was I might find some old junk to play with for a while…" she said then burst into a smile. "Which in a way I did…" she added, pointing back towards The Oegopsida.

I may not be fast on the uptake on occasion, but things were starting to fall into place. "So, I'm guessing our good Captain No One was using the whaling station as a base of operations?" I suggested. It seemed a logical conclusion. I knew enough about logistics to know a ship the size of The Oegopsida needed regular places to put in for supplies and it wasn't like Verne could just sail her into any old port. Even the laxest harbour master is going to raise an eyebrow at a thousand foot of war machine surfacing at their quayside.

Picky of them, I'm sure.

"Not as such but close enough. Verne has supply dumps here and there around the world in the kind of places no one ever goes. Remote desolate places, like the whaling station at South Georgia. Which is frankly about as remote as it gets."

"Still, that's some happy coincidence Verne happened to be there when you arrived," I said, smiling, and somehow missing the irony that my own presence on his vessel was due to an even more unlikely coincidence in many ways.

"He wasn't, but I found a large stash of supplies under tarpaulins in the old whaling huts. Food, fuel, machine parts, all carefully stored and hidden. So I knew someone was using it as a supply dump and figured all I had to do was wait. Besides, what other choice did I have, the penguin fetishists weren't going to be resupplied for six months, and the BAS ships wouldn't be back that way for a year. It struck me whoever was using the old whaling station as a surreptitious supply base was probably my best bet for getting off the island."

"I thought you only took supplies for a week?"

"I had but there was plenty to eat, food, fuel and machine parts, remember…" she said, grinning. "So I stayed at the whaling station for a couple of months until The Oegopsida popped up. Quite literally popped up, as it happens, which gave me a bit of a fright. I hadn't been expecting a submarine. I'd spent most days scanning the horizon for airships. Then up The Oegopsida pops out of the ocean while I was cooking myself some chicken of the Antarctic."

"Chicken of the Antarctic?" I asked because I am on occasion a tad slow. "There's chickens in the Antarctic?"

Hettie rolled her eyes at me. "Yes dearest, millions of them. They wear little tuxedos."

"What?" I asked and then as light dawned, I added, "Oh…"

Hettie laughed at the pained expression crossing my face, then winked at me. "Nice to see you're as gullible as ever, Hannibal. No, I wasn't eating the damn penguins. I was just dipping into the captain's stores. There were plenty of dry rations among the supplies. Even in summer it never gets much above freezing down there, the mountain valleys are glacial, well packed supplies last a long time and I fished in the little harbour on the warmer days. That said, I'd probably have tried penguin eventually, just for a change," she said and grinned at me.

"How did the captain feel about you stealing his supplies?" I asked.

Hettie shrugged at me. "I'd barely made a dent in them. Besides, it would've been churlish of him to complain about me stealing them. He's more or less a pirate to start with."

"Okay, so Verne and his crew shows up... how did you know they wouldn't kill you for tampering with their supplies. You must have suspected they would be smugglers or pirates or something of that ilk?"

"I didn't but what was I gonna do...? Hang around with the penguin watchers and hope I'd get a ride on the supply ship? It seemed worth trying my luck. Besides, I was sure I could handle myself if things turned nasty," she said, which was probably an understatement, knowing Hettie. "But anyway, when his nibs showed up, I offered my services as an engineer, to pay for the supplies I'd used, don't you know... Just until they could drop me off somewhere more civilised. That was what, six months back. Verne took me on as an engine hand, then a few weeks later he promoted me to chief when he realised I was teaching the guy who had the job before me how to do his job right."

"How did that go down with the bloke you replaced?" I asked.

"Meh, we had a few words. He wasn't very happy about it but I convinced him it was in his best interested to accept his change in circumstance," she said with a wry smile.

I raised an eyebrow at this and gave her a hard look. I knew Hettie too well not to know what 'a few words' and 'convinced him' probably meant.

She shrugged at me. "His jaw healed well enough. It was his own fault, he should have ducked… Besides, the captain had already made the decision. Verne's very progressive. He believes in a meritocracy and I'm as good an engineer as he has ever had aboard this tub."

From anyone else, I might've considered this last to be bragging. In fact, it was bragging, but as this was Hettie there was a fair chance it was also true. All the same, I'd one question that I still felt needed an answer.

"Okay, so you start working for Verne, but you must know he's a pirate, I mean you knew that before you even joined his crew and you're… Well, you're not. You're an English woman, you stand for the national anthem, you were an officer, you took an oath to the crown and what not… How can you just turn pirate?"

She gave me a withering look. "And where did that get me? South bloody Georgia among the penguin fiddlers that's where. All because some toffee-nosed prick expected me to consent to marry him? Like I should be grateful to be considered for the privilege of being Mrs Piggy. Sod that. The captain lets me tinker with this beast of his and as far as he and the rest of them are concerned I'm just one of the crew. No one gives a damn what I have between my legs, or what I don't have, come to that. The only thing that matters here is what I know and I don't have to pretend I don't hear the sniggers behind my back because I'm a girl carrying a spanner."

"No one ever…" I started, but my words fell away in the face of the vehement stare she gave me.

"Of course, they did. Even you idiots in the club. 'Good old 'Spanners'', 'she's one of the chaps'… oh sure, I was one of the chaps alright, whenever I was stood at the bar buying a round. But the minute I was out of sight, I was 'the chap who wasn't a chap'. The 'filly in trousers'. The regiment couldn't wait to shove me off to the south pole because I became inconvenient in the eyes of the old school tie brigade. My CO was a member of 'The Ins & Outs' you know, on the committee and everything. That didn't stop him throwing me under the trolleybus, did it? All chaps together, right up until it actually matters, when I actually needed someone to stand up for me… Not for my honour, not because I'm a lady, not because some poxy gentlemen's code dictated they should, but because I really was one of the chaps… Oh no, ship me off to the Antarctic and dump me with a bunch of penguin lovers, because I had the temerity to refuse a proposal and made things awkward for the brass…"

There are times when the wisest course of action is to say nothing. I, you may not be surprised to learn, often forget to adhere to this advice. My mouth has a habit of running off ahead of my common sense. For once, however, I took the wisest course and said nothing in the face of the hard stare Hettie was giving me. Not least because I knew she was right.

After taking a moment to compose herself once more, Hettie smiled again and continued. "The captain's a pirate, which pretty much makes me a pirate too. But do you know something, Hannibal, I'm happier here, on this ship, than I have ever been anywhere else in my life. I'm valued here and just one of the crew. Chief engine monkey at that. All I have ever wanted was to be the chief engineer on my own ship. So, to be frank, bugger 'The Ins & Outs', bugger England, bugger the Royal Air Navy, bugger Old Brass Knickers herself, bugger the whole bloody lot of them. If the occasional bit of piracy is the cost of that happiness… Well, pass me the rum and yo fucking ho, my hearty."

In fairness, I couldn't fault her logic and said as much. It wasn't like I was labouring under any pretentions of loyalty to the crown myself anymore. So what if Hettie had become party to a bit of piracy? Hell, that's not as bad as half the things on my docket now, is it?

Cigarettes stubbed out, and conversation with them, Hettie escorted me further into the base. We passed guards stationed here and there at doors which seemed fairly random, but my natural curiosity was muted for the time being. Hettie's revelations helped with that, as it gave me much to dwell on. I had precipitated her change in circumstances as she said. If I'd never escalated the whole cheesecake affair into a duel between me and Piggy then maybe it was true that she really could've managed the situation more delicately…. Even if delicate was never a word anyone associated with Hettie Clarkhurst.

Eventually she walked us to a corridor lined with numbered doors, which put me in mind of a rather severe hotel. The kind of corridor you would expect to find in a hotel that doubled as a secret base in the heart of an active volcano, at any rate. Then finally she came to a halt outside a room with the number seventeen on the door.

"You're in here, get yourself some rest, and wash up. The doctor's holding a dinner for the captain and senior crew members this evening," she told me. "I'll knock you up when it's time to go."

"I'm invited?" I asked, somewhat surprised by this.

Captain Verne, I concluded, must have had a higher opinion of my worth than I'd imagined. It did make sense though. After all, I'd been the captain of my own airship, however briefly and as captain of The Johan's Lament, I held a certain rank. And of course the long established precedent in military circles was that naval ranks be they of the sea or the air were interchangeable in the chain of command. While my captaincy had been brief, and not entirely successful, I remained just as much a captain as Verne himself. As such, the doctor inviting me to dine alongside my fellow captain made perfect sense. Indeed, now I thought about it, I should've been offended that I'd never been invited to dine with Verne aboard The Oegopsida.

However, now wasn't the time to dwell on breaches of protocol. Verne was not a proper military man after all. It was probably no more than an oversight on his part and one he and the good doctor sought to correct now.

Yes, I thought, I would be the bigger man, damn it. I would make no mention of Verne's lack of courtesy. Besides, he was French after all, and the French invented the words faux pas... It was beholden of an English gentleman to forgive such lapses. I would be gracious, I would greet Captain Verne and this Doctor Musk as they deserved, as a gentleman should. I would make no mention of my earlier mistreatment at Verne's hands. No, not at all, I would let this invitation be his apology and accept it in the manner expected of a man of rank, a man like myself...

"Not exactly," Hettie said.

"What?"

"Well, you weren't mentioned as it happens. The captain just told me to sort you out some quarters then leave you to it," she said. "But I'm invited, and I need an escort. And well... Frankly while you're a bit of a blow hard, and most of the time you're neither use nor ornament, you're pretty enough when you've showered and had a shave. Your uniform is in there, by the way. They washed and repaired it for you. I dare say you'll scrub up nicely enough and make for a bit of arm candy if nothing else."

Then she gifted me a wink, smiled and pushed my door open for me before turning and stalking off down the corridor. Meanwhile, I stood in the doorway watching her go, feeling a little cheap and a tad dirty as I tried to work out if she was pulling my leg or if I should feel insulted.

CHAPTER 14

Henrietta's arm candy

My East India Company Aerial-Navy uniform had seen better days. It had, however, also seen worse. Just as Hettie had informed me, it was freshly laundered, and someone had taken a needle and thread to the worst of the damage. Thus, while I remained far from enamoured of the EIC uniform, it felt good to be out of the drab overalls worn by The Oegopsida's crew, and into something more fitting.

I was also pleasantly surprised to discover someone had stocked my assigned guest quarters with a full toilet kit. Clean towels, a fresh bar of soap, hair oil, a small pair of scissors and shaving kit that lay by a small sink in my room. Best of all, however, a newish cutthroat razor, a blessing since my previous trusty old throat slasher was currently at the bottom of the Indian Ocean. It was with no small glee that I tested the razor's blade, found it acceptably sharp and spent a good twenty minutes or so trimming away at my beard and shaving around it until I'd neatly trimmed it all back to my preferred moustache and tightly cropped chin. Admittedly, I would've cheerfully killed for a little wax, which was noticeably absent, but I did at least feel a tad more presentable as I towelled off before taking my time to dress properly.

I took a moment to take in my image in the small mirror over the sink, and damn if I didn't cut a bit of a dash. I'm aware that's an awfully vain thing to say, but a man should present himself to the world how he wishes the world to perceive him. If the world sees a well-presented officer, the world will assume he is just that and a gentleman to boot. Of course, I doubted even for a moment that I would fool someone like Verne. He knew enough about me already to have formed his own opinions. But our host, Doctor Musk, was a different matter and starting off on the right foot with him seemed wise.

Also, to be entirely honest, I discovered that as I was Hettie's date for the evening, I'd no wish to let her down. Though this realisation came as something of a surprise even to me.

There was one fly in the soup however. The scabbard loops on my belt remained noticeably absent of a scabbard and a blade. Just as the white leather holster on my other hip remained bereft of a trusty service pistol. However, despite being unarmed, I felt like a British officer once more, and there is a certain armour in the self-assurance that lends a fellow.

Also, I had a new cutthroat and that was a comfort of a kind. However, when I tried to slip the ornate razor into the small leather sleeve on the inside of my boot, it refused to fit as the handle was too bulky. That hidden sleeve inside my boot was of course not part of my uniform, but I've made a habit of having such a sleeve sown into every right boot I'd owned since I first acquired a pair officer's boots in a brothel shortly after I received my first commission. There is quite a story behind how I acquired those boots, but I'll tell that another time. As I said, however, this particular cutthroat had a rather ornate handle of sculpted silver and just wouldn't fit where it was supposed to. Annoyed by this, I determined I'd have to trade it for a more mundane workaday razor when I got a chance and slipped it instead into a jacket pocket. A slightly more conspicuous place to keep such a weapon, and one that entirely ruined the line of the jacket. All in all, even without a sword and pistol, I felt prepared to meet the world head on, and now I had at least one weapon about my person.

Once shaved and dressed to my satisfaction, I was at a loss as to what to do with myself. It didn't seem wise to go exploring on my own. I was unsure of Verne's good graces and knew little about our host, Doctor Musk. And so, I lay on the bed, thinking over what little I'd been told about Musk, yet in doing so I came up blank in terms of insights.

Yes, I'm aware that's hardly a shock, thank you so much for that.

I tried not to think too deeply about the story Hettie had told me. It struck me as odd that the Foreque-Wright's had gone to so much trouble to get her out of the way. I'd have thought old Piggy's greater concern would've been getting even with me. I was the one who pushed him into his disgrace after all. But doubtless it was easier for them to go after Hettie. It didn't sit well with me in any regard and I tried to push it out of my mind, not least because I seemed to be the cause of her misfortunes. Even if she had landed on her feet in the end.

I must have nodded off for a while because the next I remember I was being awakened by a loud knocking at the door of my room. Followed by the dulcet tones of Hettie shouting the suggestion I should 'get my arse in gear' with her usual brand of subtlety.

I gave myself a last once over in the mirror, and almost as an afterthought moved the cutthroat to my trouser pocket. It really did ruin the line of the jacket. Then I ran my hands over my hair to smooth it down a little, and encouraged my beard to remain neat, once more bemoaning inwardly the lack of wax.

"Today would be good, Hannibal!" Hettie shouted once more.

Honestly, I swear, the woman had no idea how much effort is involved in a chap looking his best. *Does she think it all just falls into place on its own?'* I asked myself. But so as not to try her temper, I ran my fingers through my hair one last time and then opened the door. Beyond which I saw the most surprising thing I'd come across so far on that damn island…

Henrietta Clarkhurst in a dress…

Hettie, as I may have remarked before, has always been a girl of ample figure. This is not to say she was overweight, you must understand. No one who spent as much time as she did working with heavy machinery is ever going to run to fat, but what she was for want of another word is solid. Broad shouldered, with the kind of hips built for childbearing or riding horses, and a bosom for which a word like ample is something of an understatement. I'd no doubt Hettie had been the terror of the hockey field back in her school days. Indeed, she'd have made a better prop forward than most of the Rugley school pack had in mine. What I am saying here is that Hettie is a girl who is not merely strong in the willed department. I've known a few blokes who fancied themselves as pugilists who wouldn't have lasted three rounds in the ring against Hettie. She's a big, solid girl, with a big, solid personality to go with it. Yet despite this, Hettie remained very much a woman. And when she could be bothered to wiped the engine oil from her face and do something with her hair, a damn attractive one.

Actually, that does Hettie a disservice, she remained a damn attractive woman when she was up to her elbows in engine grease, but hopefully you see the point I am making. That point being that when Hettie decides she wants to be Henrietta for the evening she can outshine a room full of society debutants just as easily as 'Spanners' could out swear, fart and arm-wrestle a tap room full of engineers.

The thing is though, you tend to forget when you spend time around Hettie that Henrietta is hiding beneath a layers of engine oil, dollops of grease and soot-stained overalls. So when Henrietta appears before you… Well… It bowls you an unexpected Yorker.

Henrietta Clarkhurst in a dress. Her hair up, with little ringlets framing her eyes, a low-cut corseted dress making the most of her 'assets' while showing off the rest of her curves. Bright eyes framed with mascara and eyeshadow. Dark lipstick and a touch of blusher replacing oil smears and soot stains. Little dimples in her cheeks that appear as she smiles. She is a force to be reckoned with…

Particularly those dimples.

"Henrietta, you look…" I started to say. But never got any further than that as her eyes narrowed and she bit me off before I could say further.

"Oh stow it, you arse. Captain told me to make myself presentable as it's a formal affair. I haven't dressed up for you, so don't be getting any ideas," Hettie, who was definitely not being Henrietta, said.

I took a breath and raised my hands up in the universal sign of surrender. "Okay Hettie, I was just going to say you look…"

"Of course, I do, what did you expect? Really, Hannibal, you're such a bloke at times," she berated. She reached out and brushed some imaginary lint from my lapel, then sniffed , and with a touch of cynicism continued, "I suppose you'll do, you're decorative enough in a uniform, even if you're a little too skinny…"

"Skinny?" I retorted.

"Oh, enough with you. As I said, it's a formal affair, so do be on your best behaviour, Hannibal. Speak if you're spoken to and laugh politely at their jokes by all means. But for god's sake, keep your opinions to yourself. I'm quite sure no one will wish to hear them. Remember, you're just there to look pretty. Oh, and do try to smile. I don't want you embarrassing me," she instructed.

"Yes, Hettie," I said meekly, because what else could I do?

"Henrietta. This is a formal affair as I said, please try to keep that in your pretty little head, Hannibal. Honestly, it's not all that complicated even for you," she admonished further, then offered me her arm.

"Of course, Henrietta," I said, taking it.

I wasn't entirely sure how serious she was being. Perhaps she was making a point of some kind. But I was certain that while I might be calling her Henrietta this evening, she remained very definitely Hettie underneath that ball gown.

CHAPTER 15

The fate of mankind

"Miss Clarkhurst, Captain Verne tells me you're quite the engineer," Doctor Musk commented somewhere between the first course and the second. He was sitting at one end of the table, while the captain had taken up the seat at the opposite end. I suspect this was a rather deliberate arrangement, so each could lay claim to the head of the table. But the effect of the arrangement was the cold tension between also laid upon everyone else present, including myself.

There were eight of us in all, including the doctor and the captain, myself and Hettie. Opposite us sat a man and woman who were introduced as Hue and Letti Packard, a married couple, both Babbage scientists working on Musk's great project. The Oegopsida's first officer, a Dutchman called Crowther, sat alongside me and seemed intent on keeping his own council, or else he was such a dull conversationalist that I can't recall a single word he ever said. Opposite Crowther and nearest to the captain was a demure woman in her early forties who was clearly of Japanese descent. She was introduced to me and Hettie as Madam Verne, the captain's wife.

That definite chill in the air around the table got just plain frosty when it came to the captain and his wife. They exchanged few carefully polite words, and those mostly in Japanese, a language Verne appeared to be fluent in, unlike anyone else present save his wife. Admittedly, with my somewhat eclectic ear for languages, I had picked up a few isolated words of Japanese in my short time in the land of the rising sun, but, true to form, the words I had picked up were of the 'coarse' variety, so I was as much in the dark as everyone else in regard to their private conversation. That said, I raised an eyebrow at one point when she uttered something along the lines of 'Kuso yarō', which if I am correct is a somewhat vulgar reference to the captain's parentage··· Of course, it might have been something else entirely. My grasp of even my own elective Japanese struggled towards rudimentary, though the look it drew from her husband suggested I wasn't entirely mistaken.

Shortly after she uttered that particularly descriptive comment, around the time we were finishing the first course, it dawned on me that Madam Verne couldn't have been aboard The Oegopsida for some time, or she and Hettie would've been acquainted, yet both she and I were introduced to Madam Verne when we arrived. It was then I realised that it had been Doctor Musk not Verne himself who introduced her. I kicked myself for being slow on the up take but now it had occurred to me, I started to notice the odd glances being shared between her and our island host, glances which when noticed caused a scowl to cross Verne's otherwise impassive visage.

By the end of that first course, I'd determined a guess as to the nature of the rift between the two men sitting at opposite ends of the table. Madam Verne, it was clear to me, had been resident on the island for some time. That much I was sure of. Beyond that, of course, a gentleman doesn't speculate on the marital affairs of others, but then I'm not entirely a gentleman. Suffice to say, I was near certain that Madam Verne and the good doctor had been enjoying some extramarital dalliance, just as I was equally certain that the captain was aware of their affair. This explained why he'd been reticent about visiting his former base of operations, and why he was far from happy asking the doctor for assistance with his daughter.

Further ungentlemanly speculation on my part was diverted as the first course was cleared away by a couple of stewards and Musk engaging Hettie in conversation.

"The captain is most kind, I'm sure," Hettie replied, her tone of voice a very un-Hettie-like home counties tearoom accent, as refined as you like.

"Ah, but the good captain has never been one to give undue praise, have you, Verne…?" Musk said, a smidge of needle in his voice. "If our good captain says you're a fine engineer, Miss Clarkhurst, then a fine engineer you undoubtedly are."

"She is that. Few could learn all there is to know about The Oegopsida in so short a time," Verne interrupted, not wishing to be outdone. Between the two of them, they managed to make Hettie uncharacteristically blush, but then praise being lavished on her skill with machinery was about the only thing that could ever make Hettie blush in my experience.

"That is indeed impressive. Tell me, Miss Clarkhurst, what would it take to tempt you away from our good captain and persuade you to lend your expertise to my own endeavours?" Musk inquired playfully, eliciting a disgruntled grunt from the opposite end of the table. A reaction that I suspect Musk sought to provoke, judging by the eyebrow he raised in the captain's direction and the sly smile that crossed his lips.

"Really, Elonis, are you trying to steal my crew for your ridiculous project now?" Verne asked, or rather demanded, irritably.

Madam Verne, despite her natural Japanese reserve, looked decidedly uncomfortable and said something sharp, in Japanese, to her husband who cleared his throat to respond. A look passed between them that was hard to read. It was however enough to make me reconsider my previous assumption. Whatever had driven a wedge between the two men, and she was definitely at the heart of it, it was not perhaps some petty infidelity. There was more to it. A rivalry of the heart may be bitter, but this seemed to have deeper roots.

Musk smiled thinly at the captain before turning his gaze towards Hettie and winking at her. I only caught the gesture as I was sitting beside her. He turned his gaze back to the captain and asked, with a greasy sheen to his words, "I'm sure, Verne, you'd never stand in Miss Clarkhurst's way if she found my 'ridiculous project' as you put it, intriguing?"

He was slick, I will give him that much, as slick as an oil spill.

Verne for his part was clearly struggling to maintain his composure but before the captain could say anything, however, Musk sank back into his chair and continued. "Besides, you know as well as I do, recent events have only highlighted the need for my 'ridiculous project'. The British and Russian Empires at loggerheads, China and Japan's nasty little war intensifying… You've heard what happened at Hiroshima, I'm sure. Or does life in that marvellous craft of yours keep you far too isolated to keep up with world events?"

At the mention of Hiroshima, I paled slightly. My own memories of that event were far too immediate even after all that had happened since.

"Elonis, it would be pleasant not to be reminded of one's brother's crimes," Madam Verne interrupted, sharply, with a look on her face that could've curdled milk. It took me a moment to put that together. Then I remembered my Bad Penny, Madam Verne's step-daughter, had called 'The Brass Warlord', uncle. Yamamoto had been the mastermind behind the Hiroshima bullet train gambit. The train I'd inadvertently found myself trapped upon a few months ago. The same Yamamoto who was ultimately responsible for the death of almost half a million Chinese troops and Japanese civilians.

Unsurprisingly, I suppose, casual references to Hiroshima didn't sit well with his sister. While some of his countrymen no doubt thought him a hero, there isn't so much as a tart's honour between war hero and mass murderer when it comes down to it.

For myself, I decided there was some wisdom in not mentioning my own part in that holocaust. Albeit that the involvement had been inadvertent. Besides I could still remember the brightness of the flare as the city went up, the smell of burning ash on the wind, and the hopelessness I felt on that hillside, watching a vision of Hell on Earth.

"My apologies, Madam Verne. It was an ill-considered example," Musk said, though his tone suggested he was somewhat disingenuous. "But be that as it may, it remains an example of mankind's ultimate fate if we are to remain trapped upon this singular globe. Man will ever make war upon man and do so with ever greater weapons. Humanity's is a sad history, littered with violent destruction. Oppenheimer's theorem dictates it is and always will be thus. Hence the requirement and urgency of my 'ridiculous project' as your husband so colourfully puts it…"

"What's Oppenheimer's theorem?" I found myself asking, partially in hope of leading the conversation away from Hiroshima. For my pains, I was rewarded with a sharp kick to the ankle curtesy of Hettie, annoyed at my impertinence no doubt. I coughed to swallow a yelp of pain and threw Hettie a wild look, but she ignored me and assumed every appearance of having found something interesting on the ceiling.

"Ah yes, Captain Smyth, you're a military man, are you not?" Musk inquired, and to avoid a further kick from Hettie, I merely nodded in the affirmative. He smiled his oily smile again, at me this time. Then appeared to consider this a moment before continuing with his diatribe on what I suspected was a favourite subject of his, seeing as how he placed himself centre stage within it.

"Then I'd think perhaps you, more than anyone here, would understand the theorem. You and those of your ilk have always sought bigger newer weapons to better fight your wars, have you not? Greater and more efficient means of waging conflicts. Bigger airships, bigger guns, bigger… explosions? What is the phrase… oh yes, weapons of massive destruction…"

"You must forgive me, Doctor. I'm just a simple soldier, well, airman. I go where ordered and do what must be done. The why is for wiser heads than mine… But in essence, yes, of course. Britain must strive to stay ahead of the Queen's enemies as her enemies will undoubtedly strive for the means to defeat us," I answered in a manner befitting an officer of the empire, which of course I wasn't anymore.

Personally, it must be said I was all for avoiding bloodshed whenever possible. Particularly if the blood being shed was likely to be mine. Frankly I was past caring about Old Brass Nipples' enemies, not least because I was doubtless counted as one of them. But it is a basic military philosophy, to stay ahead of the game. No one wanted to be on the team armed with pea shooters facing howitzers. Possessing overwhelming force when facing the enemy is, I've found, a great comfort to the military mind.

"Just so, Captain Smyth. The British Empire is a fine example of my point. An empire built on the devastating use of force, that maintains its influence by its willingness to revert to barbarity whenever it deems such actions appropriate," Musk said.

"You expect us to take a knife to a gun fight?" I retorted, feeling my heckles rise at the tone of this accusation. "I hardly consider it barbarous to quell unrest by the most efficient means available. The empire is built on peace and stability. Sometimes it goes a little far, I'll grant you, but in the end our advanced weaponry, airships, land citadels and everything, enforce the peace and it's through them the empire thrives for the good of all."

Doctor Musk smiled, then waved my defensiveness aside. "Yes, of course, such is the mind-set of the military, and a commendable one among those in uniform, no doubt. But, you see, that same mind-set is in essence the heart of Oppenheimer's theorem. Oppenheimer was a physicist first and foremost, would you believe, but in later life he dabbled with moral philosophy. Through the study of physics, he came to believe it would be possible to create weapons of such power one solitary bomb could turn whole cities to ash. Weapons that unleashed the power of the atom."

"But isn't an atom the smallest thing possible?" I asked, mostly, if I am honest, to push the conversation on from cities turning to ash. Such an event was no mere speculation for me, Hiroshima was still raw. I was also, I'll admit, morbidly intrigued by the conversation, despite my usual ambivalence to scientific conjecture. "It doesn't sound like something you could destroy cities with…"

"You are misinformed on both counts. Though no one has ever attempted to make such a weapon. Not with any success at any rate, thankfully. Many believe Oppenheimer came the closest. They say he went mad in the end, though I would posit instead that he became very, very sane. He burned all his notes reputedly, though there is some conjecture they survived and there are many who seek them even now. All that is truly known is that Oppenheimer gave up physics late in life and took up philosophy instead, and of course, his theorem. Copies of it are hard to find as certain governments saw fit to suppress this later work. They were less than fond of much it had to say on the nature of governance, as well as a general treatise on humanity's propensity for violence. It is the final chapter that holds the key to his theorem, however. In essence, it states his belief that mankind will ultimately destroy itself in its never-ending quest for greater weapons of war. Humanity, he theorised, would eventually create the means of its own destruction. Furthermore, having created such a device, mankind would prove to be incapable of not using it."

"That's ridiculous," I said. "Even if such a weapon was created, no one would ever be mad enough to use it."

"Oh, MAD is exactly what they would be. Mutually Assured Destruction… Some would consider it the ultimate deterrent. If you use your weapon of mass-destructive force on us, we will use ours on you. But that is the tactical philosophy of the insane," Musk said with obvious belief.

"Or the end of war…" one of the Packards said, I forget which.

"Tell that to Hiroshima," Musk rebuked, and Madam Verne visibly stiffened once more. "No, Packard, the history of mankind tells us that there will always be someone in power prepared to take the risk. Think of it from their viewpoint. One bomb, just one airship, over an enemy's capital and you win a war in a single shot. There will always be those who argue doing so would save the lives that would be lost in a protracted war. Better to give the blankets to Indians, as our own countrymen once decided," he added and both Packards went pale.

I can't pretend I understood the reference, but I could venture a guess. Both the Packards and Musk had American accents and that former country's Indian wars retained a brutal reputation, even if that reputation paled in comparison to the horrors of its civil wars.

"I see," I said, though I didn't entirely. "But if you're proposing that mankind is doomed, what is this project of yours that will save them?" I asked, preparing myself for the kick under the table that never came. Hettie, it seemed was wondering what the Doctor was up to on the island as well.

If I am honest here, my interest was minimal. Musk reminded me too much of those other mad scientists, Gates and Jobs, which didn't bode well. That said, compared to those two, he had something more of the personable showman about him. He was oily and slick, but he had a way about him that made the ridiculous seem somehow reasonable, if only you listened to him long enough. I later came to realise Musk was more a big ideas man than anything else. He left the actual mechanics of his ideas to those he employed. But, god save me, did the man have an ego as big as his ideas. If I could get past the overwhelming urge to punch him in the mouth, I could've almost liked the man. But a few minutes in his company always had me balling my fists for some reason.

I think it was the smile.

"It struck me several years ago that the solution to the Oppenheimer theorem was obvious," he explained, a tad wild-eyed. "But one must admit that what is obvious to oneself is not always so obvious to others. The answer is Mars, Mr Smyth, Mars…"

"Mars?" I and Hettie asked in tandem, both of us genuinely taken aback.

"Indeed, Mars, Miss Clarkhurst, for if mankind is to survive itself, he must expand beyond this single world," Musk explained, clearly delighted at grabbing Hettie's interest.

"But how does 'man' get to Mars?" Hettie asked, with an odd stress on the word 'man' that I doubt anyone else caught. Musk certainly didn't, which amused me more than it should because I knew he was walking a thin line with her. Hettie was a woman of many little foibles on occasion. For all she was one of the chaps, she could also be very much the suffragette.

"It's simple enough. I am building a gun that will fire him there," Musk said plainly, and if I didn't know it before, it was then I knew then the man was quite mad.

"You're going to shoot a gun at a planet?" I heard myself asking, bemused at the ridiculousness of the suggestion.

"Of course not, Mr Smyth," he said, laughing with an odd sort of amusement, and for a moment I thought the whole suggestion was just that, an ill-conceived jest, but then he continued. "It would be impossible even with a dozen Babbages to calculate such a trajectory. I am sure you as a former gunnery officer would agree. Mars is simply too far away, too small a target, and gravity has too firm a hold upon this Earth for us to achieve the velocity that would be required for such a shot."

I couldn't argue with that logic, not that I'd any wish to do so. I wasn't sure if I should be laughing along with him but I found myself doing so. Hettie also chortled slightly, but my laughter tailed off as I realised the others present had remained entirely stoic.

"What then?" asked Hettie, urging Musk to explain further, which of course was what Elonis Musk desired most in my opinion, a willing audience.

"Why it is simple enough, Miss Clarkhurst. The gun I'm building here is tasked with shooting capsules to the site where we will build a gun to fire us to Mars."

"Okay, and just where would that be?" I asked and got the kick under the table I expected for interrupting.

"Why, the moon, Mr Smyth. Upon this island I have built a howitzer capable of firing a moon-shot," he said to us, smiling that odd smile as his skin glistened under the lights in an off-putting way. Then he leaned back into his seat and held out his hands like a magician at the end of a card trick. Ever the showman… He repeated himself and stressed each word. "A Moon-Shot…"

CHAPTER 16

Doctor Musk's enormous weapon

"That," said Hettie, with a mix of longing and awe, "is one enormous weapon…"

It was hard to disagree.

We were standing on a small observation platform, built into the side of the mountain. Me, Hettie, the Packards and Musk. Verne had declined to join us, it was clear that he considered the whole idea of shooting a gun at the moon ridiculous. Something 'best confined to works of fiction', as he'd put it the previous evening. Doctor Musk had laughed off Verne's dismissive tone, saying something along the lines of 'you would know, Jules…' and insisted the rest of us join him after breakfast for a tour of his facility.

So, there we stood on a rickety metal gantry sticking out of the side of the volcano, staring up at the barrel of an enormous gun.

The gun proved to be what I'd mistaken from The Oegopsida's conning tower for a weird rock formation sticking out of the mountainside, obscured as it had been at the time by mist and cloud. It is somewhat difficult to get across the sheer scale of Musk's howitzer, but let me try. The barrel was a good thirty feet across at its peak. The bore was twenty-five. As it ran down into the mountainside, the barrel became wider still. A second sleeve bulked it out to maybe forty feet and a third near where it entered the mountain was closer to fifty. I guessed at the reason for these second and third sleeves. On a normal howitzer, they'd act to absorb recoil, and prevent a blast burying the gun into the ground. Guns mounted on airships used the same principal. But it was the sheer scale of Elonis Musk's gun I found almost impossible to comprehend. The barrel extended upwards at a steep seventy degrees to the horizon, some two hundred and fifty feet or more. There wasn't, we should all be glad to know, another gun like it anywhere in the world, but then no other gun had been constructed to shoot something out of this world in the most literal of senses.

Yet, all that said, I still found it impossible to accept that even a weapon of this size could shoot a payload to the moon.

"How the hell do you load it?" I heard myself wondering aloud, as much from professional interest as anything else. I was, after all, trained as a gunnery officer, which gave me a certain interest in the practicalities of such devices.

"It loads at the breach, Mr Smyth," one of the Packards told me.

I leant out and looked over the safety rails and down the sheer drop towards the jungle canopy below. The barrel entered the mountainside below us as one great solid lump of metal. The breach must therefore be inside the mountain itself in one of the hollowed-out caverns, the barrel entering through the rock almost seamlessly. Just a narrow gap between the mountain and the barrel itself. This struck me as odd as there seemed no way to alter the angle of the gun, either vertically or horizontally. For the life of me I could not conceive a way of doing so. Fixed emplacements were damn foolish on an airship in my opinion, though they were used for the largest weapons as you needed to control the kick back so front facing cannons by nature were given minimal axis of movement. But you could move an airship... how the Hell did you move an island?

"How the Hell do you aim it?" I asked no one in particular.

"In some regard, Captain Smyth, it is not designed to be aimed at all," Doctor Musk explained, his voice almost dripping condescension.

"Really? In my experience, you generally need to aim at a target to hit it!" I argued, chaffing slightly at his tone, but Musk merely smiled in return, the kind of smile people gift you when they know they are smarter than you.

I felt that same overwhelming urge to punch him in the mouth again, not least because I was reminded of too many science lessons back at Rugley. There, the clever types took every opportunity to make us sporty types feel belittled. In later years, looking back, that always struck me as rather foolish of them, given the next lesson was invariably physical education, but then the most intelligent people are often also the most stupid in my experience. I was preparing for a snappy reply when Hettie blunted my venom somewhat by proving that Doctor Musk was not the only clever-clogs on the platform.

"Oh, of course, that's why you needed to build it so near the equator, isn't it? The rotation of the earth itself is the x axis, and your y axis is the plane of the lunar orbit," Hettie said.

I wasn't entirely sure what she was driving at. While I understand the trajectory calculations required to drop shells on the unfortunate enemies of Old Seldom Amused, scaling them up to shoot a projectile at the moon wasn't covered in my class on field gun ranging, strangely enough.

"Exactly, Miss Clarkhurst," Musk replied brightly, clearly delighted at Hettie's interest.

"And of course, the Earth spins fastest at the equator, so it will increase the orbital speed allowed for the escape velocity required to produce the slingshot effect that Von Braun posited," Hettie went on, with a certain giddy enthusiasm.

I vaguely wondered who Von Braun was but decided not to ask and further display the holes in my education. Though I was flexing the fingers of my right hand unconsciously, as some lessons from my old school had stuck with me.

"Precisely," Musk replied once more before glancing in my direction for a second and adding, "It is wonderful to see someone has a solid grasp of the physics, my dear."

Just one punch in his smug face would have made me feel so much better, of that I was sure…

Hettie, however, preened at what she took as a compliment to her rather than a back handed insult aimed at yours truly. She was also clearly enthralled by the subject at hand because she let the 'my dear' go by without comment. Any other time someone 'my deared' Hettie, they would've been lucky to get away with no more than the sharp end of a scowl.

"Also, of course, by locating here, there is a reduction in the sheer ballistic thrust you require, but even so to reach escape velocity you'd need… what did Von Braun speculate… eleven thousand…. No, it was in bloody metres, wasn't it, what's that in feet··· Thirty, no thirty-six…"

"If we had constant thrust, yes, but what we actually need to achieve is closer to forty-five…"

"Surly you'd encounter stresses beyond the hypersonic barrier?"

"Have been accounted for, though there are some issues you may be able to…"

And so, they went on. I would be delighted to give you a full accounting of all the technical details the pair of them discussed, but as you are probably aware by now, the only thing smaller than my understanding of technical gobbledegook, is my interest in it. So, I ceased to listen, leaned on the railing, and stared off into the jungle below us, and wondered if it was too early to open a hip flask.

I also lamented my lack of a hip flask, full or otherwise.

Some ten minutes or more passed on that gantry before Doctor Musk led us through some heavy steel doors and down into the bowels of the mountain. The doctor himself was still talking enthusiastically to an extremely excited Hettie, while one or other of the Packards would occasionally chime in with some minor detail or other if Musk misspoke. They were very careful when they did so. 'The good doctor of course means…' 'Twenty-two thousand per square inch, I'm sure you recall, sir…' and other carefully worded corrections.

I vaguely recalled Verne's description of Musk as 'a big idea's man' and realised what he'd meant was Musk cared more about the ideas than the details, which didn't strike me as a good trait in an engineer.

Our route down into the mountain took us via a steep metal staircase that wound down the through the rock some hundred feet or more. It was the same staircase we'd climbed early that morning, but we passed the doors that led back the way we had come and descended deeper down into the bowels of the volcano. Eventually, just as I started to think the staircase was going on right down into Satan's backyard, it ended at a set of doors that opened out into the largest cavern I'd seen so far and, as the doors opened, a wave of heat washed over us.

There was a moist quality to the air, much like that of the rainforest that covered most of the island. Yet here in the confines of the cavern, it felt several degrees hotter, a whole lot wetter and stank of sulphur, which did nothing to dismiss my Satan's backyard theory. I didn't take long, however, to detect the source of the stench. A geyser of steam erupted out of an open iron pipe sunk into the cavern floor. Noisy fans mounted by the roof of the cavern kicked in as the machinery tried to compensate for the change in air pressure the plumes of volcanic steam caused.

Several of Musk's overalled labourers were working away around the floor of the cavern, trying to manoeuvre a second pipe over to the first with block and tackle cranes, clearly trying to link them together to funnel volcanic steam around the chamber. Whether this was a planned piece of engineering, or something had gone askew it was impossible to tell. But Musk himself looked unconcerned, unlike the Packards who both rushed off to supervise the operation. Supervision which judging by the scurry of workers was much needed.

This new pipework wasn't alone. There was a tangle of tubes and conduits running all over the chamber Weaving all around the place in ways that made little sense to me. But this mass of piping was a minor distraction compared to the huge mechanical contrivance that sat in its centre, boxing off a whole section of the cavern. There was something vaguely familiar about it, but it wasn't until we reached the main floor that I recognised it for what it was, a mechanism with which I was intimately familiar, though never on this scale. It stretched from the floor of the cavern some forty feet upwards and lay at a steep angle. A huge section like a hinged door big enough to drive a truck through lay open, held aloft by enormous pistons. Beyond which was a curved tube with yet another set of doors in it. I found myself staring at it fascinated and horrified in equal measure. The mechanism was the breach and what lay within it was the shell the gun was designed to fire. The Moon-Shot itself.

"So, you see, Miss Clarkhurst, the capsule sits in the breach and we prime the a chamber below us with a mix of oxygen and nitro-glycerine. We then tap off the release system for the magma well below us and allow the pressure to build up until we reach the critical point and then funnel it into the compressors and ignite," I heard Musk saying above the noise in the cavernous room. Remarkably enough for once, I could grasp some of the concepts involved. Which would've pleased me if I hadn't found them so utterly bloody horrifying.

When I was a child, I had a spud gun... I know, I digress, but stick with me. There is, for once, a point to this digression...

When I was a child, I had a spud gun. Several actually, but my favourite was perhaps the most basic of all of them. I loved it simply because of that simplicity. Basically, it was nothing more than a cylinder you primed by pulling the trigger handle out. Then you simply drilled the nib of the barrel into a potato and gave it a twist to pull out the shot. And that was it, your spud gun was loaded. All you had to do then was point it at some unsuspecting target and pull the trigger back. The mechanics were as basic as you like. The trigger forced the cylinder to compress the air trapped within it until the spud bullet flew out of the end.

Then of course you laughed and ran round the corner so your victim didn't know who had shot a little pellet of raw potato at their exposed skin. And ran a little further if you had caused Billy White's dad to drop his bottle of Brown when you shot him, as that was a whack round the ear you didn't want to suffer. It was, as the saying goes, all fun and games, until someone loses an eye and no one ever lost an eye to a spud gun bullet.

Well, that is no one except Lenny Longbottom, and in fairness, was it my fault he turned his head when I was shooting him in the back of the neck at point blank range? Besides he was only blinded for a couple of days. Frankly he got off lightly compared to me after his mum told my mum about it and she gave me an educational hiding.

After that incident, spud guns were considered contraband in my old mum's gaff. She hurled my favourite one in the fire and made me watch as the tin turned black and started to twist up in the coals. "Oh, stop your beefing. If you want it enough, you can reach in and grab it," she'd told me. "No? Then we shan't be having another of those damn thing in the house, will we? Or next time I'll make you pick it out…"

She'd meant that too, she was hard at times, hard but fair… Well, occasionally fair at any rate. Of course, she was on the gin at the time, and I got a new one as soon as I could. But still, I never let her catch me with one again and never found one as good as that first one. They were all too complex and broke easily.

But anyway, childhood reminiscing aside, that is essentially in simple terms what Musk had built into the volcano on that small island east of Java. The spud was the capsule, the piston was the barrel of the howitzer and the charge was being primed by an active volcano, by the geothermic pressures of the earth itself.

As for the moon, the moon was Lenny Longbottom's eye…

And yes, I know that's an over simplistic explanation, but it's ostensibly that what he was talking about.

"It must take an age to build up that much volcanic gas?" I found myself asking and instantly regretted doing so. Even as I said it, I just knew what was coming.

"Several weeks, yes, but you're in luck, you have arrived only a few days before we launch," one of the Packards informed me, coming back over from where the new pipe had been forced into position and was in the process of being bolted together.

"Oh, good." I said with feeling and not a feeling of joy, I can tell you. I'm not psychic by any means, but right then I was having a premonition. I mean it was all there before me, after all.

I was a guest on an island that was basically a volcano that my hosts were using like a giant pressure cooker to fire a ballistic capsule at the moon in a few days' time.

I mean, what could possibly go wrong…?

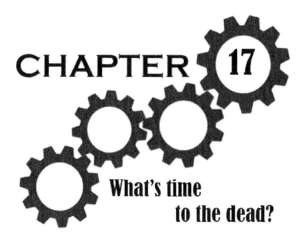

CHAPTER 17

What's time to the dead?

I took my leave of the tour party not long after this. Hettie was keen to see everything, and Musk was clearly in his element, expounding on 'his genius' for want of a better word.

The words I'd have chosen would've been 'his bloody lunacy' but let's stick with 'his genius', shall we?

I'd been both befuddled by the technology and bored in equal measure for the most part, between abject terror. And so, instead of sticking around to have the 'flight elevation thrusters', 'oxygen regeneration chambers', 'guidance gyroscopes' and a whole load of other gadgets further explained at me, as I understood about one word in three, I decided my time would be better spent investigating a sample of Hettie's latest batch of engine room hooch. Just as a matter of quality control, you understand.

Preferably somewhere beyond the confines of an active volcano.

Claiming tiredness I attributed to the injuries I was still recovering from, I entreated Doctor Musk to let me leave them to their tour, and he was kind enough to have me escorted back to the living quarters. He cared nothing about impressing me anyway. It was clearly Hettie who he wished to enamour of his grand project, something he was managing to achieve. She was like a child in a sweet factory being offered samples. The refined home counties accent she'd adopted the evening before had lost some of its polish, and been replaced with engine grease. I've seldom seen her so happy, save when she was ten shots into a drinking contest and everyone else had slipped beneath the table.

Luckily, my guide sauntered off as soon as he'd delivered me to the living quarters, so I decided I needed some fresh air. An earlier part of our facility tour had included the wide veranda outside the main complex where most of Musk's staff ate their meals, so I headed that way, having liberated a jam jar of Hettie's finest I'd previously sequestered in my room.

Not long after, I was perched on a wall overlooking a strip of white sand, palm trees and the ocean, with the sun on my back. The view from that wall was a vison of paradise or would have been save for the volcano with a gun sticking out on the edge of my vision. It loomed large, as such a thing is wont to do, and so spoiled the view somewhat, if I am honest.

I been there perhaps half an hour, or a good inch and a half into the jar, when I felt a sudden chill as a shadow fell across me. Something other than the volcano was looming behind and I know looming when I feel it. Hang about with Fabulous Frankie and his mob down at The Elves long enough and you learn to appreciate the talent behind a good looming. Whoever was behind me, well, they loomed so well they could weave a carpet from their shadow.

"Good day, Mr Smyth," the loomer said behind me. The voice was odd, though it would be hard to put a finger on exactly why. It had a flat quality to it, dry and, well, dusty is perhaps the word. It was an arid voice. Arid of anything that could be considered life. A voice that added to the sudden chill of its owner's shadow, and made it feel all the colder.

I turned with some trepidation.

Generally, I've found being loomed over is preferable to receiving a crack to the head. But the latter seems more honest in some ways. Perhaps because when you're struck from behind, at least you know that no one is trying to trick you.

But turn I did, and as the sun was blocked out by the bulk of the man behind me, its rays gave the impression of him having a halo of sorts. Which is the last thing you expect when you find yourself looking up at a Sleepman. There is nothing heavenly about them.

I tried to hide my unease, not least at being greeted verbally. I'd never heard a Sleepman talk before. That said, his voice was exactly what I'd have expected. More than my unease, I tried to hide my fear, that at least was easier than you might suspect. Not because I was unafraid, frankly I doubt there was anything I would've been more afraid of right at that moment than a looming Sleepman. But I'd learned to hide fear long ago, leastways when other more tempting options like fleeing do not present themselves.

Think of it like facing down a wild animal, or just a vicious dog for that matter. Showing no fear is always the key in such situations. It's important never to let them be aware you're afraid. By appearing to be unafraid, you put them on edge and give yourself one. Wild animals, Soho drunks with broken bottles, or a bloody Sleepman, it makes no difference. You must appear unafraid, so that is what I did. I stared him down doing my best impression of unshakable Englishness, keeping my upper lip stiff and letting him see a steely glint in my eye.

"There is no reason to be afraid, Mr Smyth," the monster before me said.

"I'm not," I lied, in what I considered to be a steady, convincing voice.

"I see, are you then shivering due only to the chill of my shadow? And are you stepping from one foot to the other not because of nervousness, but merely because the hot sand is burning the soles of your feet?" He said in that same arid monotonous tone he had used before. A surprising lack of implication to his tone, despite the words.

"Quite," I said, and forced myself still.

"The sand must be very hot if it is burning the soles of your feet through military boots…" he observed, and for just a moment I detected a hint of inflection creeping into his tone. Was it a sense of humour? Did Sleepmen have such a thing?

I coughed, as if to clear my throat, and took a small step back in the process, without trying to make it obvious I was putting room between us. Not that I could put enough room between us. Right then I considered the definition of enough room between us to be the breadth of the Pacific Ocean.

"I'm not what you think I am, Mr Smyth," he said, and thankfully made no attempt to close the gap I'd created. Then he took off his hat and made something akin to a gentlemanly bow towards me.

He didn't look any better without his hat. That strange metal plate I'd noted from a distance that covered the right side of his face was uglier close up. It looked to be made of blackened iron and covered his right cheek and eye, and now he had no hat, I realised it was not some kind of mask as I had thought. The metal had been screwed directly over that side of his head with small brass screws that had to go straight into the bones of his skull. It swept up beyond his eye and covered a full half of his cranium. The rest of his head was clean shaved and covered with a multitude of scars. Strangely I found this morbidly fascinating, in that I could not tear my gaze from it. I realised rather than a mask it was instead a crude prosthetic. At some point in his past, the right side of this man's skull had been shattered in some way. The metal plate had been screwed on to cover the damage. Yet I knew that was impossible. No one could live through the kind of trauma involved, surely. Losing half your skull is not like losing an arm for god's sake…

I finally tore my gaze away from his strange visage and as my 'I'm not afraid' gambit had clearly failed, I fell back on dismissive humour as a rear guard. "Well, thank god for that because I thought you were a Sleepman."

"I am not," he intoned. Which did nothing to dismiss my doubts.

"Well then, if you don't mind me asking then, what are you?" I asked, trying to keep the humour in my voice. This was, I'll admit, an impertinent question to ask anyone. I was, however, a fair way into a jar of Hettie's finest and my nerves were a tad frayed.

"Dead," he said, and if you'll excuse the term, he said this with such an utterly dead pan tone of voice I was completely thrown.

"What?" I choked.

"Dead, Mr Smyth. I have been for a long time, however, I try not to let it get in the way of moving around."

"What?" I said again, not entirely sure I had heard him right.

"Humour, Mr Smyth. I'm told it helps set people at their ease," his deadpan tones explained.

I suspect the drink was starting to get to me. Or perhaps it was a touch of sun stroke. Either way, I was now more puzzled than afraid. I also had a degree of morbid fascination about him now, if you'll excuse the term…

"Does it work?" I asked.

"Not noticeably, no."

Throughout this exchange, his expression, such as it was, was unchanging. But I guess it is hard to have an expression when half your face is missing and the rest is scarred to high Heaven. I did, however, came to the conclusion I wasn't in any immediate danger. Though, at the same time, I had a sudden desire to keep the liquid courage working, so I picked up the jam jar of hooch and took another drink. Perhaps the courage it invested had a certain immediacy, or perhaps it was the distraction of it taking another layer of lining from my throat as it went down, but that sense of morbid fascination only got stronger, the more I drank.

"Look, who are you?" I asked, as he clearly had me at a disadvantage and I wanted to even that score if nothing else.

"Gothe. Formerly Albert Gothe, deceased. I've made your acquaintance before Captain Smyth," he explained.

"You have? I'm sure I'd remember if we had met before…" I said, and more honest words have never passed my lips. This was not a man you would forget meeting in a hurry. Then I found myself asking, "Formerly?"

"That would be unlikely as you have not met me previously," he said, and I assumed he was just ignoring my inquiry about his name. That was fair enough, I decided. If my parents had landed me with such a moniker, I'd be tempted to ignore it too.

"You say we haven't met? But you just said we have. Which is it?" I asked, confused.

"I've met you previously, you've not met me before…. It's complicated," he failed to explain.

"You realise that doesn't make any sense. Right?" I said, taking another drink, which led to a mild coughing fit until I took a third. It was then I remembered my manners and offered him the jar. This he refused with a stiff politeness, and for a moment I saw an expression of distaste cross his face. As much as any expression could.

"I haven't partaken of strong spirits since my death," he explained in his deadpan tones. The drink was definitely getting to me by then, as this statement seemed fine to me. Besides, if he didn't want a drink, more gut rot for me, and frankly I felt I needed it.

"Okay… But let's backtrack to the whole you've met me but I've not met you thing. It's nonsensical, you know that, don't you?" I said with the warm courage of alcohol spurring me on.

"I believe when I first met you, I said much the same. It is however a matter of time. When we met you were older than you are now. While I was… Well, what is time to the dead. It was before now, let me just say that," he told me.

"…" I didn't rely. I was too busy trying to get my head around what he was saying. Was he claiming to be a ghost of some kind, I wondered. That, I decided, made as much sense as anything else he was saying.

"You understood such things then, but as I say you were older. I didn't, but I took you on faith, faith that has proved to be well founded. For now, our paths cross once more," he went on, which didn't help one bit.

"…" I didn't say. My mouth was probably open, but for the life of me I couldn't think of anything to say. I took another drink and then, because I wasn't sure how wise that had been, I shook my head in an attempt to clear it. And found words to say at last. "What? Sorry… Look, I don't

wish to be rude, but what exactly do you want, Mr Gothe?"
I asked him.

"When last we met, you requested a favour of me. You
also said you would not know me now, but asked me to
respect the favour all the same. It was… important to you,"
he explained, if that's the right word, because I can't say I
was following him too well.

Intrigued despite my confusion, or perhaps because of it,
I asked him the obvious question that occurred me. "And
what favour was that?"

"You asked that I look to the wellbeing of your young
lady, for you knew you would be unable to do so."

"My young lady, what young lady?" I asked him. Utterly
confused now. I was certain I had no young lady I needed
looking after for a start. There hadn't been a young lady in
my life since before the New Bailey for one thing. My love
life, regrettably, was as arid and dusty as Mr Gothe's voice.

"Miss Clarkhurst," he told me, and I almost coked with
the laughter I had to fight to keep down.

"Hettie? She is not my young lady," I protested.

"Strange, you certainly believed otherwise at the time,"
he told me, and if he was pulling my leg it was impossible to
tell.

"When?"

"I am given to believe this was in your future, though
my past. You were older as I said and you held her in some
affection. Perhaps it is simply that you were just more
honest with yourself then than you are now. Or will be at
least," he further explained, or further didn't depending on
your perspective.

"You realise this is an insane conversation, don't you?"
I said with feeling. "And Hettie Clarkhurst is not my lady,
that's for damn sure. We are friends is all, good friends,
mind you, but just friends. I mean, sure, I care about her, as

any bloke cares about his mates. But 'my lady', good god, the only person who'd find that idea more absurd than me would be Hettie…"

"I am sure you believe that to be the case, Captain Smyth. But I assure you, you were most adamant in your request and I have a debt owed to you. I shall honour that request. What worth is there in a dead man if not in his word," he said, and for all that deadpan voice of his, there was a sense of feeling behind it I found hard to credit. I realised that he truly did believe himself to be dead. Strange though that sounds. No word he said was a lie, at least in his own mind.

"Debt? What debt do you owe me?" asked my avarice and I would be a liar if I told you I didn't for a moment harbour the vain hope that debt might prove to be one that consisted of a considerable sum of money. Sadly, of course, it wasn't ever going to be that kind of debt.

"You saved the life of one who was my mistress when I could not. You pulled her from the wreck of Maybe's Daughter. Such is the debt I owe you. Such is the act I must reciprocate," he told me, which made no more sense than anything else he'd said, clearly.

"Maybe's… what?" I asked him. But it appeared our conversation had come to an end.

Mr Gothe placed his hat back on his head. Then he nodded to me by way of a farewell and turned away.

He did, however, leave me one final snippet of oddity, by way of his parting words. "In time you will know, Mr Smyth, in time…"

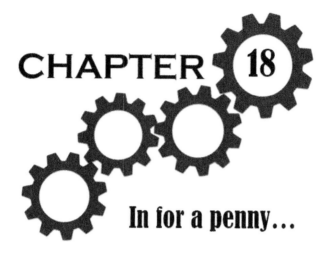

CHAPTER 18

In for a penny...

The next few days dragged by, and for much of them I put that conversation with the peculiar Albert Gothe out of my mind. Though calling him peculiar was something of an understatement. I mean, I was skipping merry along mentally as far as the whole 'I am dead' part was concerned, because the rest of the conversation had been bizarre enough. The trouble was that putting one small part of that conversation out of my mind was proving difficult... Which was why I found myself giving Hettie oddly appraising looks every time the two of us crossed paths. I wasn't even aware I was doing this until she cornered me one morning at breakfast and asked me, in her own particular vernacular, 'What the bloody Hell's gotten into you? You gawping idiot.'

I shrugged this off dismissively at the time. Not least because I didn't fancy my chances of explaining that a 'dead' man had told me, that a future me had told him, that she was 'my lady' in a conversation that had taken place sometime in the past.

Let's face it, there was no way I could say that with a straight face.

More disturbingly, I also didn't want to explain that I'd caught myself half believing there was a grain of truth to it all… Which at times I did, despite myself. There's the rub you see. There are only so many times people can intimate to you, in entire sincerity, that time travel is fact and not fiction, before you start to wonder if there is something real behind what could only otherwise be explained by a very specific sort of mass hysteria that seems to be affecting almost everyone you meet.

I'm not saying I actually believed it, but I had reached the point where I believe they believed it. I'd also come to the conclusion that while they were all clearly mad, that didn't necessarily mean they were entirely wrong, as such… But I didn't, even for a moment, want to admit that to anyone. Least of all Henrietta Clarkhurst, perhaps the most singularly grounded, practical person I'd ever met.

Hettie has the soul of an engineer, for god's sake. She is one of those chaps adept at turning the mad dreams of others into reality through the medium of nuts, bolts and common sense. Tell her you believe time travel may be possible and she'd doubtless ask you to point out which spanner she needed to use to go back to last Thursday. Then pick it up and lump you with it.

Discretion therefore being the better part of valour, I made a point of avoiding Hettie for the next day or two. Luckily, she was so busy involving herself with Musk's insane project I doubt she even noticed my absence.

A couple of times over the next few days, I was tempted to try and track down Mr Gothe again, vainly hoping I might get some sense out of him, but he'd creeped me out in so many ways I was soon dismissing the idea each time it occurred to me. In fairness, after a day or so, I'd half convinced myself he was just another mad man. God knows I'd run across enough for them in recent times. M, Gates, Wells, Jobs, Verne, now Musk... there wasn't one of them with enough marbles left to fill a bag. Gothe, I assured myself, was probably just another blasted lunatic. By the third day I'd convinced myself the most likely explanation was that he'd just mistaken me for someone else. Smyth is not an uncommon name and let's face it Smith is as common as herpes. Gothe had doubtless just imprinted his own psychosis on the world and, lucky me, I'd become subject to his delusion.

As the days passed, I managed to convince myself this was the case. What's more, Gothe had clearly suffered a great deal of head trauma at some point in the past. Having a cast iron prosthetic replacing one side of his skull told me that much. Hell, it looked like someone had shot him in the head and blown half his skull away. Frankly it was a miracle he was alive. Which might explain why he thought he wasn't. A thing like that was bound to make anyone a little loopy.

Besides which, let us be honest here, time travel was the concept that was central to everything that had happened to me in since M first walked into my cell in the New Bailey. HG Wells' insane ideas were at the heart of everything. It was hardly surprising I found myself crossing paths with yet another lunatic who shared Wells' crackpot ideas.

Well, I determined after a while, I'd be damned before I started to buy into any more of that idiocy. And having come to that conclusion, I put it out of my mind. It wasn't as if I didn't have other things to worry about. So what if some great hulk of a man believed he was dead and wanted to look after Hettie out of some imaginary debt he owed me. Hettie was a big girl, I assured myself, she can damn well take care of herself.

Besides, if it became a problem, I was sure she'd spanner the Hell out of him.

Annoyingly though, even as I told myself all this, the conversation still lurked in the back of my mind, niggling at me. I can't tell you for why. Perhaps I was vaguely remembering my own future. Pre-déjà vu if you will. The act of remembering an event that was yet to happen… I met a chef once who was full of theories on things like that. Though I'm damned if I could tell you where or when I met him. But I'm getting off track and the things that happened later, happened later, so not to digress any further…

Days dragged by, in the way days do. Captain Verne's daughter was put back together like humpty dumpty, and Hettie was busy getting herself involved with Doctor Musk's grand project. Meanwhile, between bouts of boredom, I found myself distracted by other worries. As one does when one knows an enormous volcanic explosion is just around the corner.

The good doctor was still providing guest quarters within his lair for myself and Hettie. I, however, began to feel these were uncomfortably close to an unexploded bomb. I swear the humidity inside the base was rising a little more each day. I started to hear odd creaks and the occasional hiss from pipes that sounded like they wanted to rupture under the pressure. Sure, it could've been just my paranoid imagination running wild, but trust me, you try sleeping inside an active volcano every night and see how comfortable you feel after an hour or two listening to the noise of straining metal.

After my second restless night, I'd taken to sleeping in my cabin aboard The Oegopsida. Call it cowardice if you will, I prefer to consider it an act of discretion on my part. Better, I thought, to be aboard the one means of escape when the inevitable happened, than risk it vanishing into the night and stranding me inside an erupting volcano.

It's fair to say I lacked a great deal of faith in Doctor Musk's scientific endeavour. The more I knew about him, the more he struck me as a man so in love with his ideas that he was pathologically incapable of envisioning failure. I'd met men like him before, in the military and elsewhere. Men so self-assured about their own supremacy they're unable to ever consider the possibility that their plans could miscarry. His bombastic unswerving self-confidence drove him ever onward with his projects. Which you will forgive me for thinking as a flaw in any man using an active volcano as a blow gun.

I wasn't alone in spending my nights aboard The Squid. Captain Verne returned to his ship nightly, and insisted the crew remained aboard in their down time. In the captain's case, I suspected this may have been partly to avoid spending time with his wife. Their strained relationship remained evident throughout. The only noticeable exception to the captain's dictate was Hettie, who was spending all her time examining Musk's plans and engineering. As such she was sleeping no more than a few hours a night in the stateroom the doctor had provided.

Unfortunately, my cabin on The Oegopsida was, as you'll remember, far from roomy. As such, to avoid feeling cooped up and bored out of my mind, I took to spending my days exploring the island. In truth, the impending volcanic disaster my paranoia was warning me about was just as likely to strike through the day as in the hours of darkness, but there is a limit to how long such fatalism could keep me locked up in a tiny eight foot by eight-foot room.

This was why, several days later, I found myself walking down a deserted tropical beach in blazing sunshine. As an idyll, it was one I'd long harboured, as you're aware. Admittedly, in my moments of wishful thinking, such beaches would always have a bar. A little hut with palm leaves for a roof, offering shade and a smiling waiter serving gin and tonics I could sip while admiring a bevy of scantily clad local ladies frolicking in the surf.

Sadly, this wasn't the case.

However, but for the lack of a bar and scantily clad ladies, the beach was exactly as I had imagined. Though this idyll was strained somewhat by the huge gun barrel sticking out of the side of the volcano, but I made a point of looking at that as little as possible.

This must have been a week or more after my conversation with Gothe and was not the first time I'd found myself strolling along that beach. I must have been about halfway down it when I sat down on a convenient piece of driftwood, in the middle of a swathe of white sand. I sat there a while, with my back to the mountain and just watched the surf rolling in, absentmindedly drifting off, and bemoaning the lack of a gin and tonic.

Watching the waves, it occurred to me that this was the closest thing to paradise I was ever likely to find. The sound of the surf rolling in, the cries of a gull passing overhead. The warm sand beneath my feet. The breeze off the ocean softening the heat of the sun. I felt almost at peace with the world.

So, clearly that wasn't going to last.

"There you are, Smyth, you festering lung worm," someone shouted down the beach at me.

The voice, and I wasn't even remotely surprised by this, belonged to the closest thing to a beautiful scantily clad woman I was destined to meet on that beach. It has to be said, this vision of womanhood's voice was full of bile, rage and, I suspected, no little hate directed towards yours truly. I'd have wondered why I was the focus of such vitriol, but frankly what was the point?

Swearing silently to myself as I looked up, I saw exactly who I expected, stalking towards me, because who else could it be, breaking a moment of relative peace and harmony? Who else would turn up like a bad...

"Penny, good to see you up and about, and all in one piece again," I lied, with all the charm I could muster. Which was doubtless less than the requisite required. I've found over the years that the quality of charm needed to placate the savage beast is seldom at hand when required and in the case of Vivienne Verne, I doubt enough charm exists in the world.

But then, as I sat and watched as she marched towards me, on her shapely, newly reattached legs, I realised to my surprise that I hadn't been entirely lying when I said it was good to see her. My perpetual Bad Penny had been one of the few constants in my life since I gotten out of the cell below the New Bailey. Well, her and violent blows to the head, often administered by her come to think of it. All the same, her presence was reassuring in an odd way.

"That's not my name," she snarled back at me.

I smiled. There was something to be said for that old back and forth between us. It was almost foreplay by this point. Of course, what it was usually foreplay for was her beating the hell out of me, but it was foreplay all the same.

"Indeed... Miss Verne then, if you prefer. Tell me, what can I help you with this glorious day?" I asked, pushing myself to my feet and dusting sand off my trousers.

"Stow it, you cretin, where is she?" she demanded, direct as ever.

"Where is who?" I asked, though even as I asked the question, light was dawning on the answer. Who else could

Penny be talking about but the same woman she always seemed to be asking me about, and had been since we first met? "Ah, you mean Saffron, don't you?" I added quickly as she leered at me and a sickening feeling descended over me. I knew without doubt that the idyllic last few days of relative peace were about to become complicated, and the very opposite of idyllic going forwards.

Bad Pennys, they always turn up…

A couple of hours later, I was once more in the bowels of The Oegopsida, standing beside the bulkhead door that led to the innocuous but guarded entrance to Chamber 17:2:4. If you're wondering just why I'd agreed to guide Bad Penny down there, and let her drag me into whatever she was planning to do, well, it came down to two factors. Firstly, after they put her back together again, she once more had razor-blades for fingernails. Secondly, I knew she'd be more than happy to use those blades on me.

In fairness, I'd taken less convincing than you might imagine but it was certainly nothing to do with any residual attraction I might still hold for 'Justine Casey of the Calcutta Herald'. Neither was it related to any predilection for strong domineering women you may suspect I possess. Nor was it because of any residual guilt I might be retaining over the events that happened atop of The Johan's Lament, or for that matter anything to do with our shared experience on that hilltop outside Hiroshima… And, let me be clear, it absolutely wasn't because, despite everything, I actually harboured a bit of a thing for my own dearest Bad Penny… No, it came down to nothing more than the distinct likelihood of her gutting me like a freshly caught haddock if I didn't comply with her wishes…

You can of course feel free to believe otherwise, if you must.

"Your father has her locked up through there," I told her.

Bad Penny surreptitiously glanced through the little porthole in the hatch. She had a grim look of defiance about her. I chose not to speculate as to why her father was keeping Saffron Wells' whereabouts from her. There was every chance it had nothing to do with Miss Wells' current state of mind and a lot to do with the sapphic nature of his daughter's relationship with Saffron. Verne struck me as a man who was stiffly traditionalist about such matters. But then he was, after all, a man like HG Wells from a much earlier generation. It was also possible that despite his daughter being half psychotic killing machine, half just plain psychotic, Verne's reluctance was simply the act of a protective parent. I remembered all too well the state Saffron had been in when they brought her aboard. You could understand him not wishing his daughter to see someone she loved reduced to little more than a raving shell.

"How sure are you?" Penny asked. coldly earnest.

"I'm not, but you asked if I knew and… Well, this is my best guess. Your father implied as much when I was looking around down here a few days ago."

"Snooping around, you mean," she sneered, then flashed me half a smile, "That's why I thought you'd know. You're a weasel, Smyth, you're always ferreting around where you shouldn't for information, or something to steal. A rodent like you can't help yourself."

"I resent that implication," I snapped, despite it being ostensibly true. Then I tried to lighten the conversation with a little false pomposity. "Besides which, weasels and ferrets are completely different animals…"

She gave me a scathing look before gifting me with another of those smiles which always take the harshness out of her face. "Would you prefer I called you a stoat?"

I shrugged, dismissively. "I've always fancied myself in ermine, actually."

"You would," she said and grinned, to my relief. Not that her sudden levity fooled me any. I knew full well she could turn on me any moment.

"Look, couldn't you just ask Papa Verne to let you see her?" I asked, though I was sure doing so would be fruitless. I was trying to buy myself time, on the off chance there was a way to uninvolve myself with whatever she was about to do. I should've known better. The smile dropped from her face and a cold stare that told me all I needed to know about what she thought of that idea. It was much the same look she had given me the first four times I'd made that suggestion on the way back to the submersible.

Well, you can't blame me for trying...

"You've got me here, I don't need your help anymore. You can go if you wish," she told me. As if that was ever going to be an option. The captain was already likely to keel haul me for showing her where Saffron was held if things went south. And Penny had a habit of making things go south quicker than a dose of figs and castor oil. Besides, I suspected being keel hauled on a submersible wasn't something you walk away from. I was already in the brown stuff and all I could hope to do now was rein in Penny's worst instincts.

Hope springs eternal...

All that said, she was the captain's daughter. There was every chance the guards would go ahead and open the chamber if she asked them to. Besides, I was holding out the hope that Saffron's sanity might be much restored after several days in Verne's brig. I mean, that wasn't impossible, was it? Of course, she'd been a tad wild when we found her adrift on a slowly sinking wreck. Who wouldn't be? And yes, she'd killed everyone else who survived the crash, but M's little spider had been controlling her. She'd ripped it out afterwards, hadn't she? She was probably free of its influence now. So having spent a few days locked up in a nice cosy cell, being fed and watered three times a day, there was every chance her sanity could have returned.

Yes, okay, I know, just call me an eternal optimist…

Penny didn't wait for my answer. She turned the wheel, opened the hatch and marched straight up to the first of the two guards as they turned towards her. He was probably smiling at her beneath his rebreather. She was, after all, the captain's daughter. I'm sure his crew all knew her by sight and wouldn't for a moment have imagined she was a threat. But his passive expression changed to one of horrified surprise as the blades slid out from beneath her fingernails and she raked them across his throat.

He went down faster than the first Guinness on Saint Patrick's Day.

The second guard, doubtless surprised by this turn of events, to his credit managed to bring his weapon to bear even as his compatriot was hitting the floor, but he was too slow by half. She kicked it from his grasp with a round house before leaping onto him and sinking her claws into his neck too. It was over in seconds, less than seconds. I'd held my breath from the moment she clawed the first of them and had barely noticed I was doing so before the second hit the deck.

Both men quickly turned an odd shade of purple and lay as stiff as boards. I thought for a second rigor mortis had set in at an exponential rate as I stepped through the bulkhead door behind her but Penny, who must have seen my shocked expression, burst into a grin.

"Oh relax, Stoaty," she said, holding her left hand up before me and letting me watch the ever excruciating sight of her razor-sharp blades slowly retract back behind her fingernails. "My stepmother was kind enough to include a few improvements with my new arm. My blades are laced with a paralytic. These sods will be fine, they just ain't gonna be moving about for a couple of hours."

"Your stepmother?" I found myself asking, unable to take my eyes off the prone men on the deck, while suppressing the East End urge to put the boot in as they were prone buggers in uniform. Then something clicked in my head. "Madam Verne made your new arm. I thought it was Musk."

"Musk? He's all wild ideas and big picture. I seriously doubt he knows one end of a screwdriver from the other. Sakura on the other hand, well, she's a genius with mechanics, much like Uncle Yamamoto. That's why she's here. Musk needed an actual genius to make his wild ideas a reality. He's all charm, bluster, show, and sod all real substance… Reminds me of you a little in that way, Stoaty."

I wasn't sure whether I should feel offended or not, but her summing up of Doctor Musk didn't seem far off my own impression of the man, now I considered it. It would explain why he was so keen on recruiting Hettie. If I wanted someone to make an insanely complicated machine then Henrietta Clarkhurst is exactly who I'd ask to build it. It also explained why Madam Verne was on the island. Elonis Musk knew exactly how to charm someone with praise, I'd seen that clearly enough with Hettie. It made sense if the captain's wife could build the artful mechanics that allowed my dearest Bad Penny to walk around and murder people then Musk would want her on his payroll. I didn't doubt the lengths he'd go to in order to secure her services. He was clearly an obsessive.

"Stoaty… That's not my name," I said pompously. More to break the tension than anything else. My own that is, given what had just happened.

"Yer, well now you know how that feels," she who doubtless preferred to be known as Vivienne Verne said, smiling at me while she rooted around in the pockets of one of the guards. The other guard, whose eyes were wide open, was staring wildly up at me. I felt a weird urge to close his eyelids for him. The thought of being paralysed and fully aware terrified me. It was too close to what I'd imagined it would've felt like if M's spider had ever taken full control of my body. The way the spider in Saffron Wells' eye had taken full control of hers.

Thinking of Saffron brought me back to what we were doing, and I questioned, not for the first time, my wisdom in sticking around. But there was no helping it now. Both guards' eyes were wide open. They could see me as clearly as I could see them, even if they couldn't move a muscle. I'm ashamed to say that I considered for a moment that it would've been advantageous for me personally if Penny had just plain killed them. I'm not saying she should have done, but it's a lot harder for a dead witness to point you out in a crowd. It wasn't a thought which said anything good about me, but there you go. I never claimed to be a saint, and it was just a thought after all.

"Found them, Stoaty," Penny said in triumph, breaking my unpleasant chain of thought.

I looked over and saw her pull a ring of keys out of the second guard's pockets.

"Oh good," I muttered under my breath, but she flashed me a look that suggested she heard. Then adopting an impish grin, which would've been adorable in other circumstances, she unlocked the hatch and began turning the wheel to open it.

I sighed, resigned to my fate. In for a Penny in for a pounding, as it were. So, I stepped over the paralysed guards and helped my favourite Bad Penny pull open the door to Chamber 17:2:4.

This then, was the point where things really started to go to Hell in a handcart...

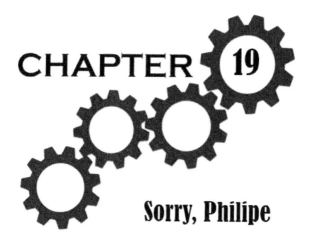

CHAPTER 19

Sorry, Philipe

Chamber 17:2:4 was bigger than I'd expected. All I'd expected was a small brig, perhaps no more than a single cell with a bed and a bucket. Instead, beyond the hatch was a short corridor that ran back twenty yards or so to a solid bulkhead. Six individual hatchways, three to a side, were spaced out down the corridor and while it might not have been the largest prison I'd ever entered, it was bigger than I'd imagined for a vessel where space was a priority. It was, however, grim. It was painted a darker grey than elsewhere, though that may have just been the lack of light. Climbing through the hatch, I reminded myself I'd been lucky Verne hadn't confined me here. If there was ever an oubliette to be thrown in and forgotten about, this was it.

The first two cells were empty. Their hatches lay open despite normal practise aboard the sub. Within were dark little rooms, lacking even so much as a porthole. I've seldom seen a grimmer place in which you could be imprisoned, and I've seen more than my fair share of such places. There wasn't even a bucket, just a hole in the corner that served as a drain. Seeing this, it struck me that if things went pear shaped, I may end up using one of those drains myself before too long. This was a far from inviting prospect, so I tried not to dwell on it. It was a prison that didn't need an entry in my good death cell guide. There was nothing good about it.

I followed Penny down the corridor and watched as she opened the next hatch at random, looked in and shut it without comment, before trying the one in the opposite wall. I caught a sight of a stack of wooden crates inside this one and my mood lightened a little. If these were storage compartments for the captain's ill-gotten gains, as I had first assumed, then perhaps there was less chance of anything major going wrong. I could always claim his daughter forced me along with her mad scheme. Sure, he might not believe me if I did, but at least I wasn't going to end up locked up down here.

It was of course the last two hatches that proved to be the actual cells. The doors had those tell-tale sliding panels, through which a guard could observe whoever was incarcerated beyond. The one on the left remained empty but to the right the last hatch proved indeed to be where Verne had stashed Saffron Wells.

God forgive me, but I wish it hadn't.

Penny opened the door, gasped and stepped through before I got a look inside. The corridor was narrow, so it wasn't until she entered that I could get close enough to see beyond the door. Within, Saffron Wells was sitting slumped on the floor, her long dark hair a straggled mess, hanging down in tresses over her eyes. They'd redressed her in fresh clothes, presumably while she was sedated, but they were already a ragged mess, as was she. It looked like she'd been clawing at her own arms and chest. Bloody trails marked where her nails had ragged at her skin. Any bruising and injuries caused by the crash and her rough, if understandable treatment, at the hands of Verne's guards, paled in significance compared with the harm she had inflicted upon herself. In hindsight that should've served as a warning to both Penny and I. We should've approached carefully and treated Saffron with caution and care. But I was too slow to pick up on those signals, and before I could say a word, it was too late. Penny rushed over to Saffron and flung her arms around her.

The sudden display of open affection and empathy from Vivienne Verne threw me somewhat. I'd known the depth of her feelings for Saffron for some time. She'd threatened to kill me more than once because of them. Right back to our first meeting on The Empress of India when she'd knocked me out for the first time with a blow that could just as easily put my lights out permanently. That night in Calcutta when she'd tied me to a bed and shown me her claws for the first time. It had been the whole reason she had dragged me off to Japan and on to that train bound for Hiroshima. Everything she had put me through all came back to her feelings for Saffron Wells. Yet, despite knowing all this, her lack of caution and the sheer openness of her display of affection caught me off guard. It was also why it took me a moment to realise what the bloody trails Saffron had left upon herself meant. A moment too many.

"Christ, Penny, she's not restrained," I shouted, and knew even as I did so, this too was a fool's error.

Up until I opened my mouth, Saffron had remained passively sat on the floor. Immobile and unresponsive as Penny fussed at her the way a lover will on finding the centre of their affection in such a state. In hindsight, perhaps we'd have been fine had I not shouted that warning. Perhaps affection and love would've won out and found some glimmer of the real Saffron Wells still flickering beneath her madness. Perhaps Vivienne Verne's compassionate embrace would've eased sanity back to Saffron's shattered psyche, and everything would've turned out differently.

Then again perhaps not.

I suspected it was too late the moment we opened that cell door. The only thing I know for sure was that Penny blamed me for what happened next. As she has told me more than once since.

"That's not..." Penny started to say, focusing entirely on the wrong part of the sentence, but she never got to finish my beratement. Instead, she was flung against the wall by Saffron who exploded to her feet with the strength of madness. I caught a glimpse of her face beneath that mass of straggled hair as she did so. Her one good eye was full of fury, telling me all I needed to know.

Saffron started screaming. A scream with primal intensity. She ignored Penny, lying slumped against the bulkhead, entirely. Everything had happened so fast even Penny's lightning like reactions hadn't been enough to prevent her being dazed by the impact. And of course, with Penny was out of the picture, I was the one standing in the doorway between Saffron Wells and freedom.

Because of course I was...

She barrelled into me and I proved to be no more prepared than Penny had. Spearing me in the midriff, she sent me flying backwards through the hatch and into the corridor. My head cracked against the opposite door. The world went...

Well, not black, but it was definitely fuzzy for a few moments.

In other circumstances I would've taken remaining conscious as a win. Hell, it had been weeks since I'd last been knocked out cold, and the ever-present concussion of the last few months was starting to be a thing of the past. But right then I'd have welcomed one of those little oblivions. It would've been preferable to finding Saffron Wells crouched over me, her ruined face inches from mine, her good eye, bloodshot, crazed and leering at me.

"Hannibal, oh my dear Hannibal, the spider ate me, it should've eaten you, but it ate me…" she half gurgled with a mouth full of blood, as if she'd been biting her tongue in the most literal sense.

Then she leaned in closer, I could smell the foulness of her breath. It smelled of decay, like rotten meat. The ruined socket of her left eye had, I knew, been stitched shut by the ship's doctor, but she had torn the bandages away and ripped those stitches out too, leaving a pit of bloody darkness that drilled into my soul.

"Saffron, I…"

"I still hear him, Hannibal. In my head. Whispering he is. Whispering. I pull out the spider but still he whispers to me."

Coward that I am, I turned my face away, trying in my panic to hold my breath and hoping against hope that my own personal Bad Penny would just this once come to my aid and pull her former lover away.

With my head was still spinning, I tried vainly to shove her away, but the strength had gone out of my limbs while I fought to stay conscious.

"I hear him, Hannibal. It should've been you, you shit of a man, but he's in my head. It should've been you," she said again. Then of all things, she leaned even closer into me and ran her bloody tongue across my face, leaving it wet with saliva and even less pleasant things, as she put her hand around my throat.

I gathered my wits enough to start reaching for my trusty cutthroat housed in the little pocket sown into my boot, but not enough to remember it wasn't there. I kept reaching for it with increasing desperation as she slowly choked me, white blotches starting to appear before my eyes. I swear she would've finished the job, and I would not have lived to recall the tale, had not she been dragged away a moment later, leaving me shaking, prone against the bulkhead, heart pounding and lungs gasping for air.

Penny, who it was that had come to my rescue, had recovered enough to pull Saffron off me just in the nick of time. But that didn't leave me in any fit state to help her restrain her mad lover. Added to which, I was sure that Vivienne 'Bad Penny' Verne who normally could've taken down a charging bull if she'd wanted to, was pulling her punches for the first and probably last time in her life. Meanwhile, I was too busy rolling about on the floor trying vainly to get air in my lungs. Mostly I only heard the struggle between them. But it lasted only moments in any regard, before Penny was sent sprawling into me as I tried to regain my footing, knocking us both prone on the decking again.

As I struggled back to my feet a second time, my natural vison was still struggling for focus, the unnatural gift of Steven Jobs however decided now was the time to start focusing properly, and through it I caught a glimpse of Saffron vanishing down the corridor. She passed through the hatch and a second later I heard a heavy thunk followed swiftly by a muffled cry. Then for a second, she appeared in the doorway once more, holding something large and heavy which she turned towards us. In my dazed state, I had no idea what she was holding, but Penny, who'd been quicker to her feet than I, suddenly dived at me again, knocking both of us back through the hatch that led to Saffron's cell, to clatter against the far wall while another heavy thunk rang out, closer than the first.

Somewhere an alarm sounded. I don't know who triggered it, or how long it took me to stumble to my feet once more. I do remember pulling Penny back to hers and muttering some kind of thanks, without being entirely sure what I was thanking her for. It was as I pulled her to her feet that I noted the mess of her new arm Saffron had made with whatever she'd been using for a weapon. The pristine fake skin had been shredded above the elbow and I could see tiny sparks arcing along the metal beneath.

"Come on, Vivienne, we need to get out of here," I said, not even realising I'd used her real name for once as I half dragged her after me, back through the hatch and down the corridor to the main entrance, my concern as much motivated by the alarms as anything. Saffron loose on the submersible didn't bode well for anyone and I wanted to get as far away from the scene of the crime as possible. Though I somehow doubted I was going to be able to just go hide in a cupboard somewhere with a bottle of brain rot until it all blew over. My favourite Bad Penny wasn't about to let me just run off and hide.

We made our way back to the main hatch, beyond which one of the guards was still lying paralysed, his shocked expression, fixed by rigour, still staring up at us. As for his compatriot… Well, the other had met with Saffron's rage and there wasn't much left of his face. Paralysis was no longer a problem for him. Nothing was a problem for him anymore.

"We need to find her," Penny said to me, an odd passivity to her tone that I can't say I liked. Vivienne Verne was many things, but passive wasn't one of them.

"Sure… You know there's going to be Hell to pay for this," I told her.

Finding Saffron Wells was the last thing I wanted to do, but a dead guard wasn't doing us any favours. I'd no doubt the captain would eventually forgive his daughter her part in this debacle, but me? Well, I wouldn't give a bent tuppence for my longevity if I got dragged before him. Every instinct I had was telling me to run, to just get myself out of there. What was that old East End mantra? 'Run fast and deny everything'. Well, it used to work well enough when I was a nipper…

Except of course there had been two guards, and while the one who wasn't dead was currently as wooden as my performance had been auditioning for the Beckets Street nativity the year one of Frankie's many uncles got us to audition for third shepherd, he was most definitely not dead.

Unlike that particular uncle of Frankie's who, while we dressed up in frocks with glued on beards, fell off St Bart's roof and got himself impaled astride the church railings. God, Frankie had mused when we recalled the incident years later, not only works in mysterious ways, but he also takes a dislike to those who go nicking lead off the roof of his house.

And if you're wondering, Frankie got the part not me. Much to Frankie's chagrin when he realised it wasn't actually a musical despite all the singing involved.

But not to digress further, the point was the guard would be able to identify exactly who let Saffron Wells free in the first place. So, there was nothing for it really but to track down Saffron before she could do more damage. For my sake if no one else's. And to do that we needed to move fast. I'd no doubt Verne's guards were already flooding down towards us. Luckily, for want of a better word, Saffron had laid a trail for us to follow. You will recall the protocol on the submersible was to seal every door behind you. Well, it turns out crazy women on psychotic rampages don't bother following protocol.

Who knew?

In any event, to follow her all we had to do was follow the open doors. Though what exactly we would do when we caught up with her was another question entirely. I'd a feeling a cheerful smile and calming words weren't going to do the trick somehow. But needs must, and with a deep sense of resignation, I set off towards the first of those open hatches with Penny. Only she pulled up short before we passed through and went back to the prone guard.

I turned to see what she was up to as I stepped through the hatch and saw Penny, sensible psychotic killer that she was, had gone back for one of the guard's harpoon rifles. As I watched her pick it up and check the load, I suddenly grasped what Saffron had shot at us with when Penny bundled us into the cell. I was suddenly more thankful for Penny knocking me flying. The thought of having one of those barbed bolts impaling me made me blanch. It also explained what had ripped the crap out of Penny's mechanical arm, even if the damage looked cosmetic for the most part.

I nodded towards Penny and watched as she pulled back the bolt action pin that slotted the next load into place. I felt a little surer of chances for a moment. True this meant she was armed and I wasn't, but at least one of us was. So I was thankful she'd the foresight to go back for the weapon. Besides which, it seemed she knew how to use the damn things. I'd of vastly preferred a good old-fashioned revolver any day. And oh, how I wished I had one. Rather than just the cutthroat in my pocket.

Penny nodded back to me, still standing over the guard she'd disarmed, the one which Saffron hadn't killed on her way past. Then, just for a second, an oddly regretful look crossed her features. Then she clicked off the safety, and pointed it down at the ridged guard's paralysed head.

She sighed audibly, frowned ever so slightly and half whispered something, just above the sound of the alarms ringing out around us. I can't be sure, but it sounded like, "Sorry, Philipe."

Then she shot him in the head.

CHAPTER 20

Death and flanges

I've killed people in the past. I've never denied that. I'm a convicted murderer, under sentence of death as I'm sure you recall, so my hands aren't exactly clean on that score. And sure, Hardacre falling to his death in my dreams time and again may be something to do with my conscience refusing to let me forget what I did, but regret doesn't make me any less a killer. Besides Hardacre isn't the only body I've left in my wake. There have been plenty of others.

I could claim most of those other deaths were a result of my service to the Crown. 'Only following orders, guv, honest!' But it was never a case of them or me. I was airship gunnery officer after all. I never saw the faces of those I was ordered to shell, but I carried out those orders. Good little soldier that I was, I never questioned the right or wrong of those orders. I just let the bombs fall where I was told to drop them.

And then there was Hiroshima...

Oh, I may not have built Yamamoto's death train, or been the one to set it underway, but I did sod all to derail it when I could've done. All I did when I rode that damn death train was try to find a way to save my own precious skin. 'Noble sacrifice? Sorry guv, not for me...' One life for many may be a fair transaction, I'll grant you that, but when that one life was mine, I chose to save it not half a million Japanese civilians and God knows how many Chinese soldiers. And sure, there may have been no way I could've stopped it, but I could've damn well tried, couldn't I?

My point, if you're asking, is there's blood a plenty on my hands. I've all but bathed in it at times. But I'll tell you this much for nothing, I've never shot someone in cold blood the way my favourite Bad Penny killed that guard.

I watched her from the hatchway, too stunned to say anything, as she calmly started back towards me. I'd always known she'd ice in her veins, but this was beyond the pale, even for her. True, I'd been pondering the problem of leaving a witness behind a moment before, but I'd have never killed the man like that.

Vivienne Verne, Bad Penny, old 'not in any way the maid', call her what you like, did it without more than a moment's passing regret. This wasn't in the heat of battle. This was no desperate act in a desperate situation. This was just a cold death, based on a cold calculation. It was murder, plain and simple and the murder of a man she knew by name.

"What the Hell?" I remember asking, trying to get my head around what I'd just witnessed, as she stepped past me and shoved the harpoon gun into my hands, the cold steel body of the weapon only making what I'd witnessed more real. I stared back at the body a moment longer. At the iron spike punched through the side of the man's skull. I stared at it as she clambered through the hatch, pushing me to one side as she did so. And as she did, I found myself pulling the loading bolt back once more, and hearing the next bolt click into position, hardly registering what I was doing, and what I was holding, as oozing blood started pooling on the deck with darker lumpier bits in it which I didn't want to think about.

Then, coughing for a second as if to clear my throat, but mostly to hold down my stomach, I turned away, because what else could I do. I turned, stepped through the hatch and followed my own personal Bad Penny as she set off ahead of me.

What else could I do?

"She's heading for the loading doors," Penny said, as we passed through to another companion way. We were making slow progress because after the first door I started closing hatches behind us. Penny had given me a hard look about that, but I'd gathered enough of my wits to realise we didn't want anyone following the same trail we were. Penny didn't actually complain, so I guess she'd come to the same realisation once she saw what I was doing.

Not that I cared what she thought, right then I felt numb. I was acting on instinct. Self-preservation, one minute to the next. At one point along the way, I toyed with the idea of shooting Penny myself. You can condemn me for that if you like, hell, I'll agree with you if you do, but I was certain if she was cold enough to kill one witness to our little blunder, she was damn well cold enough to kill me for the same reason. Not for the first time I found myself wondering just what had happened to her to make her the way she was. I'm not talking about the physical stuff. Though I'm sure losing the better part of three of your limbs before having mechanical replacements grafted onto you was trauma enough. But plenty of people lose limbs and don't turn in to psychotic assassins. There was something else, some other part of her that was damaged, some part that even a mechanical genius like her stepmother couldn't repair.

Now though wasn't the time for such speculation, besides which there were more pressing questions on my mind.

"If she gets off the sub then where she going to go?" I asked, though in truth it was as much morbid speculation on my part as an actual question. "We're on an island."

Penny just shrugged, stepped through the next hatchway and pushed the body of some unlucky crewman who'd crossed paths with Miss Wells out of the way as she did so. It wasn't the first body we'd come across. Nor was it to be the last.

But where could she actually go?

What did she want come to that?

What could a crazy woman possibly want on a volcanic island with a huge gun sticking out of the side of it?

"Oh Christ!" I swore as we reached the loading bay doors. There we found the bodies of three more crewmen. I assumed they were dead anyway, just because of the blood pooling around them. Even if they weren't, they were going to have to wait for someone else to come along to staunch their wounds. I wasn't sure what the hell she was doing, but I knew this would only get worse the longer Saffron was free. I was suppressing the urge to run and hide, and as urges go, it was a strong one. But right then, the fear of what not stopping her might mean for everyone, including importantly me, was winning out over the urge to make myself scarce. Call it an adrenaline-fuelled lapse in judgement, but fight was winning out over flight right at that moment.

Of course, there was also the nagging feeling Penny could turn on me at any moment and was almost certain to if I started to flee. I might be the one holding the harpoon rifle, but I wasn't fool enough to think that would make a damn difference if it came to that.

There was also the small matter of feeling a certain responsibility for the deaths Miss Wells was leaving in her wake. If I hadn't led Penny to Saffron, none of this would be happening. So, a little part of me was driven by a need to repent for this latest stack of sins. Between that and the desire not to join the ranks of the dead, I kept going.

I'll let you decide which of those urges was stronger.

I peered out round the loading bay doors and out into the base itself. The bodies we'd found were not alone. Saffron must have killed two or three more poor sods on her way through the sub bay. But there the trail went cold, as there were several exits from the bay she could have taken. I cursed under my breath and tried to guess where we should go next. Alarms were sounding everywhere now and in moments people would be scrambling through the base like ants. Added to which I didn't doubt for a moment that Captain Verne's guards wouldn't be far behind us.

"We need to find her. If we don't…" Penny shouted as she joined me at the entrance.

"She'll kill more people, yer… I'm aware of that," I replied, trying not to let panic show in my voice.

"No, if others find her first, they'll kill her," she insisted.

"Seriously? Look at what she's doing, Penny. She needs to be stopped," I said with feeling, trying to ignore the wild look it drew from her.

"If I can talk to her, calm her down…" Penny replied, too far gone for her habitual response to my use of my nickname for her. Her fear for Saffron gave a strangely vulnerable edge to her voice I wasn't used to hearing.

"Calm her down? She's not going to calm down, Penny. Look at them," I said, pointing at the prone bodies in the sub bay.

"It's not her fault," Penny said, and the bloody murder was back in her words. I should've backed off right then, but my own blood was up and my common sense was off having a dirty weekend in Brighton.

"Perhaps not, but what about bloody Philipe back there? That wasn't her fault either," I accused.

Penny scowled at me and for an instant I thought she was going to lash at me with those claws of hers. Damaged though her arm was, I was damned sure those would still be working. With my cursed luck, they were bound to.

"Don't shed any tears for that arsehole, he had it coming. Why do you think he drew such crappy duty?" she sneered, not a slither of regret in her voice.

"Crappy duty? Oh, I'm sure he was a lousy sailor but he didn't deserve to die like that," I snapped

"My precious father's a pirate, Hannibal. He might swan about pretending to be a noble merchant prince or whatever but he's a pirate when all is said and done," she said with a bitterness I'd not expected. "His men are pirates. Killers. Thugs. That arsehole back there was one of the worst of them. He wouldn't have batted an eyelid at doing what needs to be done, so spare me your outrage. Perhaps he didn't deserve to die like that, but he's dead and our secret's safe, for now…"

I hated the part of me that thought she was right. Not that it mattered much the way things were going. I started to argue, but didn't get far.

"I don't have time for this. We need to find her. Where would she go?" Penny asked, a note of desperation creeping into her voice. She walked across the gang plank and started looking around the submersible bay for anything that might give her a clue which way Saffron had gone.

I followed, meekly if I'm honest. Staring at bodies ripped open by harpoon bolts. Bolts fired by the twin of the weapon I was carrying. It struck me then that this was perhaps not a time to be carrying such a gun, as Verne or Musk's guards could appear at any moment. Men likely to shoot first and ask probing questions later. For a moment I thought about to dropping it behind some crates, but then I decided the reassurance of a weapon outweighed the suspicion holding it would place on me.

It was as I came to this realisation that I caught a glance of someone standing on one of the gantry ways that ran around the edge of the bay. I nudged Penny and motioned up at the man staring down at us silently. I got the impression he had been standing there waiting to catch my eye, about the same moment I realised who it was. Gothe, in a heavy black trench coat despite the temperature prevalent in the base, which was more suited to tropical fatigues and short sleeves, as you may expect inside an active volcano. Our eyes met and it felt creepy, but then everything about Mr Gothe creeped me out. He still looked too much like a Sleepman for him not to.

He didn't say a word, or shout down, or anything. Instead, he just raised an arm and pointed to the doors on the eastern side of the bay. Doors which led to a set of stairs that I knew led down deeper into the mountain towards the part base I knew reasonably well, the bit I had toured recently in the company of our host. The corridors beyond that door led down to the main breaching bay, down into heart of the mountain, and down to Doctor Musk's enormous bloody weapon…

Because of course they did…

"Hettie," I heard myself say, though I couldn't tell you why I did so.

Well, that's not entirely true, I knew why. It was because she would be down there, working on the moon-shell for Musk. Where else would Henrietta Clarkhurst be but elbow deep in machinery, messing with flanges, lubricated gussets, ring expanders, shaft clamps and the odd greased nipple.

You know, I've always wondered about engineers…

Hettie had tried to explain to me what she was working on for Musk when we shared a meal on The Squid one evening, which occasionally involved me trying to avoid choking as every one of those terms had come up. It was one of the few times I'd seen her in the previous few days and even then, she'd just been grabbing a quick bite between tinkering sessions.

What hadn't helped was that she was all very Hettie about it, which is to say loud, boisterous and demonstrative. At one point, she'd explained how she had been using an orifice gauge to try to figure out what was causing a build-up of back-end wetness leading to a lubrication failure. I found myself thankful the lingua franca aboard ship was French at that point, though many of Hettie's hand gestures hadn't helped. She was robustly proud of herself for coming up with a solution for one of those niggling little problems you come across when you try to shoot a projectile at an ancient satellite once worshiped by pagans and considered proverbially to be made of green cheese.

Frankly, it sounded like Hettie was having the time of her life with Elonis Musk's pop gun. So I knew damn well she would be down there helping with the project. This was clearly why I'd thought of Hettie when the ominous Mr Gothe pointed us in that direction.

I just didn't know why I'd said her name, and why I felt a hole in the pit of my stomach as I did so, but then I never claimed to be the sharpest knife in the back.

Regardless, without further thought I set off for those doors with some urgency, and Penny fell in behind me. I don't know if she'd actually seen where Gothe had pointed, but she followed me all the same. Possibly just because following me right then was better than standing still.

As we ran down the steps and barged our way through the double doors, I heard angry shouts behind us in French. Verne's guards had reached the loading bay, I assumed. Other shouts mingled with them in English, the prominent language spoken by Doctor Musk's men. The inevitable followed, misunderstandings, bodies from both sides, wounds inflicted by a harpoon rifle, no one really in charge, itchy trigger fingers. It was a powder keg back there and all that antipathy between Verne and Musk, well that kind of thing trickles down to the guys with guns. I heard the sound a harpoon rifle makes when it fires a bolt. Someone screamed in pain. And as the doors rattled back into place behind us, a mass brawl, with an indelicate sprinkling of gun fire broke out.

Another siren wailed and the corridor was plunged into darkness for a moment until the lights flickered back on but now tinged red. We pushed on deeper into the mountain and, turning a corner, I almost stumbled over the body of some poor sod whose only remaining purpose in his quickly expiring life was informing us we were headed the right way. Not that he needed to talk to do that, a steel rod buried in his chest did all the talking that was required.

With a mouth spewing blood, he weakly begged for help, but there was little we could've done for him, even if we were so inclined. If he was lucky, someone else might come along and get him some much-needed medical attention but I didn't fancy his chances. But then I didn't fancy anyone's chances including my own the way things were careering downhill. The fighting behind us spoke ominously of things getting out of hand, and in my experience, no one switches the lights to red because they think it jollies up the place. I shrugged a useless apology to him as I stalked past and tried to push away the guilt leaving him in our wake inspired.

I didn't have time for guilt, somewhere ahead of us HG Wells' daughter was murdering her way towards Elonis Musk's ridiculous weapon and the closest friend I still had, if not in the world, certainly in this hemisphere. Saving some poor sod who got caught in the crossfire was too far down the list for me to worry about. I'd left enough bodies behind me, what difference did one more make? Besides, my plate was full. Pitched battle behind me, a crazy woman ahead of me and right by my side was my own personal psychopath, Penny.

'Still', I thought to myself, *'things can hardly get worse…'* Of course, I was wrong about that.

As we moved further down the corridor, a crackling voice came over some loudspeakers above the sound of the sirens.

+++ Breaches in pressure containment alpha seven three through six +++

+++ emergency venting in progress +++

+++ all non-essential staff evacuate to safe zone beta three +++

I had no idea what was breaching, but I didn't need to know to be sure it didn't bode well. As for where safe zone beta three lay, well, I didn't know that either, but I would give you a pound to a bad penny it lay somewhere in the opposite direction to the one I was headed.

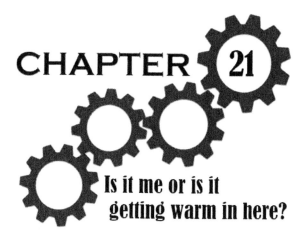

CHAPTER 21

Is it me or is it getting warm in here?

As we moved through the maze of corridors, there were more bodies, more sirens, and a running commentary from our friend with the microphone that didn't bode well, as we progressed further into the heart of the volcano.

+++ Breaches in pressure containment alpha seven three through eight +++

+++ Emergency venting in progress +++

+++ All non-essential staff evacuate to safe zone beta three +++

"That was three through six a minute ago," I said to Penny as I trailed along behind her. She wasn't slowing down, if anything she picked up the pace. A moment later, we burst through another set of double doors and out onto a gantry that overlooked the breeching chamber.

If she'd heard what I'd said, she gave no indication. I doubt she cared. She'd one goal, catch up to Saffron, that was all that mattered to her. Not that it would've made a difference if she'd replied. I know what she would've said… 'No one is keeping you here, Smyth.' I knew because I was saying it to myself. But it wasn't true, Hettie was keeping me here. As much as I wanted to turn tail and make for the nearest exit, there was no way I was leaving Hettie behind.

I'm sure you're surprised by that; I was surprising myself. But damn it, there is a line, even if the line's a crooked one…

The gantry we'd stumbled onto was the same gantry I'd stood on a few days before when Doctor Musk had given us the tour of his facility. But unlike that day, what I saw down in the chamber was anything but ordered workers building machinery. Instead, there were great plumes of steam bursting out of pipes, and workers anything but calmly scattering in all directions. Two of the workers, ones smarter than the rest if I was any judge, ran past us as we emerged, coming from the iron stairway that descended down to the breeching chamber itself. They paid us no head, despite me being armed and Penny looking like a dose of Hell about to happen to someone. If anything, they tried to knock us out of their way in their haste to get out.

They weren't alone. Others down below were also swarming out of exits, those who could at any rate. Some lay prone on the ground, shot or caught by explosions of volcanic steam or shrapnel from piping, it was hard to tell. The plumes of steam everywhere made it hard to pick individuals out. Not that we took the time to take it all in, we just headed for the stairs. Besides, it didn't take much thought to figure out why everyone was running, even if I hadn't had to duck under a burst of scalding hot sulphurous steam that erupted from one of the pipes by the stairs. The cause of that little breach was equally obvious, the harpoon bolt embedded in the piping told its own story.

We fought our way past more fleeing workers, one of which Penny shoved away into another plume of stinking steam. When he turned back around, falling to the stairs, his face was burning, flesh melting away from bone.

I've little doubt if my old school pastor was right about the existence of Hell then it is there I'm bound when I finally cash in my matchsticks, given all the crap I've done in my life. But truth told, I doubted the worst corner of Hell had a patch on that breeching chamber that day. But if it is, well, it makes me glad I'm a confirmed atheist.

God help me…

We got to the foot of the stairs without being further molested by dint of me brandishing the harpoon rifle at anyone who got too close and Penny just leering at them. I suspect it was Penny's leer that did the trick. The whole floor of the breeching chamber was wreathed in a fog of scalding steam by this point. I was grateful once more that I was wearing my solid airman's boots as I could feel the heat through them. It wasn't unlike walking through low lying fog, if the fog was trying to burn your skin off.

About then, the tannoy sounded again, the voice on the other end sounding panicked. I can't say that I blamed them.

+++ Breaches in pressure containment alpha six two through twelve +++

+++ Emergency venting… Repeat emergency venting in progress +++

+++ All staff evacuate … Repeat all staff evacuate +++

"Whatever we're doing, we better do it fast," I shouted above the rising screams of steam as we headed across towards the breeching chamber itself. The breaching doors, almost thirty yards across, were still held open by huge pistons. The Moon-Shot capsule was still in place, the bullet in the breach, if bullet is a term you could use for something five stories high. A smaller hatch that led inside it lay open, with a set of retractable ladders still attached.

It didn't take much of a guess to figure out where we would find Miss Wells. No more than it took to guess where I'd find Hettie. Where else would they be but inside the Moon-Shot itself. It wasn't like it was in a primed and ready, rifled gun barrel, pointed at the moon, waiting for a volcano to go off, or anything...

Judging by the sirens, and clouds of super-heated steam, I'd a sinking feeling, I was already too late.

We headed for the Moon-Shot while the whole chamber seemed to be disintegrating around us. I was running now, not that it would matter, I was sure. *'So much for Gothe's pledge to help me save Hettie,'* I remember thinking bitterly. Not that I'd time to wonder where he'd got to, but if the extent of his help was pointing the way from a gantry in the sub-bay then it struck me he wasn't really holding up his side of whatever bargain he thought he'd struck with me.

+++ Evacuate +++ Evacuate +++ Chamber priming underway +++

+++ Evacuate +++ Evacuate +++ Chamber priming underway +++

+++ Evacuate +++ Evacuate +++ Chamber priming underway +++

The damn tannoy was on repeat now. Whoever'd been on the other end of the microphone had doubtless taken their own advice and set up a recording. But it wasn't so much the 'evacuate' that worried me, it was the 'Chamber priming underway'. I had flashbacks to climbing aboard that train in the railway sidings at Nagoya. At the time I had no idea I was boarding the 10:30 to Hiroshima. In comparison to our entering the breeching chamber, I looked back on those few innocent minutes before me and Bad Penny were locked inside the death train with pleasure. At least on that occasion I'd no more clue what was about to happen than a tourist in Trafalgar Square patting his overly stuffed wallet when there were pick pockets about. Which in the case of Trafalgar Square is just about always. There in the breeching chambers on the other hand, I was damn well certain I knew what was going to happen to that Moon-Shot and anyone still inside it in a few minutes' time.

I am sure some might welcome an opportunity to travel at ridiculous speed to an interesting new place. Frankly though, I was willing to pass on the opportunity if I had any say in it. For one thing, I'd no reason to think that the Moon-Shot's arrival at its destination would be any less dramatic than the one I narrowly avoided in Japan.

Not that I expected the damn thing would ever arrive…

As we got to that hatchway, Elonis Musk of all people stumbled out of the stream filling the chamber with an ever-thickening mist. He was wearing what looked to me like diving gear, though diving gear reinforced with many metal straps. Under his arm, he carried a brass diving helmet, the type with porthole-like windows for the wearer to see through, though the design of it seemed not entirely right. But what did I know about diving suits?

"Mr Smyth? Miss Verne? What are you doing here? Was this your father's doing, Vivienne? Why has he attacked my people? Does he know what he has done?" Musk started demanding, his eyes wide, pupils dilated to Hell and back. I'd seen pupils like that before on opium addicts, yet he seemed lucid enough. Well, lucid enough for a man wearing a diving suit in the heart of a volcano on the verge of erupting. Which is a questionable kind of lucidity, it has to be said.

"It wasn't Verne," I snapped. "But never mind that now, what's happening?"

"Wasn't Verne? What do you mean, 'Wasn't Verne'? Who the Hell was it then?" Musk raged, grabbing my arm.

I wasn't in the mood for an extended argument. I just wanted to get inside the Moon-Shot, find Hettie, then get her and myself the hell out of there. If I could stop Saffron Wells' crazed rampage into the bargain, well, that would be all to the good, but frankly I was counting on Penny for that part of the bargain. Everything was going downhill fast and now I had this idiot grabbing my arm. I just reacted, shoving Musk away from me and swinging round the rifle. I only meant to threaten him with it, but as he tried to push it away, I felt compelled to punch him. I didn't pull the punch and it sent him reeling backwards, falling over his own feet and down into the sulphurous mist. I didn't wait around to see him get back up. I just plunged on through the hatch, shouting out Hettie's name as loud as I could.

After clambering through, I found myself inside a spacious compartment, but one that was laid out with the deck at a weird angle. I couldn't get my head around why that was until I realised the Moon-Shot was effectively lying at around sixty degrees to the horizontal. In the middle of this compartment, a ladder passed through a hole in the floor, if the Moon-Shot was standing on its end. It ran through the whole compartment and up through a hole in the ceiling to one above. Equipment lined the walls, locked into place between heavy padding that covered everything. While at the far side of the compartment, two chambers held full diving suits like the one Doctor Musk had been wearing. This further confused me. Were they expecting to land in water on the moon?

Yes, I know… It became obvious when I'd time to think about it. But I wasn't thinking entirely clearly right then. I was stressed and pressed for time.

"Hettie?" I shouted again, trying to scramble up the incline to the ladder.

"Up here," came a shout from above us, and I leapt the rest of the way, catching myself on the ladder as I did so but managing to wrap my arm around a rung. Abandoning the harpoon rifle, I started climbing, not sure what I would find when I scrambled through the hatch to the upper compartment. Penny grabbed the ladder behind me, and was soon climbing on the opposite side, hanging upside down to do so.

As I neared the top, I saw Musk arrive at the outer hatch, his face a burning crimson of rage, or more likely a burning crimson of steam fried flesh. He looked far from happy, not that I cared. He was the last person I gave a damn about right then so I ignored him and scrambled up through the hatch to the next compartment. Then, as I awkwardly found my feet on the inclined floor, I found myself looking upon a sight I should've known to expect.

I'd just spent half an hour or more fighting my way through a lunatic's lair to save Hettie and there she was. Exactly where I should've expected to find her… Standing over the prone body of Saffron Wells, a hefty monkey wrench in one hand. The monkey wrench which had clearly been most recently used to give Saffron Wells a damn good spannering.

I felt a damn fool, I can tell you that for nothing. I mean, since when did Henrietta Clarkhurst ever need someone to save her?

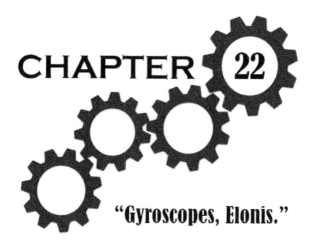

CHAPTER 22

"Gyroscopes, Elonis."

"Hannibal! Oh perfect. Well, I guess beggars can't be choosers, you're better than no one," Hettie said to me, roundly ignoring the prone body of Saffron Wells laying at her feet. She placed the monkey wrench to one side with some reverence and started grappling her way over to the far side of the chamber.

All too aware of who was climbing up the ladder just behind me, I risked a closer look at Miss Wells and was relieved to see she was still breathing, which was something at least. Whether that ultimately would prove to be a good or bad thing was another matter, but it held off the inevitable a little while at least.

I was still struggling to get my footing right on the steeply inclined decking when Penny came through the hatch behind me. She saw Saffron prone on the floor and let out a guttural scream of equal measures, rage and anguish. So, I braced myself, which wasn't particularly easy at forty-five degrees, to get between Hettie and the second psychopathic female killing machine she'd the misfortune of coming across that day. I was also suddenly horribly aware of the fact that I was the one who'd brought the latest one to her door, or her Moon-Shell, or whatever this damn thing was.

A flash of unbridled hatred crossed Penny's face, hatred aimed squarely in Hettie's oblivious direction. Hettie wasn't even looking Penny's way, she was far too busy trying to unhook a panel on the far wall. I very nearly panicked, though given everything that was happening, I believe panic would've been an entirely reasonable reaction. The sound of an explosion outside didn't help matters, but mostly I was close to panicking because I'd placed myself between an outraged Bad Penny and someone I cared for. I don't think I could've stopped her, or even slowed her down worth a damn, had she gone for Hettie right then.

I won't deny that I could've done with a stiff drink at that point. Hell, I would've taken a bottle of Raki, I'd have drank vermouth, egg nog, anything in fact, even that foul smelling French liquor in the odd shaped bottle you'd never drink. The one that someone gifts you one Christmas, the one you pass on to your cousin for their birthday. The bottle that a few years later someone else gives to you, and you just know it's the same damn bottle that's been doing the rounds of your friends and relatives for years. Ever unopened. Ever passed on… But right then, I'd have popped the cork and guzzled it like my old mum on London Dry…

Penny's eyes virtually flashed with rage as she stared at Hettie. Barely contained rage, fuelled by hatred. But for once she ignored her basest violent urges and instead dashed over to where Saffron lay, collapsing to her knees before Miss Wells, cradling her head in her arms.

"She's alive," I heard her gasp, relief in her voice, as she started stroking her lover's hair.

"Of course, she's alive, I wasn't trying to kill her, girl," Hettie said over her shoulder. "I just needed to stop her doing more damage. She's done quite enough as it is." She said all this in the matter of fact tone Hettie always adopted when she was focused on a problem. She didn't even turn towards Penny as she said it, utterly absorbed in whatever she was trying to do.

"You better hope she stays that way," Penny snarled back.

"Oh, spare me the melodramatics, lass, I've things to do," Hettie said dismissively, then muttered more to herself than the rest of us something along the lines of, "Daft bint made a real mess of this…"

Penny, if she heard this, let it pass. She was focused entirely on Miss Wells, displaying the kind of affection I would've never credited her as possessing for anyone.

Hettie, meanwhile, had dismissed Penny from her thoughts entirely. She was too busy growling at a maintenance cover she was fighting with, as she tried to remove it. I took a step closer and saw the cause of the problem. A harpoon bolt had hammered into the panel and was wedged in, preventing her from removing the cover.

As the ladies were each engaged with their own obsessions, I felt a sudden wave of relief wash over me. Bad Penny wasn't about to kill Hettie right at that moment. Even though she had just called her 'lass' and 'girl' in quick succession, something I doubt anyone else would've gotten away with for a second. Her focus was all on Saffron. Hettie, meanwhile, was messing with machinery, or trying to, which struck me, even in these circumstances, as the most normal thing in the world.

I felt for the moment at least, that I could breathe safely…

That wave of relief didn't last, of course. A moment later, the realisation of where I was and what was happening came back with a vengeance, helped on by another small but nevertheless worrying explosion somewhere outside that sent vibrations through the deck plates. This brought on a sense of clarity to the situation I was in, and of course, panic…

"Hettie, we need to get out of here," I shouted.

She huffed with clear exasperation, then without even turning to look at me, she replied, "Out of the question, old boy, now get your skinny arse over here and give me a hand. I'd be better off with a crowbar to be honest, but you'll have to do."

"Hettie…" I argued.

"Now! Hannibal, I don't have time to repeat myself," she barked with the authoritative tone she wheeled out to make anyone do as they're told. It was somewhere between governess and sergeant major, with just enough of the home counties thrown in to give it that upper-class edge that expects to be obeyed.

Years of military training caused me snap to it, without further thought. I scrambled over alongside her, put my hands where she told me to put them and, between us, we pulled that damn panel free, the harpoon bolt still stuck through it. What lay beyond was a mess of pipes, wires and a bank of valves, many of which had been smashed by the bolt Saffron had shot through the panel. Several of the shattered valves were sparking, and there was a smell of burnt carbon. Looking at it, I had the horrible feeling a fire would erupt in that rats' nest at any moment. I couldn't make head nor tail of it, but that should come as no surprise. What I was sure of, however, was we didn't have time to fanny about trying to fix that mess, and the impulse to follow orders waned enough for the urgency of the situation to reassert itself in my consciousness.

"Hettie, this isn't somewhere we want to be right now," I said, calmly emphasising each word. Which just about made me a poster boy for restraint right then.

Hettie ignored me, reaching into the mess and tugging at a broken valve until it came free of its housing. This she examined closely before throwing it aside. Then she reached in once more and pulled out another while making a tutting noise under her breath. The same tut I swear engineers get taught on their first day at technical college. Then she threw that one aside as well. I'd no idea what she was doing, indeed I was less than convinced that she knew what she was doing right then, beyond stalling for time.

When she dragged out a third valve, as I got more irritated, itchy feet syndrome setting in, she held the valve up to the light and examined it with a practised eye. Nodded to herself. Then rammed it back into the socket she removed the first one from. Then whistling tunelessly in a distracted way, she pulled a couple of wires free of their housings and started twisting them together, despite the alarming spark they made as she touched them together. Somehow all this caused the other sparks in the box to cease and the valves to start lighting up with the little glows I'd expect to see from them if everything was working properly.

"Well, that's bypassed that, which is a start," Hettie muttered. Not that I was convinced that ripping out three valves and replacing one of them in another socket could ever fix anything. I must've commented on this in some way though I'm damned if I remember. But she turned to me and added, "The others were just redundancies, we can manage without them. This whole ship is a little over engineered to be honest. If I'd had the time, I could have stripped out half the sub systems that Madam Verne put in.

Woman's a genius but she'd build a steamroller to flatter a mole hill."

Having said this, Hettie started repeating the process she'd just been through with another set of valves. This time the second valve passed her muster and was used to replace the first one.

"How much damage is there?" a new voice said from the hatchway, a voice that was rasping slightly so I didn't quite recognise it straight away. Doctor Musk must have taken a lung or two full of steam outside when I'd sucker punched him.

My knuckles still stung, but I didn't regret punching the twerp for a moment.

"Enough, but nothing I can't fix it," Hettie shouted back to him. "Check the gyroscope guides!"

Musk didn't answer directly. He was instead taking a moment to survey the room and take everything in. His eyes were slightly wild, though that might have been the sulphur. "I can look at…. What is Saffron Wells doing in my ship?" he asked, though there was a surprising lack of passion to his voice. He seemed more curious than angry. Later, when I had time to think, I came up with a few theories about Elonis Musk. I don't think he was actually emotionless. Far from it, in fact. I believe it was simply that he experienced emotions in the wrong order. Or to put it simply, Elonis couldn't process anger if his curiosity got in the way. He was the kind of man who would pull something apart to see how it worked, be it a clock, an engine or an animal. I doubt he would even register the difference. His curiosity beat every other emotion he ever felt hands down, be it empathy or anger.

Given I'd just dumped him on his backside in a fogbank of super-heated sulphurous gas, these emotional shortcomings were probably a good thing. For me at least.

"Gyroscopes, Elonis," Hettie barked back at him in 'that voice', her hand inside the bulkhead, twisting more wires together and crimping them off.

I had to suppress a chuckle. Despite everything that was happening. I realised that this might well be Doctor Musk's grand project. We might well be standing inside his vision, his Moon-Shell. But right then, Hettie was the one in charge and it would take a braver man than him to argue with her.

The good doctor nodding to Hettie, and ignoring the rest of us, he began climbing up to the next level. Which, genius though he might well have been, was undoubtedly the cleverest thing I ever saw him do.

Having a moment to gather my thoughts, I glanced over to the corner where Penny was still cradling an unconscious Saffron. She was still stroking Miss Wells' hair affectionately in a most un-Penny-like way, her face wrapped with concern. I found myself staring at her, watching tears well up in her eyes which had nothing to do with the wisps of sulphurous smoke snaking through the hatch.

There was a heavy thud below us, and for a moment I thought something else had gone wrong. Hettie must have seen the concern in my face because she shook her head and told me, "That will just be Mr Gothe, bringing in the last of the supplies."

"You know Gothe?" I asked, though why I was surprised is anyone's guess.

"Of course, he's the pilot," she told me as she screwed up her face in the way she sometimes did when she was focusing on a task. "Interesting man."

"What?" was all I managed. I'll admit that wasn't going to win any awards for insightfulness.

"He's got some strange physiology," Hettie set about explaining while further fiddling with the cluster of wires and valves behind the panel, barely pausing in her work. "Elonis made him pilot because of the oxygen reserve. It's odd really, you know he just turned up on the island one day a couple of years back. Even Elonis doesn't know where he's from."

"He just turned up?"

"Apparently, but that's not what's strange about him," she said, handing me a piece of brass, that was some form of coupler, to hold for her. It felt alarmingly hot in my hands and I started juggling it between them.

"I've talked to him, strange isn't the half of it," I said with feeling, and she snorted with laughter.

"Did he tell you he's dead?" she asked, as if this was the most normal question in the world, while taking the coupler from my hand and shoving it forcibly back in place.

"How did you know?"

"Because he says that to everyone… Thing is though, it turns out he is. Near as damn. He doesn't have a heartbeat as such, barely breathes, and his blood's more like oil but thicker. Weird, I know. But anyway, that makes him the ideal pilot for this old bird," Hettie explained, as if this was the most normal conversation in the world, between frowning at the coupler, pulling it back out, reversing it and ramming it back in place.

"What?"

"Well, like I said, oxygen reserves. As Mr Gothe barely breathes, we cut down on the air recycling needed to support the three of us."

"Three people, in this thing?" I asked, but even as I did so, I got the niggling feeling I'd missed something important in what she said.

"Gothe's the pilot. Then there's Elonis, of course, and the engineer. I mean, you'd have to be a complete buffoon to try this without an engineer on board," she said with those wonderfully matter of fact tones I knew so well.

"I thought Musk was an engineer?" I said, then for other reasons, I asked another question bugging at me about this whole situation. "And when did you get on a first name basis?"

Hettie laughed off the latter and answered the former. "Doctor Musk is what you might call a grand thinker, rather than a doer. I mean, don't tell him this but I think everything would run smoother if he stayed behind, but what are you going to do? It's his ship. Anyway, he needs a real engineer to handle the complicated stuff. You know, making things actually work…"

"Ah, so that's why Verne hates him. He's got Madam Verne tied up in all this. Where is she anyway?" I asked, thinking light had dawned on me, but yes, as you probably realised quicker than I, I was still being dim at this point.

"She'll be on The Oegopsida, I shouldn't wonder. Truth told, she was never all that keen on the idea. Between you and me, I think she's more interested in theory than getting grease under her fingernails," Hettie said, with a disparaging edge to her voice. As if this was the worst thing she could say about anybody. Which in Hettie's world view was probably true.

For my part, I was still confused. In my defence, there was a lot to take on board, what with a volcano beneath us, Saffron's rampage, and us standing in the world's biggest artillery shell. A shell about to be shot out of the world's biggest gun, at the moon.

"So, if Madam Verne is not the engineer?" I started to ask and right then it dawned on me…

Yes, I'm slow, we covered that.

"Well, she stepped down when I arrived, and I took her place," she said, with a beaming smile. As if she had done no more than volunteered to take over a cake stall at a Cotswolds village fair…

Somewhere beneath us, the volcano rumbled.

CHAPTER 23

The thing about Hettie Clarkhurst

"Are you flaming crazy?" I asked, with genuine sentiment.

In response to this outburst, Hettie laughed. In the circumstances, I think this did little but confirm my hypothesis.

"This is why I've been so busy this last week. I've had to learn everything about the Moon-Shot Madam Verne could teach me, as quickly as possible. Good thing too, considering what your mad friend over there just did," she said, pointing an oily finger in the direction of the still unconscious Saffron Wells.

My Bad Penny was still cradling Saffron on her knees, stroking her hair and looking to be in a state of shock. If not for everything else that was happening, that might have worried me more than anything. In all the time I'd known

Penny, even when we stood on the hillside overlooking Hiroshima after the bullet train, I'd never before known Vivienne Verne to look lost in events. I'd never seen anything really faze her. God knows she'd been unpredictable in the past, but right then I dreaded to think how she might react to whatever came next.

Penny must have felt my eyes upon her. She raised her head and our gazes briefly locked. I could see the barely held back tears. What I couldn't see was her usual defiant barely held back anger. Instead, she looked resigned to whatever fate had in store. For some reason, that made me shiver despite the heat, and I turned back to Hettie.

"You're actually considering this?" I asked rhetorically, it was obviously the case. Henrietta Clarkhurst never backed down from a challenge.

"Well, that's all I was doing, just considering it, but I don't have much choice in the matter now," she said with a tinge of resignation. But I knew her well enough to recognise the core of excitement in her voice. She glanced over at Saffron and Penny, frowned for a moment, then turned back to the panel, forcibly pulling the harpoon bolt free of the cover and dropping it to the floor. "Your friend back there, well, she's made the decision for me. She screwed up the equipment managing the pressure build up below. Now all the safeties are locked out and we can't tap off the build-up. So, the gun's gonna fire sooner than expected. Now in fact. There's no other option if we want even a slim chance of containing the blast. There is sod all we can do to stop it."

"That doesn't mean you need to be in it," I said, but I knew I was fighting a losing cause. Hettie's mind was set.

She wrestled the housing cover back into place and started screwing bolts back in, glancing up at me while she used a spanner to tighten them up. "Unless you can find someone else who can compensate for the shredded guidance system on the fly in the next half hour, I sort of do."

"Rubbish, you can run, just get out of here and let Musk worry about his damn bullet," I snapped, not even aware I'd raised my voice at her doing so. By rights she should have snapped back. She should have been angry at my presumption. Berated me for even thinking I had a wit of influence over what she decided to do. Instead, when she replied it was in a calm, measured tone resigned to the hand fate had dealt.

"You don't understand, Hannibal…" she started to say, only to be interrupted by a shout from above.

"Miss Clarkhurst, I think you better look at this, the gyroscope's… Just come look," Musk shouted through the hatch, an edge of panic in his voice. This did little to inspire my own faith in Hettie's chances of survival, or my own.

My mood must have shown in my face as Hettie gave me a hard look, then tightened in the last bolt. She shook her head at me and made her way over to the ladders. I started to follow but she waved me back, nodding back towards Penny and Saffron. "See to your own mess, old boy. I'll be back in a moment," she said as she started to climb.

I watched her for a moment, then took her advice and scrambled my way over to Penny, still nursing the conscious Saffron. "How is she?" I asked as I knelt beside them.

Penny turned to face me, her eyes red from held back tears. She looked vulnerable and shaken, not at all the Bad Penny I was used to. She'd found a wet cloth somewhere and was cleaning blood and dirt from Saffron's face.

"She seems peaceful," Penny said quietly.

She seemed half dead to me, but I didn't say that. How could I?

"We are going to need to move her," I told Penny. Though I had no idea how we would accomplish such a feat. I couldn't see how we could manhandle her down through the ladder hatch. It would have been hard enough for the two of us to get her through the outer one. Difficult and time consuming, far too time consuming. I had a distinct feeling we wouldn't want to be in the breeching chamber when the gun went off. Hell, I didn't want to be inside the mountain when that happened. I'd prefer to have been hundreds of miles away, sipping cocktails out of coconuts... But what I wanted and what I was going to get, were two different things.

Penny shook her head at me. I suspected that, despite everything, she was still lucid enough to know carrying an unconscious Miss Wells out of there was going to be a non-starter.

"We need to wake her up," Penny told me and I was polite enough not to tell her that was a fool idea. She knew that as well as I did. The last thing we needed on top of everything else was Saffron Wells up and running amok again. That said though, what other choice was there? Well, apart from me legging it on my own and leaving the rest of them to fend for themselves.

Believe me, I was tempted. So very damn tempted. Or would have been if not for...

"Hannibal, get up here and bring my tools," Hettie shouted down through the hatch.

Nodding sympathetically to Penny, I lurched to my feet, grabbed Hettie's canvas tool bag and scrambled up the ladder to the next deck. A trickier task than you can imagine with the sheer bulk of that tool bag. Never get in a handbag swinging contest with an engineer, you'll lose... More by stubbornness than anything else, I managed to shove the bag onto the next deck ahead of me as I climbed through.

I found Hettie dealing with a strange set of brass interlocking rings. These were connected to two pivots attached to the deck and ceiling. I knew enough to know this was some form of oversized gyroscope. They were common enough arrangements on airships where they were used to make automatic adjustments to keep the keel level. But this arrangement was larger and far more complex than any I'd seen before.

I slid the tool bag over to her, while she pushed Musk back towards me, and out of her way. Looking at the gyroscope, I could tell it was stuck somehow. Which was quite the engineering insight coming from me, I know. Hettie, though, clearly knew what she was doing and started rooting around in her bag immediately.

"How are the ladies?" Musk asked me, remembering his manners, which seemed mildly absurd in the circumstances.

"They've had better days," said the master of understatement, who I may add had also had better days and wasn't really in the mood for small talk.

Hettie ignored us both and found what she was looking for in the bag, a rather large rubber mallet, with which she proceeded to apply percussive engineering at its best. Doctor Musk looked alarmed by this, which I took as more evidence he wasn't really an engineer. Bludgeoning machinery into submission is a time-honoured engineering tradition, I've found.

Regardless of his concern, a few of Hettie's well-placed blows freed up the mechanism and the brass circles started to swing freely.

Hettie paused long enough to tell Musk to go check how Gothe was getting on below before she started rooting out a large set of spanners and making more adjustments to the gyroscope. Those little adjustments that needed to be more precise than those she could achieve with a hammer. Though they involved the odd swear word unbefitting a lady and occasionally using the spanners as hammers as well. After a minute or two though, she stepped back, satisfied, and threw the tools back in the bag. Until then, I doubt she even realised I was still standing there.

"So, what don't I understand?" I asked her, referring back to the conversation on the deck below.

"That's a long list, Smyth. I doubt I've the time to go through it," she said with a smile. But she knew I wasn't in a joking mood. She gave a sigh, placed her hands on her hips and looked me in the eye. "Okay, it's like this… the shell's going to reach orbit, and frankly there is nothing I can do to stop it. Your crazy friend down there managed to set it all in motion. I'd say that was just bad luck but while there were a whole lot of things she could've damaged and not caused the damn thing to go off, she managed to damage just about everything, so I doubt it matters if she was trying to do it on purpose or not. We have to fire the gun because it's that or the pressure is going to blow the whole mountain. If it doesn't anyway."

"So, fire the damn gun then. You don't have to be in it," I retorted. I shouldn't have cared, I told myself so. But she was a friend. I didn't have so many damn friends left I wanted to lose another one. In truth though, it was more than that. More than I cared to admit even to myself. Me and Hettie, well, we'd always gotten on. We'd both been outsiders back in the 'The Ins & Outs'. Me because I didn't really belong in the officer class and her because, well, she might be one of the chaps, but she wasn't a chap, and while no one would've ever dared voice that opinion, it always hung around her neck unsaid. So, we were friends because we were both interlopers in a social set we didn't really belong to. True, there'd never been any more to it than that. She had never expressed a wish to 'spanner' me as it were, and nor had I her. There had never been anything of that sort between us. But still, a part of me, well, I'd always thought… maybe…

Hell, I've been around. There's been a lot of ladies in my life, one way or another. I can't say I've ever been much of a gentleman towards them or inclined to get too close, I was always a tad wayward in that regard. Hettie knew that as well as anyone. She'd been ribbing me about my girlfriends for years. Truth was, she was the chap I occasionally spoke to about such things when I wanted the kind of conversation that wasn't the kind of conversation a chap would have with another chap in a bar. She'd lend me an ear, call me a wazzock, and tell me to straighten myself out. She was always a mate in that way.

Yet still, despite that, there was always that maybe… No matter how I looked at it.

"That's the problem, Hannibal, I do. I told you the shell will gain orbit. But unless I can manage to keep it balanced just right when it does, it's gonna come straight back down."

"So? There's a whole lot of ocean outside," I said. "A few dead fish ain't the end of the world."

"Orbit, Hannibal, orbit… From there, it could come down anywhere. Literally anywhere. Sure, that might be the sea, but something this big hitting the sea from orbit would cause a Hell of a tsunami. And that's if it hits the sea. It might hit a land mass and cause far worse. Have you seen the pictures of that Siberian crater? The one where that meteor hit a few years back, hundreds of miles of devastation and it wasn't a third of the size of this damn thing even before it burned up on the way down. You want to imagine how much damage this could do if it came down on Paris, or Munich or bloody London, for that matter, because I don't."

"But," I started, futilely, Hettie was in full swing.

"But nothing, old boy, it's going up and it needs to stay up. It needs to do what it was designed to do. And I'll need to be inside it to make sure that happens."

"Why you?"

"Because there's no one else. Elonis bloody Musk can't do it, Gothe can't pilot it and do running repairs at the same time. I have to do this, Hannibal. It's not a matter of choice. I have to," she told me with the kind of determination she used to reserve for drinking competitions at the bar. Hettie never backed out of those either, and inevitably won. I knew then there was no way I was going to talk her out of it. Her mind was set, and when Hettie Clarkhurst sets her mind to something, you just have to accept it's going to happen.

Bereft of other choices, I did the only thing left I could do. Terrified though I was at the idea and as much as I would sooner have dangled my privates in a piranha tank. God knows I'm not the hero type…

There comes, however, a time in every man's life when he's just got to do, what he's got to do.

"Fine," I told her, "if that's the case, I'm staying."

CHAPTER 24

Goodnight my darling

"Oh, don't be such a cretin," Hettie said with a laugh. For the sake of my much-battered pride, I hoped she was laughing with bitterness, not exasperation, but I suspect the latter. Shaking her head, she explained, "I told you… There's oxygen for two plus Gothe and no more, so even if you were serious, there's no room. Besides what use would you be? Seriously? No, Hannibal… What I need you to do is get clear, taking those two ladies down there with you."

I'd be a liar if I claimed it wasn't with some relief that I realised my 'heroic' gesture was utterly futile. Hettie was going to do what Hettie was going to do. And me? I was going to do what she told me to do. Lest I made a bigger fool of myself. I'd be damned if I was going to make matters worse by pleading with her. Besides, some big romantic gesture would be somewhat at odds with our relationship. I mean, I'm sure there should've been violins playing, and the two of us should've stepped closer in to some faltering embrace. One of us becoming misty-eyed, while the other remained steely and determined. But, let's face it, I'd have been the misty-eyed one in this scenario, and Hettie like as not would've given me a slap for being such a 'wet fish'. As such, I let it pass.

"Miss Clarkhurst, Captain Smyth, you must attend below," a voice like grit on a tombstone called up through the hatch. This thankfully cut short any further embarrassment on my part. I was uncomfortably aware there was none on Hettie's part at all. She remained her normal no-nonsense self and pushed me towards the ladder to climb down ahead of her. At least she didn't say 'ladies first' which was something of a blessing.

I'd swear I could hear her thinking it though…

I dropped down into the chamber below and found everyone was present. Elonis Musk stood against the wall with a vague look of childish glee, despite everything that was happening around him. Gothe, who was the one who had called us down, was standing grim-faced by the ladder, but that was just how his face was. Penny was still kneeling with Saffron's head on her lap, but Saffron herself was awake, if blurry-eyed, and being fed water by Penny from a steel canteen, the providence of which I'd no inclination to know.

"Miss Wells?" I inquired, having reached the foot of the ladder. I carefully made my way over to her and Penny. I was trepidatious, though I could see no sign of her earlier madness. Which is to say, she wasn't trying to kill anyone, or more importantly me. But how long that would remain the case was another matter.

She turned her gaze towards me. Her single good eye bloodshot, her ruined face was drip white, a mask of barely held back terror. With one hand she pushed the canteen aside and I saw her lips trembling. I was struck once again by the beauty she had once been. Still was in fact, for all the self-inflicted ruin she had exacted upon her visage. As our eyes met, in a rasping shaky voice, she said, "Hannibal, still with us, I see."

"Don't worry yourself over that arsehole," my personal Bad Penny growled.

"You're looking better?" I said to Saffron, ignoring Penny. It was no more than a pretty lie. She wasn't. There was also something in her eye, the way her face grimaced, and the twitching of her mouth, which told me she was struggling to hold something at bay. I had a horrible feeling I knew what that something was.

"Ever the liar, Smyth, but I appreciate it," Saffron said, then erupted into a fit of coughing. The kind of cough you get from forty a day and a life spent stoking engines. The kind of cough that they used to call a death rattle.

I smiled, weakly. To protest would've just devalued my words and pretty lies aren't worth much to begin with, even ones told in kindness.

"I can feel it, Hannibal. It's still in me, trying to take hold again," she said in broken words, once the cough had subsided.

"What's she talking about?" Musk asked behind me, as if she wasn't there. For a man so blessed with charisma, he was remarkably poor with people in general. He was much like Gates and Jobs in that respect. Geniuses all three, undoubtedly, but something was missing from their emotional make up. They could take a machine apart and tell you how each section worked, but they couldn't tell you how normal people thought or felt. I think that's one of the reasons being in their company always gave me an itch. I half expected them to try and find out how people worked the same way they did with machines.

"The rage," I told him. Which wasn't entirely true but close enough to save more explanation. I could see she was struggling with it even now, holding it back with faltering willpower. I knew she couldn't hold it back for long. I knew because I'd felt it too. That time in Wells' study, again on the cliff side at Hamamatsu, all those times the Brass Shogun made me take off Jobs' dampener monticule just to see what would happen. I knew the build-up of pressure she was experiencing at the back of her mind. The alien presence residing there, trying to take control.

But that couldn't be right, could it? She'd ripped out the spider, hadn't she? Just as mine had been ripped out by Jobs… But as I asked myself these questions, I remembered what Jobs had told me. The longer the spider remained intact, the deeper its tendrils dug back into its victim's brain, and Saffron had lived with her spider far longer than I.

Saffron must have seen the moment of understanding in my eyes. She nodded slightly in my direction. "Yes," she said. "It's still there. It burrowed too deep. I can feel it, whispering, oh but it hurts, Hannibal… It's still there, I can feel it… Moving."

I shivered involuntarily. 'There but for the grace of…' and all that.

"It wants control again. It will take over, you know this. I can't hold it back, not for much longer," she said, the struggle evident in both her words and her broken voice which strained a little more each time she spoke.

"M's spider," I muttered, feeling a little echo of that rage myself. Saffron Wells didn't deserve this. No one, not even I, deserved this… But Saffron Wells certainly didn't.

She'd been a beautiful, confident young woman, doing what she believed was right. A woman striving to make the world a better place. Oh, I'll admit, she'd been a pirate, a thief and I dare say at times a killer, but unlike me she'd been all those things for good reason. She'd done what she'd done because she believed in something, no matter how misguided that something might have been. Not from avarice, or greed like my not-so-good-self. I don't know if that makes her life a noble one, but it was noble in a way mine had never been. It struck me then that that should count for something. That in a fair universe someone like Saffron shouldn't suffer such a fate. Not when someone like me manages to avoid it. But then when is the universe ever fair?

Perhaps that's all too simplistic. Perhaps I'm just a sucker for a pretty face. But I stand by those words, as much as I stand by anything.

"I can feel it, Smyth, gnawing at my mind. It's been gnawing at it for days. For weeks. Eating away at me. I think I'm more it than I anymore. I killed them all, Hannibal. It made me kill them. Killed them, drowned them, all those people, all those people who trusted me…" she said, becoming less lucid as she did so, and I wondered how true that was. For all I knew, it wasn't the spider at all, her mind may have snapped under the strain. Perhaps Hettie giving her a blow to the head just brought her to her senses for a little while, or perhaps it had weakened the spider's grip. What did it matter what the truth of it was? I could see in her eyes the struggle going on behind as she fought to hold back the rage. But I chose to believe it was the spider, if only because that would be better, in a way. I hated the idea of Saffron being responsible for the massacre at the wreck of The Johan's Lament. Better it be true Mr Gates' spider was the cause, if only for what little piece of mind that might give her now.

"What can I do?" I asked, and even as I did so I dreaded the answer, because I knew only too well what that answer was. If her lucidity was but an island of sanity within a sea of madness, the island was sinking fast beneath the waves, and like she, I feared she would never find land again. So, I knew what her answer would be, because if I was her, if the spider's rage had taken over me so completely, I know what I'd be asking of the one who knew what I was going through. I knew exactly what I'd ask them to do and I'm a demandable coward if ever there was one. Saffron Wells, she was never that.

"Kill me," she pleaded. "Kill me now, before the rage comes back." And I felt the full weight of her plea.

"Don't you dare!" Penny snapped. "Don't you even think about it." I don't know if she was saying the latter to me or Saffron, or to both of us. It amounted to much the same in any regard.

I ignored Penny this once. Moving closer and going down on one knee beside Saffron, I felt resigned to it. To do what needed to be done. Much as I hated the idea. My hand went, of its own accord, to the top of my boot, my fingers seeking the cut-throat they knew lay within the hidden sleeve. But it still wasn't there, still hadn't been there since the fall from The Johan. My trusty old blade was still somewhere at the bottom of the Pacific.

Penny was glaring at me. She must have known what I normally kept in my boot sleeve. Known what I was reaching for. "NO!" she snarled, punching me in the chest and for a moment I thought I'd got a gut full of razors for my trouble, as I rocked back, trying to catch myself.

"Vivienne…" Saffron said, using Penny's real name like a weapon, but with an edge of hopelessness in her voice that cut through the room. "Please, Vivienne, it's the only way, my love. I can't… I can't fall back into the dark, the rage, I just can't…"

I could say nothing, and for a moment despite the calamitous noise beyond it, a heavy silence hung in that chamber. I understood, only too well, the desperation in her voice, and I felt my hand, slick with sweat, reaching towards the pocket where my new cut-throat lay, my fingers seeking the handle into which the blade was folded, treacherously trembling as they did so. Then Penny came to my rescue and took the impetus away from me, thankfully.

"I can't let him do this. He has no right," she said and I felt my inner coward's relief as it agreed with her. Yet looking into Saffron's eye, I knew it didn't matter what Penny said, for I could see no other choice.

"He knows, Vivienne, he knows what it's like," Saffron told her lover and even as she said those words, I could see she was losing the battle. An edge of venom was creeping into her words. "He knows… Tell her… Tell her, Hannibal," she continued falteringly, her breathing becoming laboured, and the blood running to her face. She was fighting it, fighting it with all she had left. Fighting but losing.

"It's…" I started to say, but my words faltered on my lips. My fingers grasped the cut-throat, and I cursed the blasted luck that meant I'd have to be the one to do it. I didn't care that it would be an act of mercy. Though sure, I could tell myself that afterwards. I'd convince myself of it. I was good at convincing myself of things, fooling myself. I fooled myself all the time. Even in the small hours when sleep won't come and I'm staring into the darkness, watching the faces on the ceiling. I'd convince myself it was a mercy. That it had to be done. That she asked me to do it. That there was no other way…

And sometimes on those sleepless nights, I'd even believe myself…

As I started to pull the cut-throat out of my pocket though, a look from Penny stopped me. She took Saffron's head in her hands, forcing Saffron to gaze back at her, her expression torn between love and bitterness. I knew she could see the pain in Saffron's face, the battle going on beneath the surface, her features twisted as she grasped at what little control she had left. In return, a strange calm came over Penny's own features, a look of resolution, born of love.

"No," Penny said to her. Vivienne Verne said to her… "No, my love. You cannot ask him, for if he were to lay one finger on you, I would gut him here and now. You cannot ask him that, my love. You cannot… But I won't make you ask me."

And she held her there, gazing back into the ruined face of the woman she loved. Then she leaned in close, whispered something to her. Something just between them. Then kissed her on the lips. A lover's kiss.

A lover's kiss goodbye.

I didn't see the blades, I didn't hear them as they pieced the back of Saffron's skull. Pushing though skin, through bone, and through what was left of her mind.

Looking back now, so many years later, I like to think there was no pain for Saffron in that moment. Or less pain perhaps, as the fight she'd been losing faded away in the embrace of her lover. In one last long kiss goodbye. I like to think there was some peace for her in those final moments. Peace for the tormented soul of Saffron Wells. Perhaps even some peace for my very own Bad Penny too, in those final moments.

Then Penny sat there, still cradling Miss Wells' limp, broken body. A tear running down her cheek, perhaps for the first, and only time, I saw Vivienne Verne weep. Grasping for some desperate peace of her own, not letting her lover go, after letting Saffron go to that final peace, the peace she had so desperately desired.

But then I was always a bloody romantic fool.

CHAPTER 25

That knotty romantic slither

"I hate to break this up, but you both need to go now. We're out of time," Henrietta Clarkhurst, the ever practical and never in any way sentimental, said.

Penny didn't move. I doubt she cared. I doubt she cared about anything right then.

"Give her a moment," I said, quietly.

"You don't have a moment," Elonis Musk chipped in, and unlike Hettie, who I could forgive for her practicality, he I hated for his inability to find an ounce of bloody empathy. I had an overwhelming urge to punch the insensitive swine in the mouth. I'll admit, this is something of a double standard on my part, but while Hettie was my friend, I can't say I cared at all for Elonis Musk. I glared at him, feeling my own anger surge. Though I suspect I just needed someone to focus my anger on, other than myself.

Standing to one side of the pretentious doctor was a dour-looking Gothe, who nodded to me. He gave me the creeps in a whole other way. He still reminded me of The Ministry's pet goons too much for me to feel comfortable around him. But if any man had a face for a grim circumstance, it was him. Which, if he was right about his condition, made an equally grim kind of sense. But that nod it seemed was meant to tell me something. What it was, I'd be damned if I knew. Save perhaps that he felt some measure of sympathy, which was more than anyone was getting from Musk.

"Hannibal!" Hettie said with a touch more urgency.

I sighed, then put my hand on Vivienne Verne's shoulder, partly to hurry her along, partly just to console her as best I could. Which wasn't a whole lot.

If nothing else, my touch was enough to bring her back to her normal self. Which is to say she rounded on me and suddenly I felt her fingers at my throat. Which I'll admit wasn't what I'd hoped for.

It's odd, the things that go through your head at a moment like that. Right then I found myself thinking of the paralytic coating she had on her razor-like nails. It struck me that this would be a stupid time to get myself turned into a statue. I also found myself fleetingly wondering what Penny would look like with snakes for hair. I guess that's what you get for a subpar classical education.

I made myself focus on important matters and grasped for words that might stay her hand. "Now Penny, do you really think this is the time?"

"That's not my name!" came her usual retort. Then she smiled, a bitter, hard, enraged smile, but a smile nonetheless, just for a second. Just a second, then her hard edge returned.

"I know, I also know you're not mad at me, Penny. You want someone to pay for this? Want to kill someone for this? Well, I can think of better targets than me. Can't you? Hell, I'll help you anyway I can if making them bastards pay is what you want…" I said, though I was just a tad disingenuous at the time, if I am honest. I was gambling that her lust for revenge would outweigh any desire she might have to die with her lover. Or more importantly kill me in the process.

If I could focus her mind on revenge, even if just for a moment, I realised, then maybe I might still get out of there alive. I felt a certain sense of urgency about the getting out part. Another bout of ominous rumbling from below saw to that.

"M!" she said, and I knew it wasn't a question.

"Yes, him. Him and his whole damn Ministry. I'll happily help you tear them apart, Penny dearest. More than happily," I told her and the oddest thing was realising right at that moment, if only right that that moment, I meant every word. It took another moment for that to sink in, to both of us I suspect…

Then finally to my relief, she took her hand from my throat. By which time I was almost smiling at the thought, if I'm honest. Unleashing a vengeful Bad Penny on 'M' and The bloody Ministry. Why… that was a thing to find joy in, even if it took a tragedy to bring it about.

"But," I told her, once I judged the idea was firmly rooted in my favourite psychopath's head, "but, my dearest Vivienne, we can't do that unless we get out of here first. So, I think we need to leave now."

As I said this, I took a step back as I got to my feet. I kept my eyes on her though. I was all too aware how fragile this situation was.

Gently Penny rested Saffron's head down on the decking, and after smoothing out her hair one last time, she too rose to her feet before turning to match my gaze once more. I had the sense that she was sizing up my commitment to her cause. I couldn't blame her for that. I doubt she bought my sincerity. I wasn't entirely sure I bought it myself.

"What about Saffron?" she asked, her voice half breaking. I glanced over at Hettie who subtly shook her head, telling me what I needed to know. There wasn't a hope in Hell of us getting clear carrying the body. I knew we were already cutting it fine as it was. My urge to cut and run was overwhelming in all honesty, and when it comes to cutting and running, I've a lot of experience.

"We'll never get clear with her," I said gently, but the look Penny gave me suggested that wasn't an option, there was no way she was going to just leave her there. I started thinking fast, desperate for inspiration, and somehow came up with one thing that I might get her to agree to. It was the only gambit I had. Though in honestly it relied on something I didn't even believe was possible. I was convinced that everyone we left behind in the Moon-Shot was as doomed as poor Saffron had been. Though I was trying hard to believe otherwise for Hettie's sake. But when you have nothing left to play but a crappy hand, you may as well play it in hope, if not expectation.

"Penny," I said, and saw the snarl in her eyes as I used that name. I banked on it in fact, as if I could keep her focused with anger, I may just have a chance to push her through this. "It occurs to me that someone as special as Miss Wells deserves to be buried somewhere special. Well, I can't think of anywhere more special for her to be laid to rest than the moon… Can you?"

I told you I was a romantic at the core. Oh, I may bury it deep, but I'm a romantic all the same.

For a second, Bad Penny's eyes lit up at this suggestion. I had her, I knew. She'd go along with it, and we could get on our way as well… Which, of course, was why someone just had to throw a spanner in the works.

"That's out of the question," Musk said in a voice so pompous it deserved to be recorded and played in parliament to show MPs how they should sound. The blow took him full in the face.

Before you leap to the assumption, no the blow didn't emanate from me. Though, right then, I'd've dearly loved to have punch him. It wasn't from Penny either, or even, despite my suspicion she was as inclined to do as I, Hettie.

No, to my surprise the blow to Doctor Elonis Musk's face was struck by the fist of someone else entirely. I also have to say it was a hell of a punch. I told myself afterward that if I ever meet him again, I'd suggest he take up prize fighting. Particularly if I could lay a few hefty bets on him first as I'd every reason to believe he could take a punch even better than he threw one, given his not exactly vital aspect.

Unfortunately, I suspected he'd never pass a medical with the boxing commission.

Gothe, for it was his punch in case you were in any doubt, stalked over to where the good doctor lay prone on the decking. Looming above him. Which was another thing Mr Gothe was good at. If there was an Olympic sport for looming, he could've loomed for Britain.

"The body of Miss Wells will be treated with nothing but respect," Gothe informed the prone Elonis, his tone of voice as unyielding as a tombstone. Then his tone lightened from granite to something softer yet just as unyielding and he turned to Penny saying, "I will see to her, Miss Verne. The moon will be both her grave and her tombstone. You will be able to look upon it each night and know she rests there, in peace. You have my word on this, for all the honour a dead man may have."

Right then I could've hugged the man, or whatever the hell he was.

Penny said nothing for a moment. She just met his gaze, staring back at the ruined half-masked face of the man. But then the smallest of smiles crossed her lips.

"Thank you, Mr Gothe," she said, though how she knew his name I couldn't guess. But having said this, without further ceremony, she went over to the ladder and with a last nod to Gothe ,she started to climb down.

Relieved, despite my sense of urgency, I took a moment and offered the man my hand. "You're a good man, Gothe," I told him, though I found myself trying to ignore how cold and oddly clammy his hand felt.

"I shall look after her," he said, and at first I thought he meant Saffron Wells, but then he reminded me of our earlier troubling conversation, "I remember the debt I owe you Mr Smyth. I shall do as you will ask me in the past."

And there was that troubling tense again. 'As you will ask me in the past.' I tried not to dwell upon it though and turned back to Hettie, who had come over to stand by the ladder.

"Well, old chap, I guess this is goodbye again."

I held out my hand to her. Chap to chap. Chap to chap who isn't really a chap, but is more a chap than any other chap I know. Hettie in turn gave me an oddly appraising look before taking my hand. She grasped it in a chap-like fashion, but then used her not inconsiderable strength to pull me closer to her, and to my utter surprise she kissed me full on the lips, in the least chap-like way possible.

For a moment I was too surprised to respond. Then, as my wits gathered themselves, and a sudden terrible sadness overcame me mixed with the strangest hit of joy, I kissed her back, as long and as hard as I could. In a moment that stretched out into oblivion…

And sorry, but you'll just have to forgive that knotty romantic slither buried deep in my callow soul for that poor man's poetry…

It was over in an instant and she pulled away, coughed slightly as she collected herself. "Right… Anyway… Now you get yourself gone. I'll bloody haunt you if you don't get out of here alive."

"Surely it's the dead who haunt the living…" I said, risking a smile, and fighting the urge to duck the punch I thought she was about to throw at me for that bit of impertinence.

She didn't answer me so much as fix me with a hard stare, that suggested it was time to depart while the departing was good. Though there was a hint of a smile that broadened after a moment passed.

"All right, guess it's time I was going," I said. I grasped hold of the ladder and slid down while my nerve held. My last sight of Hettie was of her staring down the hole after me, smiling in the most girlish way I'd ever seen Henrietta Clarkhurst smile.

It was a remarkably pretty smile.

Down below, my Bad Penny was already climbing out of the hatchway and down to the breeching chamber itself. She caught my gaze as I finally tore it away from Hettie.

"You coming, Stoaty?" she yelled at me.

I gave her a hard stare, and raised an eyebrow before I answered… Then I smiled despite everything and followed her out of the Moon-Shot. Shouting after her as I did so, "That's not my name…"

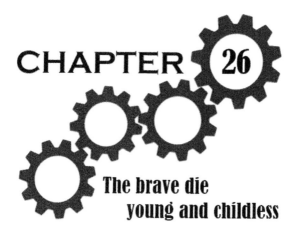

CHAPTER 26

The brave die young and childless

As my feet touched the breeching chamber floor, the hatch in the Moon-Shot slammed shut behind us with a thud. I started after Penny who was already running through the sulphur fumes of the chamber which were thicker and deeper than they had been only a few minutes before. Now instead of ankle deep, they were almost up to my waist, and even through my dense airman's trousers, I could feel the scalding heat.

We'd crossed the chamber and were taking the steps two at a time when, before we even reached the first landing, I heard a rush of air being evacuated from pistons. Risking a look behind me, which almost cost me my footing, I saw the huge breach cover was now descending into place. Sealing the Moon-Shot inside. "Too late now, Hettie..." I muttered to myself, knowing that if she, or any of the crew, had harboured second thoughts… Well, they were committed now.

I managed to catch myself despite my stumble and ran on up the next flight of steps. Warning klaxons were blaring out all around us.

Penny, of course, was faster than I. She reached the top while I was still a flight below. Which was why I found myself dodging some poor unfortunate's body she'd shoved out of her way as it tumbled down the stairs towards me. I saw the face as the body rolled past. Blistered and raw around the mouth where they'd breathed too much super-heated sulphur. Their lungs must have burned to a crisp as they struggled to breathe. A horrible way to go and given how much of the damn stuff I was inhaling, one that didn't bode well for me.

I caught up with Penny on the overlook. She was trying to force a door open which had sealed shut when everything finally went to hell. It made me glad she was with me. Without that inhuman strength of hers, I could never have opened the damn thing. Between us, but mostly because of her, we managed to force it clear of its hinges. I helped her push it over the side and we were off again, running down red lit corridors. The air was at least of slightly better quality there than it had been in the chamber. Though for how long that would remain the case was anyone's guess, and I had no intention of hanging around to find out.

Then as we came to the next set of sealed doors the blaring klaxons finally squealed and died. The silence they left behind was eerie for the few moments it lasted. But then I found myself wishing the klaxon would start up again, if only to mask the ominous deep rumbles that replaced it. The ground started shaking beneath us and parts of the ceiling fell around us, as we fought in unison to open the next set of doors. This time we only managed to make a gap a foot or so wide. It was easy enough for Penny to slip through but for me it was a tight squeeze. As I forced my way through, the rumbling and shaking intensified, making it hard to keep my footing as the base started to collapse around us.

"The volcano," I remember saying at some point, which earned me a withering reply from Penny that I can't recall. I guess I deserved whatever she called me for stating the obvious. What I didn't say, and didn't have to say, was that the volcano was going to erupt all too soon if it hadn't started doing so already. My lungs felt like they were burning inside me and all the exertion mixed with the sulphur in the air meant that wasn't a figure of speech.

We pushed on.

The next few minutes are a blur. I remember passing several bodies on the way, more than were caused by Saffron's rage-fuelled rampage. Falling rubble, and the fire fight in the sub-bay did for most of them, I suspect. Some of them might still have been alive, just trapped by rubble and if they were lucky knocked unconscious, but I would be buggered before taking the time to check on any of them. It wouldn't have helped in any event. About all I'd have achieved would be dying with them.

You may wish to condemn me for that, but think on it a moment. Bravery and selflessness are fine traits, I'm sure, but evolution has always been on the side of the coward. The coward is the one who runs rather than dies a valiant yet pointless death. The coward is the one who survives to bring forth the next generation. The brave, the selfless, the heroes, they die young and childless. Your ancestors are not the ones that stayed behind and held the line so others could flee. Your ancestors are the ones who ran the fastest when the Mongolian hordes descended on their village and I'm damn sure they didn't stop to help those that fell by the wayside. Your very existence is proof of that…

That is, I'll grant you, an ugly way to consider one's forefathers, but since when was truth the prettiest of things?

Explosions seemed to be following on behind us, and I was sure by now the whole base was imploding. I found it hard to credit that Saffron Wells alone could've done enough damage to bring about this catastrophe. Unless of course the whole place had been balanced on a knife edge to start with, which of course it had been. An active volcano isn't something you just harness but Doctor Musk's hubris knew no bounds. He had tapped into the titanic forces of the Earth itself. Tried to harness the power of Vulcan for his own purpose, that of the great enormous weapon he was so proud of. I found my only surprise was that it hadn't gone off half-cocked months ago. Just as I was sure Elonis Musk would have remained confident of his own genius even now as everything exploded around him. Smug bastard that he was.

We got to the last corridor, the one that led to the submersible bay itself, just as the roof caved in behind us, trapping anyone still left in the heart of the base. There, in truth is my vindication for running by and ignoring the wounded and trapped. Though I can't say it made me feel any better about doing so. Cowards may survive and live on, but they always have the guilt to contend with afterwards. I guess that's why we make heroes of those that stay behind and help the trapped and wounded... As if the pride we feel for them for their sacrifice negates our own guilt somehow.

'We must live on, for those who gave their lives, that we may live ours...' and all that... As we try to gloss over our legging it sharpish when the chips were down.

Our relief at our last-minute escape was short-lived. We burst through the doors into the submersible bay seeking salvation, only to find it empty. The Oegopsida had scarpered back to the ocean, leaving us behind. We were being hoist by our own petard, all considered.

Penny stared at me, her expression one of shock. Personally, I wasn't surprised. Of course, her father had ordered The Oegopsida out to sea. Besides which, the captain probably laboured under the misapprehension that we were both on board. Not that I suspected he wasted a thought on myself, but Penny was after all his daughter. You'd have to assume even a cold fish like Verne would've thought twice before leaving her to her fate.

Judging by the bodies in the sub-bay, he may well have ordered the ship out even before the mountain started erupting. The fight between The Oegopsida's guards and Musk's had been short and bloody. I doubt he waited on anyone when the klaxons started sounding. The tunnel back out to the sea was after all an ancient volcanic vent. I wouldn't have hung around either if I thought there was the slightest chance of the caldera going up and trapping my vessel inside the mountain.

Franticly, I ran over to where I'd seen a couple of small launches tied up previously. Boats small enough to make it through the tunnel on a low tide. But I swiftly abandoned that idea when I saw the water level. I doubted there was more than a foot of clearance the length of the tunnel. Someone had tried regardless, and one of the launches was smashed to ribbons in the mouth of the tunnel. Some poor sod was floating face down in the water beside it.

"We need to get to the beaches," I shouted to Penny, pointlessly as it happens as she was already running for the exits. I charged after her, almost stumbling as another low rumble rocked the base and a chunk of roof fell to the deck where I'd been standing only moments before. Luckily, I caught my footing and kept moving, hoping against all expectation we could escape the base before the gun was fired, the mountain blew, or both. Hope which was slipping away by the second.

I don't remember much more of our run through the base to the eastern side of the island. It was chaos. Two maybe three more tremors hit us in the process, and I heard numerous distant explosions. Some poor sod got impaled on some iron work right in front of me as a gas pipe burst, flinging him down a hole which an earlier tremor must have ripped open in the concrete floor. I'd swear it was one of the Packards but I didn't linger long enough to be sure.

We got out to the beach among a crowd of a dozen or so other survivors who had fled in the same direction we had. Most were just milling around aimlessly. Glad to be free of the building and feeling safer in the open. Clearly these were unaware of the most basic rule you need to follow when running away from a catastrophe. Keep running.

My survival instincts were more carefully honed. I knew with the certainty of the coward we were still too close to the base. With so much damage within and the mechanisms for containing the gun's blast ruptured or just plain destroyed, when it went off there was every chance the exhaust would be venting straight out of the building.

I grabbed Penny's arm and got her to follow me further down the beach. I kept moving despite the fact my legs were burning and my lungs crying out for respite. I'd no idea how far away would be far enough. In fact, I'd a morbid certainty that there would be no far enough when the mountain itself went up. I'd give up on ifs by then. The volcano was going to erupt with the certainty of a prep boy's pimple, and no more pleasantly.

We'd reached the end of the beach when the gun finally went off. We were probably two miles away by then. We might as well have been standing in the breeching chamber, considering the noise. The shockwave that followed sent us both off our feet. I've never, and hope to never again, heard the like of it. I suspect they heard it in India, Hell, I suspect they heard it in London. I witnessed the death of Hiroshima, but it was a whisper compared to the sound of Doctor Musk's weapon going off. Though I was a damn sight closer on this occasion.

There was an eruption of fire out of the barrel that I rolled over just in time to see. But I didn't see anything come out. For Hettie's sake, I could only hope I'd missed the Moon-Shot flying off into orbit, because if they'd misfired, they were most certainly dead.

I stared up at the burning exhaust still pouring out of the end of that enormous barrel for moments after the blast. The flames were almost blue, hard to see against a clear sky, but the smoke rising out of the barrel above them was dark as pitch and would soon start to blot out that sky. It was already seemed to be getting darker, but perhaps that was just my imagination.

I stumbled to my feet and offered my hand to Penny, risking a look further down the beach towards the entrance. There, no one was moving. The shockwave could only have been worse nearer to the base itself. But despite the encroaching darkness from the barrel's smog and the ringing in my ears, I remember thinking to myself, at least we're safe. It's over, the gun's gone off and the volcano's stayed intact. I found myself thanking the god I didn't believe in and Old Iron Knickers' legendary libido. Amazed but thankful that the release of pressure caused by the gun firing had been enough to temper the volcano itself.

I stood for a while, catching my breath and it seemed to me my old friend The Lady had dealt me another healthy dose of underserved luck. So like the good little gambler I am, I made a silent promise to raise a glass to her and play a hand of cards next chance I got. When I did, I swore to myself, I would make many outrageous bets, just to keep her happy and on my side.

We'd made it, we were safe...

It was of course then, just as I was thinking this, the ground shook with another tremor. A tremor longer, deeper, and more violent than any that had gone before. Nature, it seemed, was not going to be out-done by some petty man-made contraption. The tremor went on, loose rocks rolling down the mountainside towards the beach. Animals fled out of the dense undergrowth, a flock of birds that had just settled back on the tree tops burst into the air, and the side of the mountain blew out.

I was deafened again for the second time in as many minutes, as the base side of the mountain collapsed in on itself and in a wave of heat, smoke and violence, lava rushed through the holes that were left in the wake of the collapse.

We ran into the surf, and kept running until the sand beneath us was gone. Then we swam out into the bay. Already exhausted, lungs aflame with smoke and sulphur, we swam because to do otherwise was to die. With the thunderous noise of the eruption behind us, we swam in the only direction that mattered, away.

Fire rained from the sky. Bursts of steam were sent up as flaming rocks hit the ocean around us. The volcano shattered what remained of the base, and flung wreckage everywhere. By no more than luck, some of the wreckage was the kind that floated. At some point before my legs gave out, I found myself clinging to a large piece of wood. I've no idea what it had been, all I cared was that it was there. Penny was swimming close by and must have seen me, so before long we were both clinging for bitter life to whatever it was, rolling up and down in the waves, watching nature's firework display.

How we had managed to make it out? Well, I have told you what I remember. Truth told, I'm not sure how much of it is true. Mostly we'd just run and kept running. Then swam out to sea when there was no land left to run on. Hope was now a chunk of wood and only so long as my arm could hold me to it.

The eruption slowly calmed down while we watched, the initial violence of it all simmering down after an hour or more, but in the way of these things it was to carry on for months to come. We were in the water for, well, I'm not sure how long, an hour, maybe two, when salvation in the form of Penny's father arrived from beneath us and for the second time in a month or so I was rescued after a brush with death by Captain No One of The Oegopsida.

This, it struck me at the time, had all the hallmarks of becoming a habit. But if you're going to form a habit of being rescued from an impending water doom, it struck me it isn't a bad one to form. Of course, avoiding impending watery dooms in the first place would probably be a wiser move, but what were the chances of that with my luck?

CHAPTER 27

Redemption from on high

Not too long after this, we found ourselves sitting in the galley, heavy blankets draped over our shoulders, trying to ward off hypothermia. I felt wrecked, a feeling not helped by nervous exhaustion and lungs full of more sulphur than you get in a lifetime chain-smoking Capstan full strength. The thrumming of the engines, and the gentle vibrations in the deck plates were little comfort as The Oegopsida steamed westward towards Java, away from the ill-fated Krakatoa Island.

Captain Verne had picked up some other refugees from the island. Though it was surprisingly, or perhaps unsurprisingly, few. I was back in a jumpsuit with a squid insignia on the shoulder, as was everyone else. My precious old Bad Penny was sitting silently, making even less effort to engage than I was. Neither of us had seen the captain himself. His first mate had brought us down to the galley and told us we were to wait there. Penny hadn't argued any more than I had. I'd have worried about that, but we were both too damn tired.

We sat in silence, nursing bad French coffee. Frankly, I'd have killed for a cup of my old mum's tea. In a mug, of course, stewed within an inch of its life and with so much sugar in it you could stand the spoon up. But coffee was all the galley served, so coffee it was, in tiny little cups.

Time passed, and I didn't feel much more alive, though my eyes had stopped stinging from sea water and, having coughed up half a lung or more of sulphur-infused spew, I was starting to breathe easier. Eventually one of the bridge officers entered the galley and made a bee line for us.

"Monsieur Smyth, the captain commands your presence in the communications room," he informed me. I think it was one of the first lieutenants. I never caught his name.

"Et moi?" Penny asked him, and received no more than a gallic shrug as a reply.

I glanced at her, as I got to my feet, wondering what was going through her mind. I can be a callous swine, self-centred and self-obsessed for the most part, but it occurred to me then I'd been sitting there shivering, worrying about Hettie and ignoring Penny for hours. My feelings for Hettie were complicated to say the least. I feared she was dead, and I'd every right to fear she was dead. But I still had hope. No matter how slender. Penny, meanwhile, knew the one person she truly cared for was dead. There was no ambiguity about it, not least because in the end, she'd been the one to kill her. Albeit in an act of compassion on her part. I realised I couldn't imagine what was going on in her head right then. She'd a shallow look in her eye that made her seem empty, as if all the fire had gone out of her now we were safely aboard The Oegopsida.

For a moment, I found myself dwelling on Penny, wondering what she'd do now. Would she follow through with her plan to revenge herself on The Ministry and M? Or would that all be too much for her. She seemed lost and for the first time I think I realised how young she really was. How small and weak she seemed sitting in that galley. A petty young woman, little more than a child, whose life had already been shattered in more ways than one, even before this latest disparate chapter. She was the daughter of a distant father and, I had to assume, a birth mother long gone. Certainly, she'd never spoken of her, not that we'd ever been what you might call close of course. And now, the love of her young life was dead, and by her own hand no less, and just when she probably needed him the most, her father had sent, not for her, but for an itinerant mercenary, someone who at best she despised.

I risked half a smile of sympathy in her direction. In return, I received nothing but a blank lifeless stare. Not even a bitter threat or an icy insult, both of which would have been typical of our relationship previously. I felt strangely perturbed by this, but shrugged it off and followed the lieutenant through the hatchway.

The communications room was a small offshoot of the bridge. Verne was there talking in French to someone through a headset. Madam Verne stood silently at his side, studying something on the bank of instruments before them which lit the room in a strange green glow.

I was waved to enter by my escort then left standing behind him in the dimly lit room. A few minutes passed with me listening to one half of a conversation, in a language I was vaguely familiar with at best. I heard Musk's name a couple of times, but picked up very little. Then the captain handed the headset to his wife before turning to face me.

"Mr Smyth, your powers of survival continue to astound me. I should ask what part you had in Miss Wells' escape, not to mention the events her rampage set in motion… But I shall not. I have no doubt my daughter was involved. Her obsession with Miss Wells I know only too well," he said plainly, his face betraying little emotion, though I got a hint from the lilt of his voice that this conversation was not going to be the end of it. But he was putting it on one side for now, which was something.

"Captain Verne, I…" I started to say, but he cut me off.

"This is not the time, and you don't have any," he told me sternly. For a second, I'd visions of him throwing me off the ship. I rather worriedly found myself wondering if they would surface first or just shove me out of an airlock. I wasn't sure which would be the worst fate. But of course, he'd just pulled me out of the ocean an hour ago. While it's true I suspected my rescue had much to do with my being in the vicinity of his daughter, putting me out on my ear to drown now would at the very least be ill-mannered. Verne was a stickler for manners.

"I regret…" I started once more.

"I'm sure you do, Monsieur, but I brought you here because someone else wishes to speak with you, and while I care little for you, I respect them greatly. Time is something of a luxury in this regard, so we will speak of your future aboard my vessel later," Verne said, then placed his hand, with some affection, upon the shoulder of his wife, and said something in Japanese.

She nodded in reply and relieved herself of the headphones before handing them to me. I watched, slightly bemused as the two of them exited through the hatch and left me alone in the communications room. Though I did note the hatch remained open, counter to all protocol.

I was a little narked by this, because despite everything, it seemed a tad insulting. Feeling slightly ruffled, I turned towards the console, pulling the headphones on. It was only then I saw the source of green light was yet another of those damn screens William Gates designed. I had a momentary shiver, as I looked at the fuzzy imagine, wondering whose eyes I was looking through, or if there was just some random camera somewhere sending signals back. Whatever it was, the image was indecipherable green haze on top of a darker green haze. All I could tell from the image was that it seemed to be the inside of some room or other but it was impossible to make out details. Then after a moment, it resolved slightly and I realised a figure was standing in the foreground, or rather not standing exactly… Whoever it was seemed to be bobbing about as if they were submerged in water. I put that down to the fuzzy nature of the imagine, which was matched by the static that was all I heard through the headset and equally indecipherable.

After a moment, the figure seemed to move closer to the camera. Then there was a shadow that I realised was someone's hand slapping at the equipment in the time honoured fashion of frustrated operators everywhere. I doubted that was going to help much but a moment later it turned out the percussive repairs were being done with a professional touch.

"Hannibal, still on the mortal coil, I see. Well played, old lad." The voice of Hettie Clarkhurst crackled through the headset, while a ghosting image of Hettie in all her green screen glory resolved itself through lines of interference.

This, of course, was a moment for mildly heroic nonchalance. You know the kind of thing, a feint of indifference. Events passed off with a mildly cunning witticism. The kind of off the cuff remark that expresses no surprise in what the less heroic would have considered an unexpected turn of events…

"Hettie?" I asked the fuzzy image, completely failing to vocalise any of the above.

"You were expecting Old Brass Knickers?" came the reply that didn't.

"I… You're alive… I thought… I was sure…. You're alive!" I said, and felt a chill run through me that had nothing to do with a couple of hours in the ocean. While I'd hoped she'd survived the shot, faced as I was now with unexpected proof of her continued existence, the enormity of how slim that hope had seemed came down on me all at once.

"Yes… Look Hannibal, I don't have much time. We achieved orbit, but I'll be in the Earth's shadow in two minutes and before we're back round again, we slingshot. So, put your disbelief on the back burner. We need to talk," Hettie said between the squeals of static that cut over her.

She slapped the equipment at her end again and the imagine cleared up a little more. As it did, I realised suddenly she was indeed floating. Not in water, but in the air. Free of terra firmer, it appeared gravity ceased to have an effect, which was the strangest of things to witness, as her hair had escaped her perpetual hairband and was floating freely around her.

"You're going through with the rest of this lunacy?" I asked incredulously.

Hettie laughed. "Lunacy, good one!"

"What?"

"Lunacy, from the root Latin Luna, meaning of the moon… Oh, you weren't being heroically nonchalant, with a cunning piece of wit…?"

I said nothing, I wanted to say, 'No, I mean the crazy idea of using the Earth to slingshot a tin can at the bloody moon.' But for once, I realised nothing was the best thing I could say and actually managed to say nothing… Unfortunately, that left a hole in the conversation where my part should have been, so a moment passed before Hettie decided to fill it herself.

"Any-who, look, we don't have time for this. I've only a few moments before I'm out of range, and I need to tell you something. I should've told you before, but it never seemed the right moment."

"Okay."

"It's about that guy you killed, Harding."

"Hardacre," I corrected.

"Whatever his name was. The one you claim you killed in self-defence. Anyway, listen…"

"Hang on, you knew about my trial? I thought you… I mean, I assume you didn't…"

"Of course I knew. I mean, it wasn't big news or anything but it was in the papers," she said, and managed to sound a little offended.

"But you were in the Antarctic," I said, partly to cover my foolishness.

"That was months ago. Do you think Captain Verne doesn't keep up with the news? I knew. I knew about it before we picked you up. But that's not important. I knew before that, I just had no way to warn you."

"I, what? I don't follow." And I didn't, this was Gothe all over again…

"It was a setup, don't you see?"

"It…" I started to say, then stuttered into silence. I wanted to explain that whatever she thought had happened, and bless her for even entertaining the possibility I was innocent, I wasn't, but I couldn't bring myself to be as honest with Hettie as I've been with you, dear reader. I knew what I'd done. Hell, I relived it most every night. I saw Hardacre plunge through the bomb bay doors to his doom, time and time again in my nightmares and sometimes I swapped places with him. The memory of his murder was still fresh as a daisy, I assure you. As were the memories of being caught in the ordinance bay as I threw the sergeant to his doom. But I found myself unable to admit that to Hettie. If she was gracious enough to believe I was innocent, then I was happy to let her do so. I can't say I care greatly about what most people think of me, I don't care much for what I think of myself, but I'd go to my grave happier knowing that Henrietta Clarkhurst didn't think me an utter shite.

"It was Piggy," she told me, before my silence dragged on.

"Piggy… what? I don't follow…" I said, feeling more confused than ever. Then suddenly a nagging thought returned once more from the recesses of my mind. Charles Fortescue-Wright, old Piggy from 'The Ins & Outs'. Hettie had told me the lengths he'd gone to in order to exact his revenge on her. All for the effrontery of turning down his proposal. Yet that was what had led to our embarrassing duel on Hampstead Heath. It seemed bizarre he'd exacted no such revenge on me, now I thought of it once more… I felt a sudden chill all the way to my bones that was nothing to do with hyperthermia.

"He was behind my getting sent to Antarctica, remember, him and his family connections," she prodded, though light had already started to dawn.

"I remember. I can hardly forget, but…" I said, and that 'but' just hung there, waiting for what suddenly seemed all too obvious.

"Well, for you he went with a more direct approach. He knew you'd be up to no good, Hell we all knew you'd be up to no good, it's part of your charm, and when aren't you? He figured out you were involved in smuggling something or other for someone."

"Redwood…" I admitted, who I have never trusted. Calling Redwood a snake was an insult to serpents, but his money was good. Almost, it now occurred to me, too good for the last lot of shipments I'd agreed to. I thought he was just sweetening the pot because of the fiasco in the Balkans. I'd claimed I needed to lay low after that, though in truth I'd been trying to fleece him for extra shekels on the back of it. Hell, I'd patted myself on the back for pulling the wool over his eyes when I got him to double my fee. I never considered he had agreed to that all too quickly at the time.

"Redwood was a stooge for Maitland Fortescue-Wright. Piggy's father. Turns out Maitland is some important bod at some Ministry or other. They turn a blind eye to some of Redwood's activities and fund a few of them. So, anyway, they got Redwood to convince Hardacre he'd give him a bigger slice of the pie, as long as he helped cut you out. He was told to attack you. They'd cooked up a deal with another RAN officer to take over the smuggling operation and he was supposed to catch you in the act. Hardacre would claim he'd 'caught you smuggling' and they would get rid of you, the way you got rid of Hardacre. Luckily for you, this other guy turned up a little late, and didn't have the stomach to just do you in."

"Maythorpe?" I asked, though it was more exclamation than question. I'd tell you I'd never trusted Maythorpe either, but that would imply I'd ever given him a second thought. He was no more than a puffed up blowhard... This couldn't be right...

Then I remembered just how outraged Maythorpe had been when he stumbled across me on The Empress of India. Not to mention how much effort he went to in order to be rid of me in Egypt too. I'd dismissed it at the time as no more than his usual stuck-up indignation. It made a horrible kind of sense, if he'd struck a deal with the Fortescue-Wrights. He was sure I was a loose end that had been tied up at Tyburn, with a noose around my neck. As that wasn't the case, his new smuggling operation would be in jeopardy… Avarice, it made sense to me, more so than simple moral outrage. He must have thought things with Redwood had gotten fouled up. What with me still being in the land of the living… It explained the strength of his resentment towards me on Captain Singh's bridge.

It all made a horrible kind of sense. I mean, I'd wondered why Hardacre turned on me the way he did. True enough, I'd assumed greed was behind it, but I'd never pegged the man for having much ambition, or being a thinker. At the end of the day, that was why I'd employed him in the first place. I should've known he'd not come up with the idea of betraying me all on his lonesome.

"Hang on, Hettie, how do you know all this? I didn't know all this!" I asked her.

"Because the Captain of the Shackleton let it all slip. The arsehole was full of himself. When he started explaining why he was shafting me, he got carried away and told me how they shafted you too."

"The Shackleton? Oh, the survey ship. But how did he know?"

"He worked for Piggy's father. Maitland's ministry was funding the whole enterprise. There's something they're after down there. Anyway, Captain shit for brains was pissed with me. He didn't appreciate some of the things I'd done to screw with his ship. Man had no sense of humour… Anyway, I guess he wanted me to understand just how deep in the shit I was and I guess he thought telling me how they were going to screw you over was just jam on the scone. What he didn't tell me I managed to ferret out with Verne's help. Wells and Verne have people everywhere, there's not much they can't find out for you, if you ask them nicely."

"Why would you go to all that effort for me?" I asked, my confusion honest, but not helped by my mind spinning away with it all. There was something else she'd said, though

I couldn't grasp it, something that tied everything together. Some little detail I was missing, nagging at me.

"Because we're friends, Hannibal, you bloody arse. Captain Dyer let slip what Piggy's old man had planned for you and... Well, I remember what you did for me, daft as it was. Look, long story short, you're not a murderer, Hannibal, you never were. Do you see? It really was self-defence and you can't be faulted for that, can you...? Besides, I thought you were dead, at first anyway, and I thought your name should be cleared. Then Verne told me you were still alive and had been recruited by The Ministry and that Wells was trying to turn you. Verne told --e... Oh da-n it... Sig--als goi-g to d-op any mom-nt, were e-teri-g t—shad--. I'll s-- you ar----d o-- -oy. -ake c-r- o- yo-r-elf," Hettie said, the signal weakening and interference cutting through her words. In the end, it was just static. The last syllables were just electrical noise, though for a brief moment it cleared up. And she added something along the lines of, "It's w--t you're best at..."

And with that, Henrietta Clarkhurst, of the Hampshire Clarkhursts, formally warrant officer Clarkhurst of the Royal Air Navy's engineering corp, was gone.

I wasn't sure the Moon knew what was about to hit it...

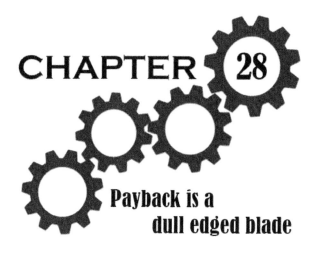

CHAPTER 28

Payback is a dull edged blade

About ten days after I was plucked out of the Ocean for a second time by The Oegopsida it surfaced again about a hundred nautical miles of the coast of southern Africa around two in the morning ship time. Those had been a long ten days, the first few of which I had spent working my way through the last of Hettie's engine room hooch, until Vivienne Verne of all people pulled me out of a self-pitying drunken stupor.

My perpetual Bad Penny, predictably, had no intention of letting me drink myself quietly to death. She wanted to hurt someone, for once however that someone was not me.

"I want to end them!" she told me, "I want to end them all!"

"How?" I asked her.

I didn't ask who she was talking about, I didn't have to. For once me and My Bad Penny were on the same page. I wanted to end them too.

As I said, it had been a long few days, and between bouts of unconsciousness I'd had time to think. Most of my thoughts were focused on Charles Fortescue-Wright. I'd determined some pay back was in order. Not because he and his father orchestrated my demise, you may be surprised to learn, but because of what they'd done to Hettie.

Strange, isn't it? The things that motivate us. Henrietta Clarkhurst would call me a bloody fool for taking up arms in her defence, she'd be right to do so too, it was how all this started after all. I'd done that before and it led to the Fortescue-Wrights making me a murderer, and they had no matter what Hettie thought.

But that as beside the point. All the events that led up to that murder happened though my own choices. As I've told you before, hell, as I told you right at the start of these reminiscences, I'm a liar, a thief, a coward and a murderer. Avarice, greed, and selfishness are all my hallmarks. So Piggy and his old man may've conducted the orchestra, but I was first violin. I fiddled my way onto that ordinance deck that night. All they did was call the tune.

Hettie though…

Hettie had been blameless. All she had ever done was turn down a suiter she'd never sought in the first place. For that, she'd been tricked into throwing away her career. For that, gotten stranded in the Antarctic. And for that, ultimately ended up being blasted out of the world itself. All because piggy-eyed Charles Fortescue-Wright thought he had the right to call upon her affection.

In short, they'd fucked over her life, for having the temerity to turn down an unsolicited proposal. The way I'd it figured, I deserved all I'd gotten. One way or another. But

Henrietta Clarkhurst... Hettie... She deserved none of what had come her way. So yes, I wanted to end them all right. Charles, Maitland, Maythorpe, Redwood and that whole cancerous Ministry of theirs. I wanted vengeance. I wanted payback. Not so much for me, but for Hettie.

Which bring me to that question I asked Vivienne Verne, or Bad penny if you prefer... 'How?'

Over the next couple of days, we came up with some idea's. Damn fool idea's. But what else would you expect. The whole thing was a damn fool exercise. The Ministry was a secretive monolithic organisation at the heart of the British government. It had its grubby fingers in everything and a grasp on power that probably led all the way to the throne itself. Between us we had a psychotic with razors for fingernails and a selfish bastard with a dull edged cut-throat.

We needed allies. Preferably the kind of allies that have even more resources than a secretive arm of the British government...

Strange as it may seem, given the impossibility of the task we had set ourselves, by the time we surfaced that night off the coast of Southern Africa we had the germ of a plan. A plan that we would go on to spend the long tedious journey around the southern tip of Africa, up through the South Atlantic and into the North talking over. By the time The Oegopsida got to Europe we had talked it all through endless times, yet in essence it was the plan we came up with in those first few days that we two unlikely collaborators decided to put into practise.

Which was why the day before we surfaced that night off Southern Africa, I went to see Captain Verne and formally offered my services to him and became part of his crew. It suited our purposes; he was after all intent on freeing HG Wells from the clutches of the Russians. Besides which, I also felt I owed Saffron Wells that much because there but for the grace of whatever deity you happen to believe in, and all that.

I was surprised how quickly Verne accepted my offer, I expected after everything that had happened at Krakatoa, he'd want to wash his hands of me. As it turned out I had Vivienne to thank for the captain's leniency. She'd told the old man I had effectively gotten her out of the volcano when it came down to it. Which isn't the whole story as you know.

Captain Verne had forgiven Vivienne for her own indiscretions at Krakatoa. Something he did in the most French way imaginable by sulking for several days before declaring, "That which is done in passion must always to be forgiven," embracing his daughter and kissing her on both cheeks. But as he had forgiven his daughter, he wasn't holding the disaster on the island against me either. Which came as a relief as I'd visions of long swims in shark infested waters being the other option likely to be presented to me.

In any event, I signed on The Oegopsida for the Wells rescue. If nothing else HG Wells free in the world once more would distract The Ministry from what me and my Bad Penny had planned for them. Them, piggy and his father.

I'd been trying to put the pieces together in the days that followed Krakatoa. But it was about three days after Hettie's message it all finally clicked into place. I'd woken from a drunken stupor inspired dream, a dream in which I was screaming curses at Charles 'Piggy' Fortescue-Wright and staring him in his piggy little eyes, when those eyes had morphed into another face, one less jowly, less pig like, but one that still held a strong familial resemblance. A face I'd known for a while and one that regularly featured in my nightmares. A face belonging to a man whose given name I'd never known. Not until then…

Maitland Fortescue-Wright. A man whose face I knew and hated.

You'll remember I said something had bugged me about Hettie's explanation. That I felt one little piece of information must link everything up… Well, I was slow, I'll give you that… It took me days to figure it out. But I got there in the end though.

Hettie told me Piggy's father Maitland was high up in a ministry. When I woke that morning, it came to me that he was higher up than she even suspected, because when it clicked together in my mind, I realised that he ran that ministry. The Ministry… Maitland Fortescue-Wright was a man I knew by another name. Well just an abbreviation as it turns out.

'M'.

I realised 'M' must have hit upon the idea of using me to get to HG Wells when he discovered the connection even I'd been unaware of. Piggy doubtless got his father to look into me in order to pursue his vendetta. Nepotism has always been at the heart of the British establishment. You can get anything done if you have the right family connections, a rolled up trouser leg, and a tie from your old school days.

To Maitland, it must have seemed like a perfect solution, two birds with one stone. I suspect Hettie's information wasn't entirely right. I suspect Maitland's plan had always been to frame me, and Hardacre would've been conveniently done away with even if I hadn't killed him myself. Once they framed me, I'd fall under The Ministry's control. His nauseating Piggy offspring would get his revenge on the upstart oink Smyth… and Maitland would get his agent without a choice, against HG Wells.

All so neat and tidy isn't it. All very neat and nasty. All very British establishment. The ruling classes survived because they were damn good at the ruling part, not because they were nice or gave a damn about the rest of us.

Well, I intended to make them regret not just killing me and regret all they had done to Hettie into the bargain. Signing on as crew on The Oegopsida and freeing HG Wells was just going to be the start of it.

If I'd not been determined of this before I was the night we surfaced off southern Africa We'd heard no more from Hettie, Elonis Musk and Mr Gothe after that last message. But for all my faults I was always goods at trigonometry, trajectories, and ordinance calculations. There was a reason I'd been commissioned as a gunnery officer after all. Between me and the captain we managed to figured out just when Doctor Musk Moon-shot would reach its target. That was why me, the captain and Penny were stood up on the conning tower that particular night. Watching the moon while drinking the captain's brandy and wrapped up in fur coats against the chill.

After the second or third brandy, so it may have been an optical illusion, I saw a huge upheaval in the lunar surface. As if it was struck by a large meteorite leaving a new crater on that much scarred surface, and we raised a glass to the three of them, and to Saffron Wells as well as she reached her final destination.

Whether it was going to be the final destination for Hettie, the mad doctor and the dead man, well, that's a tale for someone else to tell. I had other business to attend to in London, there was just a little matter of going to Moscow first…

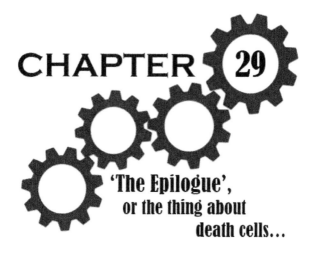

CHAPTER 29

'The Epilogue',
or the thing about death cells...

I woke in the dark, lying on a cold stone floor. I knew from the smell alone where I was, a death cell. It may or may not prove to be mine in the fullness of time, but it had been someone's at some time in the past. You develop a nose for this kind of thing. Well, you do if you're unlucky enough to spend as much time behind bars as I have over the years.

There's an entry for 'the Good Death Cell Guide right there.

Beneath the Kremlin, at the heart of Mother Russia.

Accommodation dank and devoid of hope.

Notably bleak and reeks of urine, both human and vermin.

Likely to be forgotten and left to starve to death, indeed the skeleton in the corner suggests you are not the first to whom this fate has been reserved.

9/10 it's a classic

As once again I found myself sitting in the cold and the dark, with little concept of the passage of time, save for the drip, drip, drip of something I preferred to think of as water through a vent in the ceiling. I was starting to have doubts about the plan as I sat there on damp flag stones and time passed. My head was ringing. Trying to ignore my surroundings.

I think I became a little delusional for a while. But that's death cells for you. They play tricks on your mind. I mean, I know I imagined it, but I would've sworn a small chink of light opened up in the back wall at one point. Like a doorway, where a doorway couldn't be. Then I'd also have sworn that of all things a calico cat wandered in, sauntered around for a while then stopped and looked up at me, tilted its head to one side in that inquisitive manner all cats have. Then stalked off back through that impossible doorway, which promptly vanished just as its tail slipped through.

And if that's not delusional enough for you, as the cat looked up at me, I could also have sworn I heard a voice in my head purring for a moment that said, '*Oh, it's you, sorry, I must have taken a wrong turn in the forest in the cellar, I was looking for Sonny Burbank's. Wrong cell, wrong reality, not to worry. Anyway, sorry about that, take care, Harry, I'll see you around.*'

Death cells… I tell you, there is something weird about them. They play tricks on my mind. Though I guess that should come as no surprise. Given what they are.

More time passed and sanity, for want of another word, returned. Which is to say the cat didn't…

Then finally just as I'd begun to give up hope, more than half convinced that fool plan of mine was going to be the death of me, another chink of light appeared. This one in the front wall, where I expected it to be.

The cell door opened and then, flanked by two rough-looking Russian jailers, in walked a familiar face. The face of a man I trusted about as far as I could throw him, but also the face of a man I knew would jump at the chance to put one over the British and The Ministry in particular. All I needed to do was convince him that I was all for switching sides. Ironically, as it happens, from a side I'd never really been on to start with.

I stared up at him, doing my best to present a stiff upper, while smiling a sly little smile mostly to myself. This was all the product of a dumb plan, a fool's plan, an idiot undertaking, but it had got me where I wished to be all the same.

All I needed to do now was convince him of my willingness to turn over the traitor's card. My willingness to turn traitor to Great Britain, the nation of my birth. Traitor to Queen Victoria 'Iron Knickers' Sax-Coburg herself. I must convince him of my willingness to sell out every ideal and principle as a true born Englishman. Convince him I'd betray the very notion of being a gentleman of the empire.

A tall order for some, but I'm Hannibal Smyth, Harry Smith that was. I am, as I have said from the very beginning, a liar, a thief, a murderer and a scoundrel. A man who should never have passed muster as a gentleman to begin with and as to my willingness to betray my country, there was no lie there at all…

A moment passed. He stood and stared down at me, tassels hanging limp in the dead air. Then as the tension that was growing between us reached its peak, as he was ever a pretentious swine.

Then finally he spoke, "So, Mr Smyth, we meet again!"

The End…

For the moment

ABOUT THE AUTHOR

Mark writes novels that often defy simple genre definitions, they could be described as speculative fiction, though Mark would never use the term as he prefers not to speculate.

When not writing novels Mark is a persistent pernicious procrastinator, he recently petitioned parliament for the removal of the sixteenth letter from the Latin alphabet.

He is also 7th Dan Blackbelt in the ancient Yorkshire marshal art of EckEThump and favours a one man one vote system but has yet to supply the name of the man in question.

Mark has also been known to not take bio very seriously.

Email: darrack@hotmail.com
Twitter: @darrackmark
Find out more at markhayesblog.com

Printed in Great Britain
by Amazon